SHALVA HESSEL

MARRIED
TO
THE
MOSSAD

A thriller based on a true story

Married to the Mossad / Shalva Hessel

Translasted from the Hebrew: Elhanan Miller
Contact: shalva36@gmail.com

ISBN 9781544740003

MARRIED
TO
THE
MOSSAD

SHALVA HESSEL

TRANSLATED FROM THE HEBREW BY
ELHANAN MILLER

Acknowledgments

To my dear mother and father, Yael and Hanan (of blessed memory) Schwarzman—for educating me to believe, give, love humanity, love the land of Israel, and believe in the values of Judaism.

To my dear loving husband, Yoram Hessel, thanks to whom I was exposed to the fascinating experience of Mossad life. Thank you for the support and freedom you've given me.

To my dear children Roy and Michael Hessel, who are my force, soul, and courage. How proud I am of the men you turned out to be! Please continue.

To my dear beloved grandchildren: Liam, Isaiah, Eliah, Isaac, and Daniella. You enrich my life every day. I hope you mature in the spirit of Judaism and Zionism, and continue in our family tradition of Jewish values.

PART ONE

1.

She stood with her back to the door and her hands spread out to the sides. "You're not leaving here."

"Sally," he said in a calm voice, charged with hidden tension. "Let me leave."

"Only after you tell me where you disappear to at night."

"I can't tell you."

"Why, Jerry? Who won't let you?"

"I can't say that either."

"You're playing with me!" Sally's voice rose to a shout. "If you want to meet other women just say so."

"It's not other women," Jerry said. "It really isn't."

They'd been married for a year, and despite her young age, life experience had equipped her with sharp senses. She could tell a fake if she saw one. "What's going on with you? Why can't you explain?"

Jerry's voice was steady and cool. "Give me an hour. I'll leave and return with someone who'll explain."

She knew that no pressure could force him to tell, but still she insisted. "Why can't *you* explain?"

"He'll explain that too."

Sally's eyes were full of rage. "I want to come with you to where he is. Let him explain it there."

"You can't," Jerry explained patiently. "You can't even know where it is."

"You're speaking like a character out of a cheap suspense novel," Sally shouted.

A faint smile crossed Jerry's face. "Do I get an hour?"

Sally could never withstand his smile, and gave up. "One hour," she succumbed, and moved away from the door. "But not a minute longer!"

Anger and fear made her blood boil. For months, she had been spending her evenings on the couch purchased on Petticoat Lane with Jerry's holiday bonus. It was the sole valuable item in their apartment. She had read dozens of books and watched countless TV series, waiting for him to return. Every time she asked him where he'd gone, it would be an urgent meeting at work, seeing a friend, or a lecture at the London School of Economics. As time passed, his explanations became less convincing and Sally grew more suspicious. She felt that since they had arrived in London, her husband's life was being run by something unknown and more significant than she; that she was losing control over their fate.

Sally couldn't stand losing control. In every situation, she was always the leader and the center of attention. She was raised in a National-Religious family of citron farmers in Moshav Hibbat Zion, where she was considered a free spirit. Opinionated and principled, she was a tomboy who enjoyed the company of boys and was always game for a prank. Even at

the Technion, where she was the only female computer software program-
ming student, she remained independent and was unafraid to express her
opinion at every opportunity. That's where she met Jerry, and the moment
she laid eyes on him, she knew he'd be hers.

Following a short courtship, her beauty and wit worked their charms
and they became lovers. Jerry was attracted to her joie de vivre, which
complemented his solemnness, and she loved his serious and fastidious
nature. She had wholeheartedly hoped that they could wed, but Jerry kept
announcing that marriage was out of the question. "We have no money, I
have no interest in children at this point in my life, and besides, I'll never
marry someone who hasn't served in the army." Regardless, when he told
her he was accepted to LSE, one of the leading economics schools in the
world, she knew she would follow him. Her parents objected, of course,
but could do nothing to oppose the will of their stubborn daughter who
informed them that she was traveling to get married.

She landed in London with a thousand pounds and Jerry's address
at the student residence. The following day he joined her to rent a flat.
They found a room with a common kitchen in an old apartment building, and ate a greasy and unappetizing meal at the takeaway shop across
the street. The following day, Sally applied to three software engineering
schools whose addresses Jerry had found. The tuition of all three was beyond her means. The sum she brought with her from Israel was lower than
the tuition and sufficed, at most, for two months of rent, if she ate frugally.
Winter was around the corner, with its high heating costs.

Sally met with Jerry every evening and tried to remain optimistic
and not worry him, but she was growing increasingly desperate. Her parents sent her five hundred pounds for her birthday, which extended her

grace time in London by an extra month. Now, four months separated her from the day when she would have to admit defeat and call home, requesting that her parents pay for the return ticket. Jerry tried to help as best he could, but was also making a pittance working in Israeli advocacy and was barely making ends meet. Their life together now had an expiry date and their love grew desperate.

One day, Jerry turned up at her apartment with an advertisement he had ripped from the notice board at his residence: "The Pierre Marin Fund offers scholarships to students who pass its tests. Scholarships include school tuition and a stipend." The following day, Sally arrived at the fund's offices, filled out the forms, and was told she must take a test. She tried to inquire about the subject of the test, its length, and the mark required for the scholarship, but to no avail.

A week later, she was invited back to the fund's office. In a small room, seated next to three others, she answered questions related to Judaism. She counted her blessings for being exposed at home to religious law and love of Israel, and felt grateful to her family, especially her father and grandfather—a well-known and admired rabbi—for making themselves available to her questions on religious matters. Leaving the room, she knew she had successfully passed the test.

And so it was. Two weeks later, her bank account was credited with a sum of money that sufficed for tuition and living expenses for a month. Additional sums, she was promised in a letter received by mail, would arrive every month until she completed her studies.

Letter in hand, she returned to the fund's offices. "Is something wrong?" asked the astonished secretary.

"I came to thank Pierre Marin personally for his help."

"That's impossible," said the secretary.

"Why? Doesn't he exist?"

"Oh, he exists all right." She laughed. "He's a Jewish millionaire who lives in Switzerland. You can leave a letter here, but there's no chance he'll answer you."

Sally jotted down a few warm sentences of thanks on a piece of paper, inserted it into an envelope, and handed it to the secretary.

When she stepped out onto the street, she felt the world smiling at her. The mysterious Pierre Marin had gotten her life back on track.

2.

The telephone ringing woke her from her memories. She jumped from her seat and answered the call. "It will take a bit more than an hour, but I'm on my way," Jerry said in a calm voice.

Once again, her regular combativeness leaped forward. "How much longer?"

"I don't know. We're on our way," he said, and hung up.

Who was this mysterious man on his way to meet her? She tried to recall when the first signs of oddness began to appear in Jerry's life. In fact, it happened as early as the night before their wedding. They spent the night at her apartment, and around midnight the phone rang. "It must be my parents," Sally said, but Jerry sprang up to answer. She looked at him with surprise. "I gave them your number in case they needed me," he explained.

"Who needed you?" she asked, as he got out of bed and pulled the telephone as far away from her as the cord allowed. He spoke in a low voice, whispering words she could not hear into the speaker. When he returned to her side, she asked, "Who was that?"

"Someone from work," he said. "They're looking for some document."

"Someone works in advocacy at night?"

"You'd be surprised. There are departments that work around the clock. The communications room, for instance."

"Yes, but your department isn't really—"

"My department communicates with its counterpart in Australia," he explained patiently, "and with the one in New York. The time difference requires a permanent presence."

It seemed logical, but not honest. She would have inquired further, were it not for the impending wedding that had been repeatedly postponed by Jerry, who kept fearing different things: The commitment of marriage, the financial burden, or the difficulty of raising children. Sally was able to dispel his concerns, even convincing him not to settle for civil marriage in city hall. They were married by a rabbi in the Great Synagogue of London, where a handful of worshippers were asked to stay after services and serve as a religious quorum. The rabbi curiously inspected the empty sanctuary. "No relatives? No family?" he asked.

"They're in Israel," Sally replied.

"Do they know you're getting married?"

"They do," she reassured him.

The rabbi began the ceremony and ended it quickly. "I wish you luck," he said, his voice filled with compassion.

Married life was peaceful and loving. Jerry advanced at his work in Israeli advocacy and Sally found a lucrative job as head of the computer department of British Home Stores. They still had to live frugally, but they knew that life would grow easier as they advanced in their positions. Sally was almost happy. It was only Jerry's frequent disappearances at night that spoiled her mood, and worried her.

The doorbell rang and Sally rushed to open it. Jerry entered first and began looking around, as though he was searching for something. He signaled to someone standing in the corridor, beyond the wall. "This is my wife," he said when the man entered, gesturing to Sally.

"Aaron," the man introduced himself, delivering a firm handshake.

He had a pleasant face, light eyes, and graying hair, which probably used to be blond. "Come, have a seat." Sally switched on the light in the kitchen. "Would you like to eat something? Drink?" she asked the guest.

"Tea, please."

His Hebrew was tinged with a slight foreign accent. When she lit the stove fire under the teapot, the sound of children's laughter erupted beyond the thin wall, and Aaron asked Jerry who lived there.

"I don't know them," Jerry replied. "Pakistanis or something."

"And what about the other wall?" Aaron pointed at the bedroom.

"A widow with a cat."

Sally could sense Aaron's frustration. He got up. "Let's speak in another room," he ordered.

"There's only a couch and a carpet in there," Sally said.

"We'll take chairs with us."

He left, dragging his chair behind him. A few moments later, the three were seated across each other, Sally on her couch ("out of the question," Aaron politely refused when she offered it to him) and the two men on kitchen chairs. "So, what's the story?" Sally asked directly. "Where is my husband off to at nights and how are you—" she turned to Aaron "—connected to this?"

"Your husband works for the state," Aaron said.

"I already know that. He works in the finance department in an Israeli advocacy organization."

"Not really. He's registered there, but he works for a security branch."

"Is he a military attaché?" Sally recalled a tall officer, dressed in official uniform, who was introduced to her at one of the embassy parties.

"The Mossad."

"The Mossad?" Sally called out, and immediately covered her mouth. "I apologize. It's so surprising. He's a man of financial reports, numbers, balances. Not James Bond."

"The Mossad doesn't only employ James Bonds," Aaron said. "He's—
"

"Call me Sally," she interrupted him. "And listen. I don't believe this story. If you don't only employ only James Bonds, there is certainly no reason to extract Jerry from home at nights."

"Meetings," Jerry said, mincing his words.

"Jerry holds meetings with various people," Aaron explained. "His English, his education, his knowledge—these all make him very valuable to us, to the state, and to the Mossad." Something caught his eye and he bent down to the floor and looked at the illuminated crack under the door. "What—" Sally began to ask, but Aaron put his finger to his mouth, signaling to her to remain quiet. He quietly moved to the door and opened it with one fell swoop. The widow's cat was sitting on the carpet, licking its paws. "This is silly, this paranoid game," Sally announced.

"It's not paranoia," Aaron said as he returned to his chair. "This apartment isn't suitable for you. You'll need to move away. We have a flat in Mayfair, which will do fine."

"A flat in Mayfair? How will we pay for it?"

"There's no need to pay. It belongs to us, to the State of Israel."

Sally stared at Jerry. "You didn't tell me how senior you are there."

"He didn't," Aaron replied instead. "He can't. I'm the only one who can authorize him to speak. Now you are a confidante and know that your husband is a senior employee of the Mossad branch here in London."

"You wouldn't tell by the salary," Sally commented, practical as always.

Aaron shrugged. "We're all state employees, you know."

3.

The flat in Mayfair was spacious, well-equipped, and lavishly furnished, putting Sally's favorite couch to shame. Sally was consumed by the new life designed by her husband's employers. As soon as she was informed of the secret of his work, she had to acquaint herself with the rules of being married to a Mossad official. She must be prepared for the day when she would take part in his escape, or any other sudden change to his routine life. Every afternoon after work, she would show up to the embassy for a crash course on the basic rules of Mossad work. As her British friends mingled in their regular bar, Sally gained experience in surveillance, makeup and identity exchange, encrypted communications, and blending into the surroundings. She felt as though the training accentuated her skills, summarized by her father in a sentence that had infuriated her brothers: "Sally is braver and more ambitious than a boy."

Jerry's life became easier when he didn't have to hide anything. He would leave for secret meetings, sometimes using an empty flat, no less plush than their own, nearby. That flat also offered Sally her first task in the service of the Mossad, when one day she was requested to arrive there at five p.m., wearing an evening gown. She left her office an hour before the end of work and rushed home, put on a sleeveless black dress that came down to just below her knees, exposing her shapely legs. She looked in the mirror, wishing her legs were as tanned as they were in her youth, before she relocated to London. At five sharp, she left the house and lightly knocked on the next door.

The door opened. A group of men stood in the foyer and waited for her. She recognized Aaron, standing next to Jerry, and another man she identified from the intelligence classes at the embassy. Aaron signaled to her to come closer. The other men stayed put, their faces to the door. Only then did Sally realize that it wasn't her they were anticipating, but some-one more important. "The King of an African state will arrive here in the coming hour," Aaron explained. "Three women will be escorting him, and we trust you to entertain them." He led Sally to one of the rooms, where a coffee table stood, filled with refreshments. "They'll be here soon," he said and left the room, shutting the door behind him.

Sally felt offended for being separated from the men. She walked along the walls, examining the pictures depicting English landscapes. In the closet, large sheets rested neatly folded, probably to cover the couches when the room wasn't in use. A large window overlooked the street, and she gazed through it. Beneath the building, two long Mercedes cars pulled up. A group of men wearing black suits stepped out of one car and formed a human horseshoe around the only door that hadn't yet opened. Every-one's hands were deep in their jackets, and Sally knew they were holding pistols ready to be drawn. One of the men looked up, and Sally hurriedly leaned back in. A few moments later, she could hear noise in the corridor.

The door opened and three black women entered.

Sally welcomed them in English. They answered politely and then stormed the refreshments, chatting away in an African language. Sally sat down on one of the couches and watched them, amazed. Does the king starve his wives? Judging by their full figures, he didn't. One of the women, who caught her glance, said, "The king was in meetings, and we spent the day shopping. The guards wouldn't agree for us to sit in a restaurant."

One after the other, the women left the table and collapsed on the couches, removing their shoes with a sigh of relief. An uneasy silence ensued. "What have you bought?" Sally asked in English. The woman who spoke earlier answered again. "Everything," she said, adding that the other women didn't speak English.

Silence again. Sally examined the tired women. More than anything, they wished to lie down and fall asleep. She suddenly had an idea. She opened the closet and took out the sheets used to cover the couches. She then pushed the chairs and couches away from the soft carpet, spreading the sheets over it. "Here you go," she said, gesturing to the white expanse and lying down on its corner. They slipped down to the floor and were soon fast asleep.

At night, Jerry told her, "The king's wives were very pleased and refreshed after your hospitality. The king is pleased. I think he'll give us what we ask for."

4.

"Ma," said Roy, and ran to Sally with open arms. "Ma!"

Sally knelt and held him in her arms. "Ima, say Ima." She took him by the hand and led him to the kitchen. Dinner was waiting on the table, and as he ate a slice of tomato with his fingers, she switched on the electric kettle to make a cup of strong English tea.

Two years had passed since they had returned to Israel from England, but her habit of drinking tea instead of coffee lingered on. During the pregnancy with Roy and following his birth, she had tried to cut down on the amount of caffeine she drank, and substituted the tea bag with mint leaves. But as soon as she finished breast-feeding she returned to her old habit—very strong tea with two teaspoons of sugar, a few times a day, both at home and at work.

She heard the door open and close, and then Jerry's footsteps looking for them in Roy's room and then in the living room. "There you are," he said as he entered the kitchen. He kissed them both and sat at the table. "I've received a ridiculous proposal today," he said.

"From one of your female employees?"

Jerry laughed. "No, from my boss. He offered me a three-year mission to a Muslim country, fully under cover."

Sally was experienced enough to know what full cover meant: A different identity and life story, which must be memorized perfectly over months. "And what did you tell him?"

"I said no, of course. I wouldn't last three years without you and Roy."

"And what if we went with you?"

"What?" he almost shouted. It was one of those rare occasions when he lost his cool, and Sally explained quietly, "I mean, I took the basic course in London, and have even proven myself a number of times."

"This time it's completely different," Jerry insisted.

"What must you do there?"

"Forge connections with the regime, especially with the president and administration officials, to thwart an arms deal with a hostile partner, and also—" his voice dropped to a whisper, "—follow the development of their capacity to produce nuclear weapons."

Sally was unimpressed. "It doesn't sound too difficult. You know how good I am at making connections. What's the salary like?"

"Much higher than the one I have now, but—"

"And the living conditions?"

"The population is poor, but the elite and the foreigners have servants, maids, drivers. But don't even think about it. It's unprecedented in the Mossad. An entire family never traveled to a target country."

"I've done many unprecedented things, including marrying you."

Jerry didn't even smile. "We can't go. Full stop. You don't realize how secret the whole thing is. I shouldn't have even told you about the mission," he said, his face turning gloomy.

She kissed him. "Don't worry. You know how good I am at keeping secrets. I know all about my girlfriends' affairs, about my father's business dealings, and I've never told anyone, not even you, right?"

"Your girlfriends have affairs?"

"Not a word," she said. "So are we going?"

"No. It's madness," he said. "You want another child. You'll need a doctor, milk, all sorts of things. It's a primitive country."

"Tell me, don't Bedouin women in the Negev Desert have children raised in tents?" she put her arm on his shoulder. "Look how much it will benefit us: We'll make more money, save for an apartment, we'll have a nanny and be able to have another child, you'll be professionally promoted, and we'll be doing something for our country. I'll help you make connections and we'll have us an adventure."

"*You* love adventures." Jerry groaned. "I really don't."

"You have no choice. The moment you met me you began an adventure." Sally laughed.

5.

A British Airways aircraft began its descent for landing at Benazir Bhutto Airport. Sally looked out the window at the two cities spread out beneath her: modern Islamabad with its straight streets and skyscrapers glistening in the morning sun, and Rawalpindi, which seemed to have sprung up on its own with no discernible order. Sally's face was pale, her hands tightly grasping the seat handles. She stared at Jerry, who seemed calm and secure. Even in him, she knew, uncertainty was lurking. Young Roy, who received a passport with his new name, Roy Travers, was mumbling meaningless syllables of pre-speech. Would he be able to turn those mumbles into English words? Sally wondered for the umpteenth time. For the past six months, only English was spoken around him, and he was never exposed to Hebrew. In any event, could his subconscious be tainted with a few Hebrew words he had picked up?

Queuing at passport control, they were watched by a man with a mustache and gray suit, who stood to the side. "Domestic security," Jerry explained with a whisper. At the counter, a rigid officer wearing khakis examined their passports. "What purpose have you come for, tourism or business?" he asked.

"Business," said Jerry.

"And where's the child's passport?"

"He's registered in my passport," she answered. Her accent was different than her husband's, perhaps because she was born in Vardø, a small town in Norway, as her passport indicated.

The officer flipped a few pages, stamped both passports, and signaled the Travers family through. Roy waved to him with his little hand and said, "Bye bye." The officer's stern face cracked a smile.

Outside the terminal, a car awaited them with a uniformed driver. "Good morning," he said as he opened the door. "I'm Aziz, your driver."

The drive on the highway left Sally very nervous. Jerry was silent as usual. She too, atypically, didn't utter a word. All the doubts and fears she had suppressed suddenly emerged. Pakistan has no Jews, and certainly no Israelis, and yet—so she heard—covert business transactions take place between the countries. What if an Israeli she knew bumped into her here? What if she accidently spoke a word of Hebrew? What if Jerry talked in his sleep, as he sometimes did?

The driver spoke into a walkie-talkie he held in his hand. She recognized a few words in Urdu, which she had begun to study ahead of the trip. She thought he was reporting their arrival, saying he was taking them home. Suddenly she was fearful. What were the chances he was speaking to assassins waiting for them at home? Did the Mossad officials who chose him verify his identity?

The road stretched along a lake. "We have three of these in Islamabad," the driver suddenly said in English. "The government dug them when it established the city. They cool the air in summer. Before, there was nothing here. Just desert."

"Very interesting," Jerry said in the British inflection he'd adopted.

"You can drive there. I know a very nice beach. It's meant for diplomats and foreigners—and only there can you swim in a bikini."

His light-hearted chatter made Sally uneasy. She let Jerry handle the conversation, focusing her gaze on the pinkish hills in the distance. After twenty minutes of a bumpy ride, the car entered the city. It reminded Sally of a huge collection of Lego structures. Everything was well-planned but sterile, featureless. The blue lakes glistened at the edge of every boulevard, and trees were planted along the sidewalks. The car drove into a neighborhood of plush villas and pulled up next to one. A team of eight servants stood at the entrance. Jerry and Sally walked passed them, warmly shaking their hands, as the driver parked the car in the large garage.

Life in Islamabad was comfortable, and the cover designed for the family proved itself. Jerry began his job as the manager of a profitable British import-export company. Sally began developing a social circle to help Jerry accomplish his objective, easily befriending the women of the expatriate community, who socialized with the wives of the country's political leaders. Sally would sleep for only two or three hours a night, listening in bed to the sounds emitted by the house. One night she found a baseball bat in the gym in the basement, and placed it next to her bed. She trusted no one but Jerry, especially not the servants, the food, the laundry deliverymen, or the handymen busy with the air conditioner, swimming pool, or fish pond—Jerry's new hobby.

Roy forgot the little Hebrew he'd learned. Just in case, Sally decided to enroll him at the local nursery, not the international one, fearful that one of the foreigners would pick up any Hebrew words the boy may utter. He was exposed to the local culture, learned the tenets of Islam, and would wake at dawn with the servants, watching them pray, and even reciting the prayers aloud in his high-pitched voice. The love he received from the servants was a guarantee that he would come to no harm, Sally believed. Once, she froze in terror when Roy—waving at her as he rode his little tricycle on the patio—shouted "*Shalom, shalom.*" His nanny and the gardener, standing nearby, burst out laughing. "*Salaam,*" they replied, and he called back "*Salaam, salaam.*"

Sally wouldn't allow her anxieties to run her life. A few weeks after arriving in Islamabad, she returned to her old hobby—tennis—and joined an exclusive club founded back in the days of the British. The young Englishwoman with the strange accent was soon the club favorite. Rumors of her fierce serve made waves, and she found herself invited to many matches, including with men who wished to test their strength against her.

In one of these matches she met Angela, the wife of the Spanish ambassador to Pakistan. The Mediterranean temperament they shared brought the two women together, and soon they became close friends. Angela was the second person, after Jerry, to learn that Sally was pregnant with her second child. Sally, for her part, became Angela's confidante, listening to her perpetual suspicion over her husband's infidelity. The Spanish diplomat would inform his wife of trips he must take across Pakistan on a weekly basis, while rumor had it that he would meet his secretary in lavish Karachi hotels.

Rumors were the fuel that kept the small, diverse elite of Islamabad going. Many of them were revealed to Sally by Angela. Most rumors concerned the husbands' love affairs, but some touched on political or commercial matters. Sally conveyed every shred of information she gleaned from her conversations to Jerry, as she found herself listening to countless tales of pain and misery by women who felt physically and emotionally abandoned. Soon, she realized that these women did not seek clear-cut answers but rather solace. Sally would tell the women that she heard from Jerry that the men spoke tenderly of their wives, were loyal to them, and were engaged in no extramarital affairs. Their gratefulness touched Sally and made her pity them for their loneliness.

Sally too was lonely, but it was different; a couple's loneliness. She shared it with Jerry, who, unlike her, did not join friends for dinners or tennis matches, but traveled only to his office or to social functions where his presence was necessary. His introverted nature only intensified. Unlike Sally, he found it difficult to make new friends, and preferred spending his free time at home, reading, or watching international news channels. At social events, he would usually remain silent as she spoke, sometimes too much. Once, she found herself defending Israel in conversation, and being gently kicked by Jerry under the table. Sometimes, conversation drifted to the Mossad, which people often considered the best intelligence service in the world. Sally would stare at her plate, trying to hide her pride. Often they were served non-kosher food. Sally and Jerry would move the food from one side of the plate to the other, cut it into small pieces as though to eat it, but not taste a bite. They would hide the frog legs in the lettuce salad, or declare they were allergic to clams and other seafood.

In the few times that she got in trouble, Sally's quick thinking rescued her. Once, at a high society fashion show, she sat next to a man who spoke English with a foreign accent. "Where are you from?" he asked.

"England," Sally replied.

"But you have an odd accent."

Her heart beat quickly. She said with confidence, "I'm originally from Norway."

"Norway?" said the man joyously, "I'm from there too. What city?"

"A small town, you've probably never heard of it. Vardø."

"I know Vardø," said the man, and began speaking Norwegian, a language Sally didn't speak a word of. She had to suppress her urge to escape the scene on the spot. Tears of distress welled up in her eyes, and she used them to her advantage. "My parents were killed in a car accident," she said, reciting the main elements of her cover story. "I was given to an aunt in England at a young age. If you speak Norwegian—I'll cry."

The man apologized, but to dismiss any suspicion that may have arisen in him, Sally used a tactic that had always proved itself: "Tell me about yourself," she asked, and indeed he recounted his life story for the rest of the evening.

Once, Angela warned Sally away from one of the society ladies, saying, "She's a quarter Jewish, and you can tell in her personality." Sally held herself back from retorting, "I'm entirely Jewish, and you've chosen me as your best friend." Angela continued her confession. "I hate Jews. I can smell them from a distance."

How she wanted to prove to her, the best friend she had in that distant land, that her hatred of Jews was baseless! She overcame her desire, of course, as she had done many times before. At nights, when she reclaimed her identity as Jewish and Israeli, she despised the senseless hatred some harbored for her people. Her national identity was enhanced more than ever before, and every insult against Israel or Judaism was like a stab in her heart. She couldn't fathom how people could simply hate for no reason. For the first time in her life, she realized that anti-Semitism didn't stem from some kind of flaw in Judaism, but from a sense of fear and inferiority in its enemies. In any event, when she took part in the Christmas celebrations of her Christian friends, or joined Iftar dinners on the nights of Ramadan with her Muslim friends, she felt the commonality between them and the Jews, which strengthened her belief that believers are ultimately similar.

At these festivities, she missed her childhood home. She yearned for the Rosh Hashanah, Passover and Sabbath meals, the ideological arguments that accompanied them, the hymns they would sing afterward, and the quiet that enveloped the village throughout the entire Sabbath. She missed her family so much it hurt.

Roy also sensed the lack of family. When Mossad emissaries would arrive at meetings undercover, Sally and Jerry would present them as "uncles," and he would complain time and again, "Why do all my friends in kindergarten have so many uncles, and only I have uncles that come once and never return?"

Sally was allowed to contact her relatives only every few months, when she would leave the country with Jerry and Roy under the pretext of a ski or safari holiday. They would arrive at the Israeli embassy in a European capital and rush for the telephones. Her parents knew that their daughter and son-in-law were on mission in a faraway land with bad communications, but could never imagine their real living conditions. Sometimes Sally would allow Roy to greet her parents in English, constantly wary of him uttering a word in Urdu. At times she wouldn't risk it, lying to her parents that Roy had stayed behind and was being cared for by a loving nanny. To herself, she thought she could never leave him alone in Islamabad.

Nevertheless, she was forced to do so. When she was due to give birth, Jerry was busy finalizing a big business deal and she traveled alone to the United Kingdom, where she delivered their second son alone in a cold, private hospital. The only person to visit her was a strange, solemn character who asked her what she was planning to call her son. "Michael," she answered.

The next day, the man reappeared and placed an envelope on the night table next to her bed containing a birth certificate and passport for Michael Travers. "*Mazel Tov*," he said, before asking if she planned to circumcise the baby.

"Of course," she said.

"In that case, we'll do it here in the hospital, and if someone—a doctor or nurse—notices the circumcision when you return to Islamabad, tell them that many upper-class English people circumcise their children."

She left the hospital three days after the delivery and moved to a fancy hotel, waiting for Michael to heal from his circumcision. Her only connection to the outside world was her phone calls to Jerry, in which she was never herself but Sally Travers. She regarded that period as a time to examine and hone her skills as a Mossad employee. She wondered how long she could remain in a hiding place without succumbing to the urge to break out for one moment.

As Michael slept in his crib, Sally would sit at the window looking out at the lights of London, remembering the difficult beginning she had there. She never thought of calling Pierre Marin and satisfying her twenty-year urge to thank him personally for changing her life. She repressed these thoughts, imagining the accusing stare she would get from Jerry, had he known.

The monotonous life in the hotel made Sally think about the life she would lead when they return from their mission. She realized that, unlike other women, she could not settle for the routine life revolving around home, children, dog, and work. She aspired for more than that, for meaning. She had to find an occupation that would enrich and satisfy her, fulfill her insatiable need to live and experience adventures, while meeting fascinating people in exotic places.

It was the first time she realized that a regular life bored her; that the sense of adventure that accompanied her since childhood stemmed from a need to grab life and control it, to experience thrills, to take risks. That was why she followed Jerry to England without even knowing if he wanted her; that was why she insisted he would be her husband—even though he hesitated and tried to cancel the wedding—and that was why she left for Pakistan.

She returned to their home in Islamabad, aware of her motives but also concerned. Now they were a family of four whose cover could be blown at any moment of absentmindedness. Her fear of falling prey to anxiety made her want to test her boundaries at moments of uncertainty. One day, she and Jerry were invited to a couples tennis match with the chief of Pakistans intelligence, General Muhammad al-Sharif, and his tennis partner. Sally and Jerry were better players than their rivals, but every time they "lost" a ball that landed in their court and would have reduced their score, the ball collectors would shout "out." Sally complained vocally, but the ball collectors insisted. She stood her ground until a severe stare from Jerry made her swallow her pride and let their rivals win. After the game, the two couples dined at the tennis club.

Al-Sharif was swollen with pride for defeating a European couple, and Sally felt the need to come close to the fire. When the conversation drifted to the frequent terror attacks that took place in the country, and the general boasted that a number of them were thwarted thanks to information he had extracted from suspects, Sally asked him about his interrogation methods. The general smiled slyly, looking straight into her eyes. "Believe me," he said, "I pity those who fall into our hands. We are more ruthless than the Nazis."

That night, Sally opened the special hiding place where they kept their escape passports, and moved them to her purse, along with a map indicating their escape route. The darkness outside scared her. Who knew which forces were lurking there, scheming against her and her family? She lay awake all night, sensing that something terrible was going to happen to them. At dawn, she returned everything to its original place and fell asleep.

6.

General al-Sharif lived in a fortified concrete structure in Rawalpindi, where many of the headquarters of the Pakistani army were located. He felt protected by the tens of thousands of soldiers and officers, on all of whom he collected information in his giant archive. When al-Sharif threw a party, everyone knew that despite the religious ban on importing alcoholic drinks to Pakistan, alcohol would flow. Women would not wear veils covering their heads and necks, and no one would retire to pray Isha, the evening prayer that devout Muslims would never miss.

It was also clear that you couldn't refuse al-Sharif's invitation. Ever since Jerry and Sally Travers began playing tennis with him, they were invited to every party the general held, and those happened at least once a month. Jerry was satisfied with that. Pakistan's financial elite hobnobbed with the regime heads and the diplomatic community, and the information exchanged nonchalantly was highly valuable from an intelligence point of view. Sally was worried. Al-Sharif was ruthless and unpredictable, and the looks he gave her sent chills down her spine. She was unsure if they expressed interest in her femininity or an investigation he was carrying out on her family. She felt that one wrong move could bring disaster upon them.

At the parties she tried to enjoy the diverse food, and even get carried away by the fake joviality that the general's men tried to create using upbeat music, colorful lightbulbs, and exotic flowers in crystal vases. But the waiters, wearing traditional clothes and stealthily moving through the crowd, reminded her of reality. Sally could swear, by looking at them, that they understood the cacophony of languages being spoken at the party, taking mental notes of what was being said. She made a point of not speaking too much, and was glad that she and Jerry were not seated with the foreign diplomats but with the businesspeople. That way she was distanced from Angela, who was especially chatty and inquisitive after ingesting obscene quantities of Southern Comfort.

It was at one of these parties that Sally experienced her worst anxiety attack since arriving in Pakistan. The nightmare she had feared since first landing in Islamabad materialized. A moment after being seated at the table, Sally noticed a woman at the next table wearing a long skirt and a headscarf. She recognized her immediately: It was Vivian Moyal, the wife of a millionaire that Jerry and Sally had met in London, who had since gone bankrupt in a scandal that captured newspaper headlines worldwide. "We need to get out of here," she whispered to Jerry.

"Why?"

"Vivian Moyal," she said, discreetly signaling toward her.

Jerry stared at her, then a thin smile appeared on his face. "And do you know who's standing next to her?" he asked.

Sally saw a tall man wearing an elegant suit deep in conversation with Vivian. He looked like he was in his mid-fifties. His hair was graying and his entire presence exuded importance, power, status and wealth. Extreme wealth. "I don't know him. Actually, I do. I think I saw him once…"

"You saw him in a picture. It's Pierre Marin."

Sally suppressed a cry of joy. Jerry held her wrist tightly. "Don't even think of going over there. Vivian will recognize you, and you won't be able to tell Marin anything anyway. Now we'll withdraw in an organized fashion. Squirm."

That was an agreed-upon code word that signaled to her to display visible signs of discomfort so that they could leave places where they'd better not remain. Sally held her stomach with a look of pain on her face. Jerry got up from his seat and smiled courteously at the guests around the table. "My wife isn't feeling well," he apologized, as Sally pointed to her stomach and whispered to the women around her, "Since the delivery, you know…"

As they were on their way out, Angela stood up from her table and approached her. "You're leaving so early? Problems with the children?"

Sally reapplied the suffering look. "It hurts," she said. "If it continues this way I'll have to fly back to London for treatment."

Angela stroked her arm sympathetically. "I'll call you tomorrow," she said.

A bearded man dressed in black and wearing a large white skullcap approached Pierre Marin and Vivian and said something that made Vivian burst out laughing. His bushy, unkempt beard and white cap, the *taqiyah*, made him look like a devout Muslim. But something about him set him apart from the Pakistani men that Sally met, something different yet familiar. She knew she had already met him. But where? At a different party? Maybe at some ceremony? She focused on his eyes. They stirred a distant, vague memory in her.

Angela turned to her and said, "See why I can't stand Jews? Look at them. The woman is as noisy as a fish saleswoman in the market and the man next to her, Pierre Marin, controls the entire energy market of Morocco and mines in North Africa. Now he's come to milk Pakistan too." She wavered a little, her breath smelling of liqueur. "The third one is also Jewish. They call him the Honorable Rabbi Abraham Ben David. Were it not for his American passport and ties with Pierre Marin he'd never be let in here. It's a scandal..."

Sally's feigned suffering became real discomfort. She was offended as a Jew. "Look—" she started.

"We need to go," Jerry apologized, and grabbed her arm.

In the car, Sally suddenly recalled. "Did you see the rabbi standing next to Pierre Marin?" she asked Jerry excitedly.

"Yeah, so what?"

"I know who he is. I remember. He's no rabbi, just a regular laborer who worked in the garage at the nearby *moshav* to ours. His name was Dadoshvili and he cheated my older brother, Avner, out of thousands of shekels. He replaced the clutch cable in his car and lied that he'd replaced the entire clutch. He had no beard or large skullcap back then, but his eyes are the same."

"Sometimes you surprise me with your overconfidence. How can you be sure that the rabbi standing next to Marin is this Dado-something who tricked your brother? You only saw him once in your life!"

She leaned on his arm steering the wheel. "Jerry, you know I—"

"We'll have an accident because of you," he hissed.

She let go. "You know I never forget people. His eyes—I remember them." Her voice rose in frustration. "I'm sure he's conning Pierre Marin right now, and I don't know whether Vivian Moyal is cooperating with him. They say her husband left her penniless and now she's probably desperate and capable of anything. I must warn Marin. It's the least I can do to repay him."

Jerry's face was severe, reproaching. "Promise me you won't do a thing before our mission ends."

"I'll see..."

"Promise," Jerry demanded. "Think of our children!"

"I promise," Sally said sheepishly, knowing that the urge to call Marin would not leave her until they returned home in eight months' time.

7.

The Tel Aviv that the Travers family—now reclaiming their surname Amir—returned to was different. During the years they had been away, high-rises had sprung up along the Ayalon expressway, and many cafés had opened in the city's south, filled with bustling activity.

During her first days in town, Sally felt as though she was wandering a foreign city. This wasn't just because of the changes that had taken place, but also due to her difficulty to shake the habits she had acquired in Pakistan. She hesitated to enter taxis whose drivers seemed untrustworthy, collected her children from school and kindergarten herself, and examined through the peephole every person who rang her doorbell.

Jerry acclimated faster, leaving for work at his new position—which was much more senior than the one he had before Pakistan—on his first week back. Sally got a job as computing manager at an insurance company, but felt bored from day one. She missed life on the edge, which she experienced in Pakistan, and realized once again that she could not lead a normal lifestyle. Pakistan had entrenched the "bug" as an intrinsic part of her personality, turning her from a software engineer to a determined, qualified secret agent.

The emptiness she felt was compounded by the constant need to warn Pierre Marin of the harm of the imposter rabbi. She scoured the Internet looking for details on Ben David, searching his original name first: Dadoshvili. The first result she came across was a criminal court verdict concerning fraud in a car sale. She delved into the indictment, which described a promise Dadoshvili made to sell a new Mercedes to a businessman for half the price, claiming it had been confiscated by customs and could be bought by tender. He was also accused of money laundering and tax evasion. The judge had sentenced the accused to three years in prison. There were also photographs of Dadoshvili. One displayed him clean-shaven and wearing a T-shirt that read "I love New York;" the other showed him wearing prison uniform during his appeal. Other than that, there was no mention of him.

She changed the search words to "Rabbi Abraham Ben David" and got dozens of results. The rabbi was a public relations master. His photos—him wearing a beard, black clothes, and a Hassidic black hat—appeared in dozens of websites, Facebook pages, and articles. In some of the photos, he was standing next to children, probably bar mitzvah boys. In others, he was shaking hands with Israeli tycoons, some famous and some less so. Some images captured him with people she didn't know, although judging by their clothes and the scenery, they were extremely rich.

To her surprise, his telephone number and address were available on the online telephone directory. She held herself back from calling. First, she had to better understand his relationship with Pierre Marin. No search containing both their names led to any results, and Sally realized that Vivian Moyal was the only source of possible information on Ben David. She typed "Vivian Moyal." Google immediately provided a chain of gossip articles, some more flattering than others, as well as photos of the woman. Unlike the rabbi, Moyal's phone number was nowhere to be found. She paced the apartment, deep in thought. Finally, she picked up the phone and dialed a long series of numbers.

"Advocacy Inc.," the receptionist answered.

"I'd like to speak to the press officer, please."

She was transferred without any questions asked. "My name is Sally Amir," she stated. "My husband, Jerry Amir, served with your financial department about twenty years ago. In one of the events you held, we met a woman, Vivian Moyal, and I'd like to contact her and invite her to a charity ball."

"I'm new here," the press officer replied, "but I'm sure she's registered here somewhere..." Sally could hear the sound of typing on a keyboard. "Do you know where she lives?"

"London, I assume."

Some more typing.

"Shalom Moyal," Sally remembered. "That was her husband's name."

"Shalom Moyal," repeated the press officer. "Yes, the entry is on his name, and it does mention his wife as Vivian Moyal. For some reason, they've stopped inviting them. Their home number was deleted from the registry, but there's another number here, which I believe is a mobile."

Sally typed the number on her phone, and as soon as she hung up with the embassy, pressed "send." The dial tone was delayed, and Sally knew the conversation was roaming between networks. A sharp sound was heard when Vivian's phone rang somewhere in the world, and Sally wondered where she was: A Paris hotel? A London flat? A man's home in New York?"

"Hallo?" Vivian answered in her French accent.

"Vivian, it's Sally. We met in London a long—"

"Sally, of course. How could I forget?! Beautiful Sally, the woman of Jerry from the embassy..." She spoke as though she was retrieving the information from a database. "You know, something very bizarre happened to me. It was... I don't remember when, but never mind. Anyway, I was in Islamabad at a party. You know how it is, I always travel and there was a conference there on energy. Oil and all that.... But what I wanted to tell you is that over there, at the next table, there was a woman who looked so much like you. It was unbelievable! And the man next to her also reminded me of Jerry, just a bit balder. I wanted to talk to her, but she suddenly disappeared... I almost called you in Israel, but forgot your surname. There's no chance you were in Pakistan, is there?"

"None at all," Sally said confidently. "Where are you now?"

"Hilton Tel Aviv. I came to the memorial service of my brother who used to live here in Kfar Saba. I'm so glad you called. What do you say we meet?"

There was nothing Sally wanted more. "Gladly," she said.

"The ceremony is tomorrow, but I'll be free from five. We could eat something here at the hotel."

"I'll be there tomorrow at five," Sally quickly said.

The following day she traveled to Bney Brak. She drove slowly along the main road until she noticed a fashion shop. In the window, headless manikins were dressed in modest blouses and long, slim dresses. Inside, heavyset women were trying on larger versions of the same clothes. Sally pointed at a navy blue skirt on one of the manikins and said, "I'd like that one."

The saleswoman measured Sally's body by sight. "We have none in stock. It's a size no one asks for here."

"I'll buy the one in the window," she replied.

"From display?"

Sally nodded.

The saleswoman pulled the manikin into the shop and returned with the skirt in hand. "Would you like to try it on?"

Sally identified the particular stitching of Chanel. She looked at the label. The skirt was indeed exactly her size. "No need, just pack it," she said. "Do you have a headscarf?"

"Full size or half?" asked the saleswoman.

Sally hesitated. Her family was religiously observant, but the women didn't cover their hair and she didn't know the rules. "Half," she said. An array of scarves was shown to her, and Sally chose a blue one to match the skirt.

When she returned home, Sally was wearing a long-sleeved shirt buttoned to the top. She then put on the skirt and low-heeled shoes, perfect Gucci imitations she bought in Hong Kong. Her costume was complete with the headscarf, which covered her hair that was tied behind her head. At the last moment she put her personal affairs in a handbag that resembled a Hermes bag. In Vivian's eyes, she knew, people were measured by the brands they wore. When she entered the elevator, a woman in her thirties looked back at her from the mirror, unaffected by the extremely modest garb.

8.

The lobby of the Hilton Hotel was packed. Beyond the large windows the Mediterranean glistened, and in the hotel soft and featureless music played in the background. Vivian was already waiting for her, sitting on a couch. She too was dressed modestly, but ostentatiously. Her corpulent body was dressed in a long-sleeved, shiny blue dress. A diamond the size of a corn kernel rested on her chest, tied to an almost invisible necklace. A similar sized diamond decorated her finger, attached to a thick golden ring.

Sally moved toward her, treading cautiously on the thick carpet. Vivian stood up, embracing her in a cloud of heavy perfume. "Sally, my dear, my friend, I'm so happy to seeing you!"

"To see you," Sally corrected her, and immediately regretted it. She wasn't here to teach Vivian Hebrew.

"Come, I ordered us a table." Vivian took her by the arm and led her to the café on the edge of the lobby. Vivian's mobile phone rang but she didn't respond, or even check who was calling.

As they sat across from each other, Sally couldn't take her eyes off the diamond on Vivian's chest. "I see you to watch my diamond." Vivian smiled. "It's nothing. I have bigger ones. Solly—I mean Shalom, my husband—left me nothing when he went bankrupt. But the jewelry he bought me remained."

"You can't eat jewelry," Sally wryly commented.

"I have people who take care of food," Vivian replied.

Sally knew who Vivian was referring to. Everyone knew about Vivian's connections to the King of Morocco, who kept a number of mistresses across the globe. Vivian too was not overly discreet. She bent over to Sally and said, "You probably know who—the King of Morocco. Yes, none other. But you can never tell anyone."

"Good for you," Sally said, flattering her.

"He doesn't just help with money, but also with business. What do you want in Morocco I will bring you. Oil, phosphates, textile, hotel." She put her hand on Sally's arm. "You know, I was thinking today, we can do a lot of business together. You are smart and know languages and understand money, and I bring connections. We also both believe in God and keep his commandments, which means we will not cheat each other. You only found God recently, right? You still have red nail polish on your fingers."

Sally looked at Vivian's fingers. Her nails were well-kept, but covered in transparent nail polish. "Yes, I—" Sally stuttered, "How can I put it? I suddenly realized…"

"We are all like this," said Vivian. "For me it also take time until I see light."

"I haven't seen it yet," confessed Sally. "I need guidance. That's why I called you. I remembered you always knew rabbis and righteous people."

"Great!" exclaimed Vivian. "I have exactly the man you have need. A great rabbi, a holy man. He helps many people around the world, in America, Europe, and even Japan. Big people, rich people..."

"Like who?"

"Did you heard of Pierre Marin?"

"Yes, he's very rich."

"Also very difficult and closed. He only listen to the rabbi I send him. This rabbi help him a lot in life. Save him from sickness. Alone, without operation. Only by power God give him. You can believe this?"

"That's exactly the kind of rabbi I need."

"I give you his cellular number. Private-private. Only me and maybe few others know it. Tell him I send you."

"Does he live in America?"

"No, here in Beersheba. Very modest man. Live in small house with wife and six children. You cannot go to him, he come to meet you here in Hilton." She leaned over again. "And if you need something from Marin, also this the rabbi can make. Marin know he have great spiritual power, and believes every word he say. He had very bad sickness, and the rabbi said him not to go to operation, and prayed for him. What do you think happen? Marin is completely cure! His son have emotional problems, you know, and the rabbi also cure him, and now Marin wife also become crazy, she wants to go from him, and the rabbi keep her with him..."

The admiration on Vivian Moyal's face when she spoke of the rabbi didn't surprise Sally. She also considered her naïve. But what would cause a lucid and experienced businessman like Pierre Marin to view a con man as a saint?

"So let's make partnership together," Vivian continued. "Marin wants to build stations electrical in Pakistan, and I tell him, 'I can make that.' King of Morocco send me to Islamabad and arrange that everybody talk to me, even the president. We already make first meeting with Marin in Geneva. Not so much come from this, but I have plan for him. Many plans. I just need help, Rabbi Ben David to influence him from one side and someone like you who know business on the other."

The nature of Ben David, Vivian, and Marin's connections were now clear to Sally, as was her need to warn Marin of them—the sooner the better. But Vivian had no intention of letting her go. "I give you fifty percent of all we make. What you say?"

"We've just returned from our assignment and I'd like to dedicate myself to the family and to running a kosher household. Later, I'll gladly join you. In the meantime, please give me the rabbi's number."

Vivian's face immediately assumed an expression of disinterest. "Too bad," she said, "I so need a partner, and when you call—"

"I'm sorry," Sally replied. "So, the rabbi's number?"

"Actually, I'm not sure he is for you. He is big and holy, and you only begin to become stronger. Maybe look someone in Hibbat Brak."

"Just anyone in Hibbat Brak won't do. If you want me to become more dedicated, arrange a meeting between us."

"Okay, I arrange," said Vivian in a tone that left Sally sure that no such meeting would take place. She stood up. "Take care," she said, "and don't forget me."

"Yes, yes," said Vivian. Her phone rang again. This time she took the call, ignoring Sally.

9.

As soon as she stepped into the car, Sally removed the headscarf and opened the window, allowing the wind to blow through her hair. At home, she stuffed the long skirt and modest blouse deep into her closet. She made herself a coffee and thought about what Vivian had told her. From the outset, she had known that Ben David entrapped rich men, including Marin. His connection to Vivian Moyal wasn't yet clear to her, but she had no doubt that regarding Marin, Vivian was involved; busy planning a way to take a chunk out of his fortune.

How did the two succeed in entrapping such a shrewd businessman? How did they maintain Marin's dependence on the imposter rabbi? She remembered Vivian's words: "What he tells Marin—Marin does." She couldn't rule out the possibility that Vivian was the one to weave the ties between Ben David and his victims, which she knew through her ex-husband or her current lover, the King of Morocco. Had she also activated the Moroccan secret service to inquire about Marin? If so, perhaps they had uncovered a secret that made him submit to them?

The thought that Morocco's secret service was involved in the affair terrified her for a moment. She remembered the Pakistani general al-Sharif and the balls he held, and especially the conversation where he told her, "We're worse than the Nazis." The reputation of Morocco's intelligence agency was no better. During the course that she took ahead of their mission, she learned how it made a Moroccan opposition leader, Mehdi Ben Barka, disappear after he was kidnapped from a Paris café. He was killed, his body melted in a bath of acid.

The next moment, her fear had dissipated, replaced by a sense of responsibility. Sally felt again, for the umpteenth time, that she must warn Marin away from those who had taken control of his life. To do so, however, she must show him solid proof.

It was time to make contact with Ben David. She wrote down his address in Beersheba and typed it into a road navigator on her phone. The program immediately displayed the street number and the house. "I met Vivian Moyal and am leaving tomorrow for Beersheba to see where Ben David lives," she told Jerry when he returned home.

"Tomorrow is Friday," he said with surprise.

"It's the only day I don't have to be at work," she reminded him. "I'll cook tonight, clean the house tomorrow morning for the Sabbath, and then leave."

"Just be careful," Jerry said in a worried tone.

"Why? What danger could come from a manipulative woman and an imposter rabbi?"

"Imposters can become dangerous when their disguise is torn from them and their plans thwarted, and you have no experience with such things. You haven't even—"

"I haven't served in the army. I know," Sally said, annoyed. "But how many women who did serve would have withstood the pressure of living in a target country, under cover, making connections with anyone and everyone, and even giving birth without being exposed? You know what, maybe not having served in the army makes me want to prove I can do things that women who served cannot!"

"All right." Jerry relented. "You've proven it all. I take back the army business. You don't need to prove anything, certainly not to me."

"I need to prove things *to myself,*" Sally replied. "My father always used to say that man must aspire to mend the world, and effect positive change for his environment, his community, and the people of Israel. He believes there is always hope for improvement, and that's how he raised me to think."

"This world is irreparable," Jerry moaned. "I'm going to rest."

10.

She left town before noon, when Jerry retired to the bedroom to read the weekend newspapers and the house was clean and filled with the smell of food. A cloud of desert dust rested over Beersheba and the navigator sent her car to a neighborhood of small, modest houses, as Vivian described. However, the rabbi's home could hardly be described as modest. It protruded into a public garden located behind it, and grew to become a mansion. A high wall surrounded the house, and beyond it the sound of children's laughter could be heard. Sally parked her car at a certain distance and walked back. When she passed by the gate, she noticed a surveillance camera attached to it. She crossed the street to the opposite sidewalk and walked past the house again, far from the camera. Now she noticed more details: A large mailbox with no name, an intercom panel, and metal spikes atop the wall, meant to prevent climbing. Even the house number affixed to the wall by the municipality was pulled off, leaving a light square. *Whoever comes here*, she thought, *knows his way to the house even without identifying signs.*

What now? Should she enter? For a moment, she thought of ringing and asking for an address in the area. Then she decided to say that her car had broken down and ask for help. She ruled out both ideas. No one would believe that she decided to choose the least inviting house on the block. She also decided she must not be exposed to the eyes of the rabbi and his family at such an early stage of her investigation. Her eye caught sight of a gray communications box located at the edge of the well, next to a thick tree. She removed her shoes and hoisted herself onto the box, and from there to the tree. Her childhood experience assisted her as she quickly climbed to a branch in the middle of the tree, hidden in its foliage.

When she looked down at the yard, she was surprised to find a swimming pool surrounded by a large lawn. Three children, two boys and a girl, played in the water. A woman of about forty-five, wearing a bikini, exited the house carrying a tray with sandwiches. She called to the children to come to the table, situated on the porch. The children rushed to her and their voices reached Sally, who looked at the spectacle with amazement. No rabbi would allow his wife to wear such an immodest swimsuit, all the more so an imposter rabbi, who could leave no doubt as to his level of devoutness.

She was sorry she hadn't brought a camera and did her best to capture the mother and her children in the lens of her mobile phone. Then she bent down and peeked into the home's interior. She could see a large dining room table, a sitting room, and a muted television, flashing. There were no candlesticks waiting to be lit and no scent of cooked food for the Sabbath. Evening began to fall. The wife and her children entered the home. Sally called Jerry. "I'm late," she said in a low voice. "I'm staking out Ben David's house. Something very interesting is happening there."

"Take care of yourself," said Jerry. "And don't worry. I'll eat dinner with the children."

Friday night dinner was a meaningful event at the Amir household, an opportunity for a family gathering often joined by Jerry's mother, Sally's parents, and her two brothers. Sometimes they would spend it with her parents in the *moshav*. Her father would make *Kiddush*, break bread, and oversee the traditional singing of "Shalom Aleichem," sharing words of Torah with the guests. Sally was saddened, but her sense of duty was stronger. She was also curious about Ben David's strange world.

A white Lexus approached the house. When it stopped in front of the gate, a powerful spotlight shone down on it, next to the camera. In the bright light Sally recognized Ben David, who stepped out of the car on the driver's side. His head was uncovered and he was dressed in everyday clothes. Only the beard remained from the rabbi's persona.

Vivian Moyal stepped out of the back seat. Her long dress was now replaced with a short skirt exposing her knees and a short-sleeved shirt. The rabbi's wife, who changed into jeans and a light blouse, approached her. The two kissed like old friends. Both women and the rabbi entered the house and immediately the light in the living room was switched on, and Sally could see them sitting on the couch. The rabbi squeezed in between them. Vivian clung to his body and put her hand on his thigh. The three seemed close, as though safeguarding a secret. The rabbi's wife stood up and served dinner. Sally couldn't identify the food, but Vivian and the rabbi were eating their dishes with chopsticks. Was their Friday night dinner ordered at a Chinese restaurant? Sally wondered.

11.

As she sped back to Tel Aviv on the dark Highway 6, Sally's thoughts came to a realization: The fraud and impersonation the rabbi thrived on were not meant to deceive victims living in close vicinity to him, but rather those who lived far away from Beersheba and could never know that not only was Ben David not a rabbi, he wasn't even religiously observant, and certainly not holy.

The trip to Beersheba didn't answer any of Sally's questions, only lengthened the list. But there was a way to solve the riddle, and peeking from atop a tree wasn't good enough. She would have to find a pro to work with her. She dialed Jerry. "Have you eaten?" she asked.

"Yes, it was very tasty. We saved you a serving of every dish."

Sally laughed. "Don't you know I don't eat my cooking? Tasting makes me lose my appetite."

"You'll see. By the time you return you'll be so hungry you'll—"

Sally cut him off. "I need you to help me."

"Oh well." Jerry let out a fake sigh. "That's my role in the world."

"I need your experience. I found Ben David and staked out his house. Something there is very wrong. His wife walks around in a bikini, he doesn't wear rabbi's clothes, and he drives on *Shabbat*. Guess who else drives with him?"

"Vivian Moyal," Jerry said without hesitation.

"Well, you were always smart."

"Did you take pictures?"

"Only on my phone. I didn't bring a camera. I didn't believe everything would be so exposed and cheeky."

"Okay. All you need to do is give the photos to Marin and your account with him will be closed."

"It's not enough," insisted Sally. "Photos mean nothing these days. You can always claim they were Photoshopped. I must know more, understand what they're planning, who is collaborating with them, and especially how they make Marin admire than con man Dadoshvili. When I met Vivian, she said she had a plan for Marin. I need to know those plans."

Jerry was silent, and Sally knew he was remembering a list of people he knew. "There is a way," he said finally. "We'll talk when you get here."

She spent the rest of the drive impatient. "Jerry!" she called when she entered the house.

He approached her.

"What's your idea?" She asked him in a whisper.

"You can speak normally, or even shout. The children are asleep."

"Tell me while I make coffee." She took him by the sleeve and dragged him to the kitchen. "Do you want some too?"

He shook his head. "You were right to say on the phone that photos don't prove anything now. You need quality evidence, which comes in only two forms: Testimony or eavesdropping."

"I won't get anyone's testimony."

"And eavesdropping is a criminal offense," Jerry quickly continued.

Sally thought for a moment. "But that's the only way open to me."

"Then let go of this project. Don't get involved."

"I have to."

"You owe it to Marin. I understand. But Marin is just an excuse. He is a rich and powerful man. He'll manage. What motivates you is the need for action, for thrills. Why don't you join a hiking club, learn to sail a yacht, or volunteer with battered women? You can get your thrills without breaking the law."

"I'm not looking for thrills. I'm looking for justice. I can't stand the fact that a Jew would cheat another Jew in such a despicable manner."

"Again this mending the world business?" Jerry spread out his arms in frustration. Sally could identify. He also couldn't stand injustice, but his passive and conservative personality prevented him from crossing the line to thwart it. She took his hand and said, "Do you think it's right that a Jew who donates and helps out other Jews so much would be the victim of fraud with no one to assist him?"

"I don't understand you," said Jerry, "I just don't. Let's say he helps Jews, and that one Jew pretends to be a rabbi and defrauds him, why do you care so much?"

"What is a Jew for you?"

"Oh, come on..."

"No, tell me, what is a Jew?"

"The regular things: circumcision, Yom Kippur, Hanukkah, Purim..."

"So for me," declared Sally, "being Jewish is being part of a big family, with all the responsibilities involved in that: Mutual assistance, love, and concern for each other despite the differences. That's how we survived over three thousand years and that's our uniqueness. Marin understands that, and therefore is so generous toward the needy. Doesn't he deserve some generosity on my part?"

"Speak to your father," suggested Jerry. "If he approves of this, I'll help you."

Sally phoned her parents' home and put the call on loudspeaker. "Yes?" came her mother's singsong voice answer on the other end of the line.

"Hello, Mom. I need Dad."

"Has something happened?" Her mother's voice sounded worried.

"No, not at all. It's a principled disagreement between Jerry and me."

"Okay. I'll call him," said her mother with relief.

Sally listened to the familiar sounds of her parents' home, and the approaching steps of her father. His deep voice sounded from the speaker. "What happened, my girl?"

She told him the whole story, and her father answered without hesitation. "In tractate Baba Kamma of the Talmud it says that there are seven types of thieves. The primary thief is the one who tricks other people. This rabbi steals people's trust and you must cause him to stop. If you don't do so, you'd be taking part in his deceit. In addition, there could be danger to that man Marin's life, or to the life of his wife or children. You must act as is written in the book of Leviticus: 'You must not stand idly by when your neighbor's life is at stake.'"

"But it's dangerous."

"'Agents of good deeds are never harmed,'" he quoted from the Talmud.

"And I'll have expenses…"

"Heaven will repay you."

"So you support me acting?"

"Of course," said her father. "Ever since you were young, I taught you that man must mend the world and bring about redemption. Go, my girl. Right this wrong."

Sally bid her father goodbye and hung up. She stared at Jerry, who sank into one of his protracted silences. "Okay," he said suddenly. "I'll connect you to someone."

12.

Her name was Diana, and according to Jerry, she had served in a number of target states, gathering experience in surveillance and eavesdropping. They arranged a meeting at Café Brown in Tzameret Park. Diana identified Sally in the split second she stopped to survey her surroundings. They both arrived early. "Location security? That's what exposed me?" Sally laughed. Mossad agents maintained a strict rule: They must arrive for every meeting fifteen minutes early and carefully examine the location and the people occupying it.

"Exactly, location security," Diana confirmed with an expression of someone handing out a secret password. She had a long, thin body, large brown eyes that looked at the world with the amazement of a child, and black hair in a bob cut. "So, what's going on? Jerry told me you have something interesting."

"Where do we know each other from?" Sally asked, staring at Diana inquisitively.

Diana obviously expected the question. "I've worked in eavesdropping for a few years. When I married I switched to the research department and was an analyst with Jerry. Now please explain to me what's going on and—"

"Wait. A few more details. When did you retire?"

"A year ago," Diana said. "I came to the conclusion that this job is too draining, pulling me away from my husband and children, but—"

"—but now you miss it," Sally said.

"Exactly. The children are grown, my husband is busy, and I feel empty and bored." She lowered her voice. "I even considered spicing up our sex life. Swinging and the like, you know…"

"I don't know," Sally confessed, "but I do understand your need for excitement. For me, my motivation to act is different. I'm trying to prevent harm from someone who once helped me in the most crucial moment of my life, when I was young. Without his help, I wouldn't be who I am today."

Diana leaned forward. "Tell me what you mean exactly. Jerry sounded very mysterious on the phone."

"OK," said Sally. "But first I need you to promise me that even if you don't join me, everything I say remains between us."

"I promise," Diana said, and Sally told her everything she knew about Ben David, Vivian Moyal, and Pierre Marin. She omitted the story of their mission in Pakistan, though at times she suspected Diana knew something about it. Finally she said, "So I need information that can only be obtained through eavesdropping, and Jerry said you're the best. You don't have to agree if it scares you, but remember you promised to say nothing about this."

"Nothing scares me," said Diana. "I only have a few questions. Firstly, who do you work for?"

"I work for no one. Just as I told you, this is a debt of honor."

"And when you find out what this rabbi is up to, what will you do?"

"I'll give the information to Marin."

"You said he's hard to reach."

"I'll find a way. Financially, you have nothing to worry about. I will pay you by the hour, or a lump sum, whatever you prefer."

"As I told you, I need action. On the other hand, I hate to be a sucker. I'll help you with the eavesdropping, but I want you to promise me that if and when you get money, you'll think of me too."

"I promise," said Sally, "though I have to warn you that even if money is offered to me, I wouldn't want it. This is a good deed."

"So ask for expenses only—" laughed Diana "—and write me down as your first expense."

13.

"There are several ways to eavesdrop," Diana explained in the car en route to Beersheba. "You can listen in from a distance using a directional microphone, you can plant microphones in the home or the office, you can connect to their computer or mobile phone through the Internet, and you can tap into the home telephone line, which is the easiest thing to do. I suggest we start with that. First we need to get a motorcycle."

"We need a motorcycle to eavesdrop on a phone line?"

"We do." Diana laughed. "Can't do without it."

On the main street of Beersheba, a fabric sign hung between two dusty green tamarisk trees: "Sale! Motorcycle rentals for 40 shekels a day." Diana stopped the car at a distance from the shop. "We'll walk there by foot," she said, "so that they don't identify us by the car." She was obviously enjoying every moment. "Do you have a license to drive these things?" she asked Sally as they stood in front of a row of motorcycles parked on the sidewalk.

"No."

"Then I'll drive," Diana said.

"Do you have a license?"

"No, but I know how to work them."

The word "to work" amused Sally. She drove her car to the rabbi's house and Diana "worked" the motorcycle with skill probably acquired in some course. She drove slowly, used her hand to signal at every turn, and never overtook cars like other motorcycle riders who surrounded them like bees. Suddenly she drove onto a sidewalk next to a hardware shop. Sally pulled over and waited. A few minutes later, Diana emerged carrying a heavy chain, a padlock, and a plastic bag containing screwdrivers, pliers, and pincers. Diana threw everything into the car and returned to the motorcycle. Near the rabbi's home, she stopped next to Sally and said, "Now we need to find a communications box."

"We already have," Sally said, pointing to the metal cabinet next to the tree she had spent hours on the previous Friday. Diana parked the motorcycle next to it, pulled two files out of her bag, and stuck them into the lock in a professional manner. She wriggled the files for a few seconds and the cabinet door opened effortlessly. "What is the rabbi's phone number?"

Sally read it off the note in her hand. Diana connected and disconnected wires for five minutes and then pulled a dark, square object out of her bag, connected it to something in the box, and slammed the door shut. She placed another device in the compartment under the motorcycle seat, and locked it too. Finally, she knelt next to the back wheel and put the chain through it. "Never the front wheel," she said, huffing and puffing. "It's easy to take it apart and put the motorcycle on a tow truck or even a van. To detach the back wheel, though, you need to take apart the entire motorcycle."

She tied the chain around the tree trunk, fastened the padlock, and stood up. "That's it. Let's move," she said, walking slowly toward the car. When they strolled through the Old City in search of a restaurant Diana remembered from her days in the army, she explained, "The device in the cabinet will broadcast to the receiver in the motorcycle, which will also record the conversations. The batteries in both devices should last for a week. In six days we'll come back and replace them."

Sally replied with a hesitant "Yes." Another plan was already brewing in her mind.

14.

The fork stopped in midair, above Jerry's plate. "You want to do *what*?" he asked with alarm.

"Call Marin."

"You have no proof against Ben David," Jerry said in a solemn tone. "Without proof, it's libel."

"I took a photo of him, and in a week there will be phone calls too. What more do I need?"

"You can't ruin someone's life and claim he's a con just because he doesn't observe the religious commandments, and once—when he worked at the garage—tricked your brother. I'm also not sure the telephone surveillance will produce anything. It's possible that he's careful, or doesn't speak on the phone about things that can put him in danger. You need recordings of meetings, surveillance, photocopies of documents and letters, bank transactions—all the things a serious investigation firm can produce."

"In that case we should find a serious investigation firm. Do you know of any?"

"I know a few. Many Mossad veterans started firms. But such an investigation would cost a fortune. Who will pay?"

"I don't know yet. You heard Dad: I will be repaid by heaven. Let's get the ball rolling and see what happens. I don't need a long investigation; I need no more than a day or two."

Jerry shrugged. "Well, there's Jacob, our friend from London."

"Jacob Lavie started an investigation firm?"

"The largest in the country."

"Large isn't good. He'll give the job to someone junior, a beginner maybe, and then the secret will be shared by several people..."

"What secret, Mom?" asked Michael. "You said a family shouldn't keep secrets."

"It's not in the family, honey." She patted his head. "It's a secret of friends."

"That's still a secret," Roy chimed in. "And you should tell it to us."

"All right, I promise to tell you later." She waited for them to finish their dinner and then said the magic word, "Ice cream..."

"Yay!" Michael cried.

"...in your rooms."

After dishing out large portions of frozen dessert and sending the children to their rooms, Sally sat down across from Jerry. "Shall you call him or will you give me the number and I will?"

"You call," Jerry ruled. "He always liked you." Jerry got up and walked to his study. When he returned, he was holding a note. "I still think you should let this go," he said, handing her the note. "But you do what you want anyway."

"That's true," she said, and saw a grim expression briefly cross his face.

15.

The call routing system of Thunder Investigations sounded almost human. "For management, press one," the feminine voice suggested softly, and Sally did as she said. "For Jacob Lavie, press one." *That's so like him—to be number one,* Sally thought and pressed the button once again. However, it was not Jacob who answered her, but a human secretary, and when Sally asked to be transferred to Jacob, she was expectedly answered with a query. "On what matter?"

"A double homicide," she answered. "And it's urgent."

"A double homicide," the secretary repeated with alarm, but when Jacob picked up the phone he was choking with laughter. "Sally! You haven't changed. A double homicide, huh? That joke was already old back in London."

"And it still works on your secretaries. I need to speak to you. When can I come over?"

"Right now. A double homicide requires swift action, doesn't it?"

"You have no idea how right you are."

Half an hour later, she was sitting across from him in an office overlooking downtown from the top floor of a high-rise. He was almost un-changed since the last time they met. Jacob was a short and stout man, his eyes masked behind thick glasses. She retold the story of Ben David from the start as he glanced over to the computer screen on the desk. "What I can't understand," he said without looking at her, "is why you're involved."

"Do me a favor…" Sally pleaded.

For the first time, he looked up at her.

"Leave the computer. The things I'm telling you are now the essence of my life. If you have no interest, I can go."

"Excuse me," he said, walking over to turn off the screen. He sat on the edge of the desk. "I simply can't detach myself. Everything changes so quickly: Another terror attack and another statement by a politician, and on the sidebar I have data streaming in from the stock market. I'm addicted to this."

"That also answers your question."

"What do you mean?"

"Just as you're addicted to the computer, I'm addicted to fulfilling my obligations. I've explained to you how much I owe Marin, and now I have the opportunity to repay him. The only question that remains is whether you will be a good friend and help me."

"What do you need?"

"Bank accounts, names of other people Ben David is defrauding, partners, businesses he invests in. Everything but his landline."

He raised his eyebrows. "How come?"

"I've installed an eavesdropping device there," Sally said proudly.

"You're mad. That's a matter for professionals."

"I have a professional friend."

Now he was completely focused on her, even tense. "I won't help you unless you remove those devices. You'll be sending people to jail."

"You have nothing to worry about. The device is in a telephone communications box, transmitting to a motorcycle parked nearby."

"Who's your pro? People haven't been eavesdropping like that for ten years. Today there are machines that intercept phone conversations with no risk. Get it out of there immediately. Then we'll see if we can help."

"We? I was hoping you'd handle this yourself."

"I haven't left this desk in years. I have employees and they're the best in the field."

"I don't want anything leaking out."

He stood up, circled the table, and sat on the chair next to her. "Sally," he said, taking her hand. "We've known each other for many years. I am prepared to do anything you ask, but you'll need to trust me. Let me work on this my way."

"OK." Sally sighed. "Can I at least work with you?"

"Possibly." Jacob let her hand go. "Meanwhile, your mission is to remove that thingamajig you've installed, you and your friend. As soon as you tell me it's gone—we'll enter the frame."

"You can start today. Tomorrow the box will be empty."

"*We'll* begin," he said, "and I want you to realize what this entails: It's not only tapping into all of his devices, searching through his rubbish, and following him, like you said. As far as I can tell, this is a probably a pretty big financial case. We will need to bribe people here and there to obtain information. We'll also need to install hidden cameras and bugs not only at Ben David's but elsewhere. We may need to go investigating abroad. I think it's a pretty risky matter, all in all."

"The rabbi doesn't seem particularly dangerous," Sally said.

"The law is dangerous for us, but my people—all veteran officers in special Israel Defence Force units and police investigators—are prepared to take risks and walk the thin line between legal and illegal. Do you realize you are also taking a chance, as someone who ordered the investigation and authorized the steps we will take?"

Sally was momentarily terrified.

"Now let's talk about money," said Jacob. "I don't want to make a profit on you, but there are expenses: Travel, maybe flights, hours of surveillance. Who will cover all of this? I get what motivates you, but I don't believe it's a disaster for a Jew to cheat a Jew, and I owe nothing to Marin."

Sally hesitated for a moment. "I can't pay you, but..." For the first time, it occurred to her that the information she was collecting would be worth money to Marin—lots of money. She remained adamant not to pocket any of it, but it was only fair to reimburse Jacob and Diana for their work. "I believe that when I give Marin all the information that saves him, he'll cover the costs."

"And what if he doesn't?"

"That's not possible. I intuitively know he will."

"What does Jerry say?"

"He's always supported me, and continues to support me now."

Jacob sighed. "All right, I don't usually trust people that much. But since it's you... Just get that motorcycle away from there, send me what you've already recorded, and from then on, let us do our work."

16.

The streets of Beersheba were already familiar to Sally. She drove slowly, maneuvering between double-parked cars and smoke-emitting buses. Diana, sitting next to her, handed her tangerine wedges as she peeled the fruit. "Did you take the day off?" she asked.

"Yes. If I continue this way, I'll have no vacation days left."

"And you'll have no job," added Diana.

"I'm not worried about that. No one there knows the system as well as I do."

"Now, when Jacob is taking care of things, maybe you can work more."

Sally contemplated. "I'm actually thinking of taking a leave of absence for a few weeks—"

"Stop!" shouted Diana.

Sally stepped on the brakes. "What happened? You scared me."

"Police. Park here."

The wall surrounding the rabbi's house was painted in blue flashes emitted by the lights of the police car. Two policemen stood next to the motorcycle, examining its license plate.

"We're done for," said Diana. "They'll find the eavesdropping device and track me down through the rental company."

A police tow truck overtook them and stopped next to the police car. The driver came out, holding a huge cutter. The policemen explained something to him, pointing at the chain. The driver knelt, and in a moment the severed chain was thrown into the back of the truck. The policemen helped him move the motorcycle onto the towing platform, and when he drove off they followed him.

"What now?" asked Diana.

Sally put the car into gear and followed the police car and tow truck, allowing another car to get in between them, as she had learned in the agents' course. The convoy reached the historic city center: Low houses from the Ottoman period, shadowed by ugly two- or three-story buildings covered with billboards. An empty water fountain served as a skateboard rink for children, next to a pedestrian street paved with colorful concrete blocks overtaken with merchants' stalls. The tow truck turned into a courtyard surrounding a square building, followed by the police car. Above the gate, a sign read "Beersheba Police." Sally stopped the car at a distance, and they both gazed, frustrated, at their motorcycle being offloaded from the tow truck and placed in the courtyard amidst rows of stolen or abandoned cars.

Diana frowned. "What are you thinking about?" asked Sally.

"Do you see that small gate on the left? It's meant for pedestrians and at night, if there's no guard, a motorcycle can pass through it. But it's crazy. Someone can see; there are always policemen in the station."

"I'll do it," said Sally. "We'll stay in Beersheba and come back at night."

"Are you crazy? If they catch you…"

"It's a risk I'll have to take. Come, let's find a place to sit until night."

It was four in the afternoon, and about three hours remained before the autumn sun would set. They went to a matinee in the cinema and then roamed the nearby shopping mall. Diana bought a light jumper to protect her from the desert chill outside. Sally preferred a fancy velvet jacket. Just before eight, they walked by the police station, stopping at a distance from it.

They walked along the iron fence. In the guard booth, a policeman was devouring a sandwich and reading the newspaper. There was no way for pedestrians to enter the compound without him noticing. At the edge of the fence they turned left, and turned again into the alley behind the station. A high hedge stretched along the narrow street, covering a number of metal wires. "Stand guard," said Sally and stretched her arm out to Diana. "The keys."

Diana handed her the keys to the motorcycle and stood with her back to the fence, eyeing the alley. Sally began to make her way through the hedge. The metal wires were ancient, and broke without much effort. The bush, however, was rigid and almost unbendable. She struggled to break the branches and make her way through it. "You won't be able to come back through here with the motorcycle," said Diana behind her.

"I don't need the motorcycle, only the device inside it," replied Sally. "Later we can report it stolen." She continued to wriggle her way through the hedge, finally whispering, "I'm in."

A dark character paced slowly along the building wall. A rifle hung loosely on its shoulder. "What are you waiting for?" asked Diana behind her.

"Shh. There's a guard here. I'm waiting for him to disappear."

The guard turned the building corner and Sally ran across the dark courtyard. When she arrived at the building wall, she walked along it and where it ended, she stopped and peeked at the front courtyard, which was awash with light. The motorcycle stood there, where it had been dropped off that afternoon. It seemed untouched. She crept into the courtyard, staying close to a row of cars that created a thin strip of shadow in the immense light.

When she reached the motorcycle and crouched next to it, she was fearful of standing up and opening the seat lock. She extended her arm to the lock, holding the keys. The chair bounced up immediately. She felt around inside. The eavesdropping device was where they left it. When she tried to pull it out, it caught something. Sally tried pulling it again, but was afraid to use too much force lest she break the machine, or worse, destroy the recording. She had no choice but to take a chance. She stood up, and for seconds that seemed like an eternity, stood in the light shaking the motorcycle until the device came loose. Then she dived back into her safe strip of darkness.

Her pulse thumped in her temples, but her mind was clear. There wasn't much time left. If someone noticed her, they'd be there in a moment. She advanced, crouching, to the next row of cars, ran across an illuminated passageway, and found herself back in the dark. When she arrived at the back of the building she leaned against the wall, panting in panic. After calming herself, she ran along the hedge, searching for the opening she had created. When she couldn't find it, she stood up and whispered, "Diana."

She heard no answer.

"Diana," she called out again, this time louder.

Diana didn't respond.

The dark shadow of the night guard reappeared on the building wall. He suddenly stopped and turned toward the hedge. Sally knelt, fearful, among the bushes. The guard continued toward her and stopped at some distance. Sally froze. The seconds ticked by. What was he waiting for? She heard the sound of a zipper open and then of water hitting the ground. The tension dissipated inside her, but she couldn't afford to breathe a sigh of relief. Not yet.

The guard zipped himself up and walked along the fence, his head bowed in thought. When he passed by her, Sally could smell his sweat. She held her breath and didn't exhale until he disappeared behind the building. Then she allowed herself to leave her hiding place and make her way out. The eavesdropping device made it difficult for her to break through the hedge, and she embraced it to her chest and pushed through the bushes with her shoulders. When she was halfway through, she heard a whisper. "Sally, is that you?"

"Where were you?"

"I was hiding. There are prostitutes hanging around here. I began getting propositioned, and the other girls don't seem too friendly."

"Help me get out of here."

When Sally emerged from the bushes, she saw women wandering the sidewalks. A car moved slowly and stopped next to each of them. When it came up to Sally and Diana, it stopped. Diana signaled to the car to keep driving. He flashed his lights. They kept walking and he, challenged by their refusal, drove slowly alongside them. They picked up their pace, as did the car. Sally turned onto the main road and the car disappeared in the traffic. "You can stop hugging the recording device," said Diana. "And your new jacket doesn't look so great anymore."

Sally took it off. The sleeve was irreparably torn, bloodstains covering it from the scratches on her arms. She tossed it into a nearby bin. "Let's get out of here. I'm cold."

The car waited for them where they left it, a paper note stuck to the front windshield. "An advertisement," said Sally, optimistic as always. "A parking ticket," Diana corrected her. She was right.

Sally peeled the ticket from the windshield, buried the recording equipment underneath the driver's seat, and sat behind the wheel. She cleaned her hands and bruised arm with wipes and looked at the ticket.

"How much is it?" Diana asked.

"A hundred shekels. Now let's go back to the police."

"I really don't feel like having some dumb cop fill out forms and asking me where I was and what I've done."

"Wouldn't it seem suspicious to you if a woman rents a motorcycle for two weeks; the motorcycle disappears from its parking place a week later and she doesn't file a complaint?"

Diana shrugged. "All right, if there's no other choice, I'll go."

She returned an hour later, holding a few sheets of paper.

"Stupid policeman…questions…a fine?" Sally laughed.

"He was actually handsome. We spoke about life half the time. What have you done meanwhile?"

"I listened to the radio. Did they tell you why they thought it was stolen despite the chain?"

"They didn't think it was stolen. The good-looking cop explained that an important man lives near where we parked it, and after seeing it there for a few days, he suspected someone was planning a burglary or something like that. I signed a form saying they can return it straight to the rental company and bill my credit card."

"Did he happen to mention that the important man is a rabbi?"

"I asked who he was, and he said he couldn't tell, but since we became friends he said his name was Ben David and he was a real estate entrepreneur."

"Real estate entrepreneur," Sally repeated, and suddenly jumped up. "We need to get the broadcasting device out of the communications box. It has your fingerprints on it."

"That's child's play," said Diana confidently.

They returned to the rabbi's house. Darkness engulfed Diana, and she returned to the car a few moments later with the device.

"Tomorrow I'll give the receiver to Jacob and we'll see what he finds."

"I want to stay in the picture," Diana said. "Actually, I *demand* to. I'm already emotionally involved."

Sally examined Diana's face, illuminated by the headlights of a passing car, and felt deep closeness to her. "You know," she said, "tonight I realized I'm not only married to a Mossad agent, I'm *married to the Mossad.* The sense of mission, the adventures, the responsibility..."

"Tell me about it." Diana laughed.

17.

As in their previous meeting, Jacob's eyes were glued to the screen. Now, his ears were also shut, covered with large earphones. "I'm listening to the recordings you brought, and to those we taped ourselves," he quickly remarked before Sally could scold him. "We don't know these characters yet. Can you try to recognize the voices in this conversation, for example?" He removed the earphones and pressed a button. Sally heard a ringing tone and then "Hello?" in a French accent.

"Vivian Moyal," she said immediately.

"It's us," said a male voice. "Can you speak?"

"Ben David," she added.

Vivian exchanged a few sentences in French with a man probably next to her, then said, "One moment, I go to different room."

Jacob stopped the recording. "Do you know who she's with?"

"No. Maybe you can find out through the number?"

Jacob leafed through a notepad on his desk. "The number belongs to a phone in Geneva—the Four Seasons Hotel. Our tracker saw her enter the lobby. They probably recognized her at the reception, because as soon as we asked for her they didn't even ask for the room number but transferred us immediately. We also discovered that a man connected to Pierre Marin is staying at the hotel, his lawyer to be precise. Robert Darmond, also a Moroccan and childhood friend of Marin's. Vivian may be romantically connected to him, she may have only visited his room during the conversation, or she may have even been in the room with another man, making Darmond's presence coincidental."

"I don't believe in coincidence, certainly not concerning Vivian Moyal. She's interested in Marin, and Darmond's his lawyer. There must be a scheme that Ben David is involved in here. I want to hear what she tells Ben David."

Jacob silently pressed a button.

"How?" the rabbi asked.

"Not all right. He doesn't want to meet."

"Did you tell him it concerns his wife?"

"Yes. But he thinks I ask for something and he doesn't want to give nothing. He is a difficult man."

"We're thinking of a bar mitzvah here. He will have to let go of the older son at least."

"Are you kidding? He's barely Jewish."

"Never mind. His mother wants a bar mitzvah. She's dying to see the kid and we hear from her that the children also miss her. If we bring the older one here, give him a bar mitzvah at the Wailing Wall, and he sees his mother grow closer to Judaism, he will stay."

"How is she?"

"All right, thank God."

"Where?"

"You know, at the *Lulav*."

"Does she go out?"

"She doesn't go out and doesn't want to. It's cold outside and she heats herself with the fire of Torah. She will do what we want. She even gave us, you know, the necklace she got from him."

"That's a lot of money." Vivian's voice rose with anticipation. "I want that necklace."

"You won't have it, better you don't wear it by mistake. In the meantime, we put in the safe."

"He probably say give chain back. It was his mother's—"

Ben David cut her off mid-sentence. "There's no going back. She already told him it's lost."

"And if she says to you, 'Give it back'?"

"There's no regrets and no going back." Ben David's voice rose in fury. "We already told her we donated it to an orphanage. Okay, now think about how to bring the boy here. We might have to go to court. We will send you a power of attorney from the mother, signed by a lawyer and the Swiss consul. The court will let her. That's the law all over the world. She'll ask that he come for a vacation. We'll do a bar mitzvah like we said and then he'll stay with her."

Vivian mumbled, "How smart you are, thank God."

Ben David was silent, then suddenly said, "All right," and hung up without saying goodbye.

"He has partners," said Jacob. "Throughout the conversation, he said 'we.'"

"That's how rabbis speak of themselves to their disciples. What's more worrying is the matter of the mother and child. What is he talking about?"

"Well, let me tell you some things about Pierre Marin. He hides his biography, and it was very difficult to collect all the details we found in one narrative." He pulled a thick folder from the edge of the table and opened it carefully. Inside, punched pockets, documents, handwritten lists, and printed pages could be seen. "Shall we begin?" Jacob asked.

"Let's begin," Sally answered excitedly.

"Well, Pierre Marin, fifty-five years old, was born in Morocco to a Jewish father and Muslim mother. His father worked in gold mining in Africa, and he inherited his business and became a billionaire. He is the owner of one of the fanciest yachts in the world, a palace in the French Riviera and a mansion in Gstaad, a town of millionaires not far from Geneva. He's an art collector, a man of the world, multilingual. His two homes look like museums and he even keeps artwork in his yacht."

"What kind of person is he?"

"He's difficult: Overbearing, blunt, easily angered, suspicious to the verge of paranoia. Then we come to the wife and children. He's difficult not only in business but also at home. Everyone shakes in his presence. He feels as though he deserves everything, because in his immediate circle everything belongs to him. As a young man, he married a Moroccan woman. She gave birth to two children and raised them as he traveled the world and met other women. He loves beautiful women, especially top models. His second wife, Muriel, twenty years his junior, he met on his yacht when she arrived—along with other models—to a photoshoot on his yacht for Vogue. For some reason, he took to her from all the other women around. He left his first wife and children, married Muriel, had two more children with her, and even demanded that she convert to Judaism."

"At least he's a good Jew."

"Not really. Before his father's death, Pierre promised him he'd live as a Jew, but in practice he never kept any religious commandments or visited Israel. Everything changed three years ago, when he began suffering from liver disease. The doctors recommended an operation. Vivian introduced him to Ben David, who came to Gstaad, carried out a few spiritual rituals, and recommended not to touch the tumor. It was a huge risk, since Marin was already admitted for preliminary examinations at the Mayo Clinic in the US. Surprisingly, the gamble succeeded. The tumor vanished or at least stopped spreading. The metastasis even went into remission. Rabbi Ben David—"

"Don't call him a rabbi. Do me a favor," Sally interrupted him. "Ben David is enough."

"Ben David—" Jacob continued with a smile "—became Pierre Marin's spiritual guide, demanding that his family members adopt a traditional lifestyle. Marin showered Ben David with money and asked him to also treat Muriel and his older son, Joel."

"Are they sick too?"

"In a certain sense, yes." He turned a page and continued. "Years of living with Marin didn't do Muriel any good. She started drinking and became depressive. The older boy, Joel, suffers a lot. Over the past few years—he's just twelve years old—he was thrown out of a number of schools, tried to commit suicide, and Ben David declared that if he was not allowed to treat the boy, he could become a criminal."

"And the younger son?"

"He's five. His name is Rubi and he's all right for now, cared for by two nannies. But fear not, if his mother doesn't return to him it won't be long before he too goes crazy like his brother and mother."

"Who's in the hands of Ben David."

"That's the most interesting part of this mess. At some point, Muriel couldn't take the pressure of living with Marin and fled the castle. Marin didn't know where she went, nor did the kids, and at first they suspected she'd returned to her parents in a remote town in Canada. His lawyer, Darmond, used an investigation company that discovered her in Portugal. Marin promised not to bother her, and transfers money to her every month through Darmond. From the phone conversations we've just heard, it turns out that Ben David also knows where she is, in a place he calls 'the *Lulav.*' He is in touch with her, scheming to bring Joel under his influence. Ben David and Vivian's assumption is that when Marin discovers how close his wife and son have grown to Judaism, he too will make a similar move; coming completely under Ben David's sphere of influence. Then Vivian can involve him in her business plans."

"It's not necessarily a cold country," said Sally, pensive.

"He said 'it's cold outside.'"

"It could be a figure of speech, just like he calls himself 'we.' The term 'fire of Torah' could refer to the laws of Judaism, which the rabbi's wife he referred to is teaching her, and the cold outside could be secularism or lack of spirituality. As for '*Lulav*—'" she looked at Jacob "—do you have any idea?"

"Not yet," Jacob admitted.

"We should follow the rabbi," Sally said decisively.

"We are, we are. When he's not in Gstaad, he only hangs around Beersheba."

"Where in Beersheba?"

"We have a list of places from the past week." He slid a sheet of paper across the table in between Sally's arms. "Bank Hapoalim," she read. "Market, Bank Hapoalim, post office, an apartment on Reger Street, the eye department of Soroka Hospital, an apartment on Rabin Street—he has a key, a house on Tamar Street—the bank, a lawyer's office on Herzl Street, apartment on Rabin Street—"

"His mother lives on Rabin Street," Jacob commented. "The name on the door is Dadoshvili and the neighbors say she's mean."

Sally chuckled and scanned the list again. "What do the door signs of the apartments he visited say?"

Jacob looked at the report again. "The Reger Street apartment says the Lavie family, and the one on Tamar Street says Dr. Havkowitz. Havkowitz is the registered owner. He's very old, around ninety. The neighbors say he never leaves the house."

"Chances are the woman is there," Sally said confidently.

Jacob looked at her, astonished. "You think you're smarter than my investigators?"

"Where does the word *Lulav* come from?" Sally asked back.

"I don't know; it's related to the Hebrew word for blossom."

"It means heart. *Lulav* is the heart of the date tree, or in Hebrew, *tamar*."

"Isn't it cut from a palm tree?"

"Palms are the family of trees dates belong to, as well as other fruit, even coconut trees. The daughter of a citrus farmer should take her biology studies seriously, shouldn't she? Anyway, the woman is on Tamar Street and Ben David alluded to that in his conversation with Vivian, who is also traditional and, unlike you, knows what tree the *Lulav* is cut from."

"You just have to be sarcastic, don't you?" Jacob smiled. "All right, I'll send someone over there."

"I'll go," said Sally.

"We agreed you wouldn't interfere. I don't want him to see you and identify you."

"It will happen sooner or later, won't it?" Sally blurted out as she stood up. "Let me try."

"All right, but if you're such a professional, let's see you bring back a few photos of her. We only have images taken from Vogue magazine. Today she surely looks different."

"I'll bring them," Sally said and left the room.

18.

They parked the car across the road from 55 Tamar Street. It was a single story building like Ben David's house, but much smaller. Unlike Ben David's wall-encircled home, the building was surrounded by a white fence. The gaps in the fence revealed a neglected yard. "The principle is clear," Diana said. "He chooses homes where the neighbors have no idea who lives in them."

Sally nodded in agreement. "She can walk around the house, go out to the yard, and unless you stand right next to the fence and peek in, you have no idea she's there."

"You don't know if she's there either," said Diana and straightened the lapel of her jacket, where a tiny camera was hidden. "I don't think we'll have anything to film. The place looks abandoned."

"Any idea how to find out who's there?" asked Sally. "You probably learned a few methods in the unit you served in."

"I'm an expert at connected wires and tapping into phones, not tricks. Of us two, *you're* the trickster."

"All right, let's get out of here before the neighbors grow suspicious," said Sally, frustrated. "We'll get a bite to eat and think of something."

A grumble rose from the back seat of the car.

"Brutus also needs to drink, and maybe pee," cautioned Diana. She turned around and patted the back of a giant setter dog lying there. "Soon Brutus, soon you'll get a drink."

"I still don't know why you had to drag him here," murmured Sally as she began driving away.

"I told you, he suffers from separation anxiety."

"I can't believe such a huge dog is anxious about anything."

"He's big, but has the soul of a baby."

"And you never leave him alone?"

"No. When the kids are in school and Alex is at work he rides with me, like today."

Sally slowed down next to Aroma Café. "Let's see if they'll let us bring him in."

"Never mind, we'll sit outside," declared Diana. "While you park the car I'll take him for a short walk."

A few moments later they were sitting in the front porch of the café, two plastic cups of water on the table, exchanging ideas about how to penetrate the house. Diana was already at the wild stage. "I'll pretend to be a pizza deliverer." She laughed.

Sally stared at Brutus who was energetically licking water from a plastic bowl.

"How about an electric company servicewoman?" continued Diana, "or someone from the water company?"

"That's not funny," objected Sally, still looking at the dog. "We need a brilliant idea."

The waitress brought a dish of lasagna and two plates. Brutus stood erect and sniffed the air. "Look what smart eyes he has," Diana said, caressing his head.

"You know, he really does look smart," Sally said. "So smart that he could solve our problem. If we're able to get him into her yard, we could call and ask her to let him out."

"I couldn't do that to my dog. She could hurt him or—"

"How would she hurt him? Look at him; he looks like a small horse."

"I told you, he only looks big. Besides, he could get scared and start going wild."

"That's exactly what I want to happen. Let him go wild in the yard, turn things over, cause damage, and then she'll have to open up and let us take him."

"No!" said Diana decisively.

"All right," Sally relented. "Then let's just pass by there one more time and take a picture of the house from the outside." She pushed away the plate. "It's not that good. You have some. Maybe Brutus would like some at home."

"Can we pack this to go?" Diana asked the waitress. On the way to the car she added, "I want you to understand. I'll do anything to help you, but I can't put Brutus in danger."

"I understand."

"Really?"

"Really and truly."

On Tamar Street, nothing had changed. The sidewalks were empty and an afternoon breeze swept fallen bougainvillea flowers from the nearby yards. Sally stared at the house. "Look at that." She suddenly pointed at a small door in the picket fence.

"That's the door for rubbish disposal. Do you want to push through it? You won't be able to."

"First of all, if I wanted to, I could. Secondly, if we were to open the door, take out the rubbish, throw the lasagna over the fence as far as possible, and get Brutus to jump in, we could ring the doorbell and ask—"

"Out of the question. Haven't I said that yet?"

"Stop being negative and think. If the smallest thing happens to Brutus, he can always come back through the rubbish door. Besides, the lasagna we brought for him was *my* portion. Don't you think I deserve something in return?"

Diana burst out laughing. "You're funny, do you know that? Funny and crazy." She got out of the car and opened the back door. Brutus jumped onto the sidewalk and she rushed to grab the collar on his neck.

They walked him to the wooden door, which opened without difficulty, and pulled the bin out. Diana gently directed the dog to the empty niche and Sally let him smell the bag with the lasagna. He opened his muzzle excitedly. Sally pulled the bag back and threw it far into the yard. Brutus pushed his way through the narrow gate and rushed into the yard. "Now," said Sally. She closed the wooden door and they both hurried to the locked gate and pressed the doorbell. Somewhere inside the bell sounded, but no response could be heard.

They rang again. Diana peeked through the fence. Brutus devoured the remaining lasagna. "In two or three minutes, he'll start going wild and looking for a way out," she said worriedly.

Sally rang the doorbell relentlessly.

"Who is it?" called a woman in English.

"My dog jumped into your yard. Can you open the get to let him out?"

Through a crack in the fence she could see a blind open slightly. "She's looking out," Sally told Diana.

"Brutus finished eating and is playing with the bag," Diana reported back.

The blind closed. "Now she'll come," said Sally hopefully.

She didn't come. Brutus started whimpering and after a short scurry in the yard, he disappeared behind the house. Diana panicked. "If there's no fence there, he'll disappear. How will I ever find him in the desert?"

Before she finished speaking, Brutus returned. A woman dressed in a housecoat was walking him, gently holding his collar. Even through the narrow crack, Sally could tell she was pretty, even beautiful. "Get ready to take a picture," she said. Diana straightened her lapel and shoved her hand into her pocket, pressing a button. "Everything's ready," she said.

Keys rattled and the gate opened. Brutus jumped on Diana and licked her face, hiding the camera lens. Sally pulled the collar, tugging Brutus away as she looked at the woman. Her figure was slim and tall. Two births, depression, and heavy drinking had left it undamaged. Her tired face was still remarkable. Sections of her graying hair still preserved their original blonde tint, and her blue eyes shone through her clouded gaze. "We're so grateful to you," Sally said in English.

The woman seemed embarrassed. Sally continued. "Are you new here?"

"Yeah, only a few months. You also have a different accent, not an Israeli one." She seemed happy to meet another expatriate. "Where are you from?"

"Sweden," Sally repeated her old story. "How about you?"

"It's complicated," said the woman, and Sally could pick up the loneliness in her eyes. "A bit from Canada, a bit from Switzerland…"

"We have time." She turned her head to Diana, who kept her hands in her pocket. "We could chat a little, if you're free."

"But I…" The woman looked at them, lost. "I need to go," she said anxiously as she closed the gate. "Have a good day."

"Did you take her picture?" asked Sally as they got into the car.

"Twenty or thirty photos, with and without Brutus. What do you think of her?"

"She's very pretty, very lonely, and very scared. I think it's time to make a slideshow out of the photos and call Marin."

19.

"We have no person registered under that name," the Swiss telephone operator declared. Sally couldn't find Marin's number online either, and an in-depth search only revealed a number of companies where Marin served as president or CEO. Some of them were listed on the Zurich, Frankfurt, London, and New York stock exchanges, and their annual reports were open for review. Sally delved into them. She found that most of the companies dealt with mining or mineral processing in one way or another. The majority shareholder was Cosmos Holdings, registered in Vaduz, Liechtenstein.

Was Marin behind Cosmos Holdings?

The company website displayed phone numbers of offices in South Africa, Liberia, Singapore, and Colombia. Three numbers had a Swiss country code: In Zurich, Berne, and Geneva. Sally picked Geneva, the city where—according to Vivian Moyal—she mediated a meeting between Marin and Pakistani representatives. "What matter does this concern?" asked a woman in detached politeness when Sally asked for Marin.

"It's a personal matter."

"*What* personal matter?" asked the woman.

"Personal is personal, isn't it?" replied Sally, defiantly.

"You'll have to tell me what this is about," repeated the secretary, patiently. "That's the rule."

"I have a message for him from Vivian Moyal."

The secretary was unimpressed. "You can convey the message through me."

"I was asked to deliver it myself."

"Mr. Marin doesn't speak to people without a convincing reason, and with all due respect, Madame Moyal is not a convincing reason."

The answer didn't surprise Sally. She also never considered Vivian more than so much hot air. Suddenly an idea occurred to her. "Tell him I know where the lost necklace he received from his mother is."

"*Where* is it?" For the first time, the secretary sounded interested.

"I'll tell him that myself."

"Maybe you'd like to add a detail or two, confirming you are referring to the same necklace?" The secretary's enthusiasm broke through her icy shield. "No," said Sally with more than a little gloating, "there's nothing to add. I'll give you a phone number and he can call me back."

After hanging up, Sally started on her house chores, certain that the phone would soon ring. But it only rang a few hours later, when the children had already returned from school and sat down to lunch. "Madame Amir?" a pleasant male voice asked.

"Yes," Sally replied.

"This is Pierre Marin," he continued in polished English. "I understand you wanted to tell me something."

Her heart pounded. "Yes, concerning the lost necklace."

Marin was silent.

"I know who's keeping it, and I also have additional information concerning your wife and your older son."

To her surprise, Marin remained silent. She wondered whether he was unmoved by her revelation, or perhaps just good at hiding his feelings. "Hello?" she said.

After a brief additional moment of quiet, Marin asked, "Who's keeping it?"

Sally decided to reveal another card. "Rabbi Ben David. Actually, he's not a rabbi. He's an imposter."

"Are you connected to him?"

"Not at all," replied Sally sharply. "I want to help. I owe you a big favor."

Silence again.

"Many years ago, when I arrived in London penniless, I received a generous stipend from your foundation that allowed me to exist, study, and get married. Thanks to your help, I became what I am today."

"I understand," he said.

"For a while I've suspected that you are being cheated, and the thought is making me restless. I have lots of information on the man who calls himself Ben David, on the place where your wife is, and on the way they plan to bring over your son."

"Who is 'they'?"

"The rabbi and another woman you know."

"Vivian Moyal?"

This time it was Sally's turn to shut up.

"In the telephone conversation with my secretary you said you wanted to pass on a message from her," Marin said, still in a dry voice. "I can add one plus one, as you may imagine. Why are they doing this?"

"Money," Sally replied curtly.

"All right," said Marin, his voice infused with excitement. "I want to meet you, as quickly as possible."

"When will you be in Israel?"

He continued, ignoring her question. "Give the secretary your details, please. Tomorrow morning, a first-class ticket will await you at Ben Gurion Airport for a Swiss flight to Geneva. A limousine will take you from the airport to my home. When you arrive, you can stay in my guest quarters and—"

"Excuse me," Sally interrupted him, "I truly appreciate your hospitality Mr. Marin, but I'm a married woman. I can't leave my husband, fly to you alone, and stay at your home."

Marin answered without hesitation, "In that case, give my secretary your husband's details as well."

"I don't know if he can make himself available."

Marin lost his temper. "As I said, coordinate with Madame Calderon, my secretary," he ordered. "I expect to see you and I would like it to be soon." He hung up without saying goodbye, and Sally was reminded of the recorded conversation between Ben David and Vivian. The imposter rabbi also hung up with no words of parting. Was this the behavior he learned from the man whose soul he took over?

She called Jerry's office. "I spoke to Marin," she said excitedly, "I mean he called me. I told him everything."

"And what did he say?"

"He wants me to come to Geneva tomorrow. I told him I wouldn't go alone, so he promised to buy you a ticket too. First class, no less. I just need to give our details to his secretary."

Jerry let out a chuckle. "You can't be serious."

"I'm completely serious."

"You don't really expect me to leave everything and go tomorrow. I can take a vacation in say, a month, at the earliest."

"Jerry, honey, you know how long I've been waiting for this. In Pakistan, you told me to wait until we return to Israel, and I did. In Israel, you told me to wait until I have enough incriminating information against Ben David. I waited. Today I waited for hours until Marin got back to me, and now you want me to wait until you can take a vacation?"

"They expect you at work tomorrow," he reminded her.

"I have fantastic colleagues in my department. They'll make do, and anything that goes wrong can be solved over the phone or the Internet."

"And what will you do with the children?"

"My mother will come and stay with them."

"We've ordered an air-conditioning technician for tomorrow," Jerry reminded her. "We've been chasing him for a week until he found the time to come."

"My mom will let him in."

"Will your mom also go to work for me?"

"She is actually the spying type. Oh well," said Sally impatiently, "I can't wait. I'm going to fly to him tomorrow, with or without you."

"Fly without me," said Jerry in his usual calm.

"Are you serious?"

"Completely serious. Now let me work."

Sally went to her bedroom and pulled her worn suitcase out of the closet. She folded in a satin Pierre Cardin blouse, red Diesel trousers, and a skimpy black Marni dress, which she planned to turn into an elegant evening dress with the help of a pearl necklace and a pair of Stuart Weitzman sandals. During the day she would add a black Chanel jacket and Tod's shoes, a perfect costume for work meetings with businessmen or lawyers. She trusted her ability to make casual clothes seem luxurious on her sporty and trim physique. She never compromised on staying in shape, and even while traveling the world she would do certain exercises in between flights, helping keep her muscles toned.

Sally threw in underwear and toiletries when the phone rang again. "I'll travel with you," Jerry said. "I think you're crazy, and if I don't go with you a disaster could take place."

Sally leaped for joy. "Never mind the reason," she said, "as long as you're by my side."

20.

Only later in the evening, after she had finished packing and Jerry was tying up loose ends at the office before the trip, did Sally wonder about the urgency Marin had applied in his request for her to come. His wife had been away from home for many weeks, and he didn't sound especially bothered when she told him she knew where she was. The loss was indeed important to him, but he made no effort to find it. The only thing that shook him from his subdued, indifferent mode of speech was the motive Sally attributed to Ben David and Moyal—money. Was that the most important thing for him?

When Jerry arrived, she shared her thoughts with him. "He's a man who's used to controlling money," was Jerry's assessment. "I think what motivates him now is his sense he's lost control. For a person used to perpetual success, whose orders are carried out immediately, lack of control is a trauma." He smiled.

"We've met people like that before, haven't we? A few of them work at my office, and we ran into others during assignments abroad. General al-Sharif in Pakistan, for example."

"Tomorrow we'll find out who he really is." Sally hugged him. "And thanks for coming with me."

At five a.m., a fancy car picked them up—ordered by the omnipotent Madame Calderon. At the entrance to the airport terminal, a woman awaited them in a tailored suit. *"Madame et Monsieur Amir?"* she asked, then when answered in the affirmative handed Sally an envelope with two tickets. The way to the airplane was fast and easy, and the first-class department on board greeted them with cozy seats and the scent of fine perfume. After takeoff, breakfast was served, featuring smoked salmon, Swiss cheeses and fresh baked goods served hot from the oven. The earphones emitted classical music, and Sally let her thoughts carry her away. What would she tell Marin when they met, and what would happen following the meeting? Would he listen, read the material she brought, thank her, and send her back to the airport? Would she ask him to reimburse the funds she had committed to pay Jacob and Diana? Would she have to return to Israel at her own expense?

That final thought made her angry at herself for not agreeing with Marin on the details of her return. Right after their landing, as they exited the sleeve leading from the airplane, they noticed a gray-haired man holding a sign that read "Amir." "I'm Jacques," he introduced himself when they approached him. "I'm Mr. Marin's personal assistant. He asked me to meet you and accompany you to his home in Gstaad."

"Gstaad?" asked Jerry, surprised. "That's not close."

"It's also not far," Jacques assured them. He led them to passport control, and after signaling with his finger, a special counter opened for them, where a smiling clerk quickly stamped their passports. Their suitcases were already waiting on a trolley at the arrivals hall, overseen by a porter who carried them from the plane. Jacques handed him a money note and looked at the luggage with surprise. Sally assumed he was expecting heavier suitcases from Marin's guests. He signaled to the porter to follow them to a black limousine, much longer than the one that had brought them to the airport in Israel. A driver stepped out and easily loaded the two suitcases into the boot. Jacques opened one of the doors for Sally and Jerry and waited for them to sit on a round couch, upholstered in velvet. He then lightly shut the door and sat next to the driver. For a moment, Sally could still see him through the glass barrier, but it soon turned dark and he disappeared.

"Where have you brought us?" mumbled Jerry.

"I don't know, but I feel it getting better moment by moment."

He looked at her in disbelief. "You and your optimism!"

Heavy curtains, made of fine Indian fabric, covered the car windows. Sally quickly opened them, and the rural view enveloped her and Jerry. The narrow road wound through toy houses that looked as if they were taken straight from the postcards she received from her uncles overseas. Cows, roaming the fields a short distance from the car, stared at them with wide, surprised eyes and chewed their cud. As the road wound upward, the air turned thinner and sweeter. Sally felt like she was entering a fairy tale. Five hours ago, she and her husband had left their home in north Tel Aviv—which she imagined now crowded with people and cars—and were transported, like Alice, to a green wonderland.

The hilltop grew closer. The road widened, and beds of garden flowers bloomed alongside it. The limousine stopped next to a gate made of steel and marble. Jacques lowered the glass partition. "Welcome to the private castle of Pierre Marin," he said with pride, as though he owned it too. He stuck his hand through the window and tapped some numbers on a keypad attached to a pole. The elaborate gate opened widely and the limousine slid in, its tires grinding the gravel. Beyond the wall a huge garden lay before them, ending at the edge of a steep cliff. A few houses dotted the green expanse, but their large size didn't disturb the vast surroundings. Beyond them, a great distance away, another mountain rose high. Between the two mountains lay the lush valley through which they drove earlier. "Monsieur Marin likes the quiet," said Jacques without being asked, "so when he bought this mountain he also bought the one across from it, so that no one could build there and the view he loves so much wouldn't change."

The limousine crossed lawns and orchards, where groups of gardeners and handymen were busy working. "They are part of a standing team of forty employees," explained Jacques. "Besides gardeners, we also have a pool expert, the chief of our fleet of cars and motorcycles, handymen, a chef, waiters, chambermaids, and others."

A small bridge crossed over a narrow stream that reached the end of the cliff and became a waterfall. Exotic trees grew out of the water. "It's a type of mangrove," Jacques explained. "Mr. Marin brought them from the Andes." Beyond the stream, they reached a parking area next to a four-story house. Part of it was built from reddish-brown bricks, and the other from wood and glass surfaces that created completely translucent walls. A pool was visible beyond the glass screens of the ground floor, its blue water spreading a sense of calm and leisure.

Jacques got out of the limousine and quickly placed himself in front of Sally and Jerry's door, which he opened. The house door opened as well.

A blond boy of about five stood there watching them. Behind him stood a woman wearing a long skirt and white shirt, buttoned to the neck. Sally assumed she was the nanny. The boy looked at her with his big blue eyes, wet with tears. "Will you bring me back my mommy?" he asked.

21.

A tall and very handsome man stepped out of the house toward them. He was dressed in a totally different style than the tailored suit she saw him wearing in Islamabad. It was a Versace yellow sweater with leather cuffs, stylish Cavalli jeans, and an Armani silk scarf hanging lightly around his neck, which Sally estimated cost thousands of dollars. "I've seen lots of Hollywood films," murmured Jerry in Hebrew, "but this is something else."

"This is no film," whispered Sally, "this is real life."

The man approached them and stood next to the child, placing his hand on the child's head but not caressing it. "Pleased to meet you, I'm Pierre," he said and shook Sally's hand, then Jerry's. The child watched Sally silently, examining her every movement.

"Welcome, dear guests," said Marin in a flowery tone that suited a castle owner from years past. "Before we sit down for lunch, let me take you to the guests' quarters that will be entirely yours for the coming days."

He walked to the garden and took a path that left from the parking area. Sally and Jerry followed him while Jacques tailed behind. *The coming days?* wondered Sally. *How many days does he intend us to stay here? We have children to take care of, a house to run, Jerry has a demanding job. Why is this rich man, whom no one can reach, suddenly embracing us?* She glanced at Jerry, who was busy surveying everything with a suspicious eye.

Marin walked them along a boulevard of classic and modern sculptures. Sally stopped next to one, which she found particularly beautiful. Marin stopped too. "That's part of my collection," he said without the slightest arrogance, as though he was talking about canned goods in the pantry. "There are more of these, in the gardens and inside the house."

He turned to a building that stood at the edge of the path. It too was built in a style combining old and new, which Marin particularly liked, Sally realized. It was smaller than Marin's house, but quite large in itself. On the front doorpost, a large, elaborate mezuzah shone, reducing Sally's anxiety and sense of alienation. She stepped inside, into a world of luxury and comfort, stacked with collectors' items and unique furniture that also characterized Marin's aesthetic tastes combining old and new.

In the dining room, a long rosewood table greeted her, surrounded by elaborately decorated high-backed chairs. The living room was scattered with soft and inviting couches and chairs. A gigantic television screen was attached to one of the walls, across from a fully equipped bar. Sally moved to the kitchen, where the cabinets were filled with cakes, fruit, and chocolates bearing the symbols of Europe's best chocolatiers. From the bedroom window, the mountain and the valley at its feet were clearly visible. The wide beds were covered with satin sheets and a door led to a large hot tub. The floors were covered with Persian carpets and the walls boasted paintings by Picasso and Chagall.

"I must leave you. I'll see you again at lunch," said Marin in a tone that was meant to sound apologetic but sounded like a sudden order. He walked away, as usual, without a word of parting.

Jacques shot them a smile that entirely resembled his master's. A moment of tense silence lingered between them, which Jerry cut by saying, "I guess we'll go rest for a bit."

"Monsieur Marin would certainly want me to show you his garage. He's very proud of it," said Jacques, and opened a door that led into a space big enough to host a wedding. Impeccably polished cars stood parked in a row. A Porsche stood up front, next to a Rolls Royce Phantom Coupé, a Mercedes from the 1950s and a new Ferrari.

Behind, three well-equipped Jeeps stood parked, and finally two motorcycles with the words Kawasaki and Harley Davidson printed on their fuel tanks. At the side of the garage, a ski sled stood waiting for a ride through the surrounding slopes.

"You can take any car you'd like," said Jacques. "Monsieur Marin would like you to feel at home."

"Thank you," said Jerry wryly. "I think we'll have a rest."

22.

A few minutes later, in their room, Sally asked, "What happened to you? He's going out of his way to be nice to us and all you want to do is rest."

"You've just said exactly what bothers me: He goes out of his way. Everything here is big, special, expensive, and he's been bragging about it since we got here. Even after he leaves, he keeps sending his assistant or driver or whoever it is to show us the garage."

"He didn't utter one word of arrogance."

"Don't you get it? He's leading us through his property with his expression of 'this is nothing,' as though it was all a pile of rubbish. That's the real condescension. 'I have so much and I don't even care, because elsewhere I have more.' The man lives to make an impression. Who have you gotten involved with?"

Sally tried to recall Marin's expression when they toured the house. Her intuition, which she always counted on to lead her in the right direction, signaled that Marin was benevolent. "I don't think you're right," she said. "He's just a generous man who treats his wealth matter-of-factly and wants us to enjoy it too, as his guests."

"He's offering us his cars—"

"That's a sign he trusts us."

"Why?" asked Jerry. "What does he know about us except for the fact that you called to tell him you know where the necklace he gave his wife is, and that Ben David and Moyal are tricking him?"

"Jerry," said Sally tiredly, "the world is made up of those who are untrusting and lose friends, and those who are trusting and gain friends. True, you sometimes discover you were wrong to trust someone, but you can live with that. I belong to the second kind, and so does Marin, it seems."

"He's a tough businessman, and these people aren't generous for nothing."

"Let's assume he's a tough businessman," replied Sally. "Businessmen know where to invest. He's investing in us."

Jerry shrugged, removed two shirts from his suitcase, and hung them in the closet. "In any event, we'll have to leave in two days." He groaned. "I only have two shirts and two sets of underwear."

Sally opened the window and breathed in the mountain air. "It's wonderful here," she said. "It would be too bad to leave so quickly."

Jerry sulked in silence.

A light knock on the door disrupted them. Sally opened it. A thin, bony woman, dressed like the nanny in a long skirt and white blouse, curtsied to her. "My name is Natalia. I am the chief maid. Monsieur Marin invites you to dine with him." She looked at Jerry, who was busy hanging his spare pair of trousers in the closet. "I'll wait here until you finish," she pointed at a chair standing in the corridor.

"We'll be right out," promised Sally.

A few moments later, Sally led them with measured steps toward the big house. There, too, large mezuzahs adorned all the doorposts, which were numerous. Statues stood atop marble pedestals. A decorated elevator took them to the top floor, where in a room whose glass windows opened out to the view on three sides, Marin waited at the head of a table covered in a white tablecloth.

As soon as they sat down, a row of servants began serving them appetizers in golden plates, pouring various wines into crystal glasses, and placing trays of food down before them that they could obviously never finish. Sally almost asked what would be done with the leftovers. *Would they be eaten by the servants? Did Marin donate them to some institution?* Then her mind drifted to the blond boy. *Where is he now? Why is he not eating with his father?*

"*Bon appétit*," said Marin.

"Mr. Marin—" Sally started.

"Please, call me Pierre."

"Pierre, about the matter we came for—"

Marin hushed her with a polite gesture of his hand. "We'll speak after the meal," he said, concentrating on serving himself small portions of the abundance spread before him. Jerry also served himself, but Sally did not eat. A large chunk blocked her throat. She suddenly felt that Jerry was right; something about the organized, tidy world she was experiencing didn't seem right.

23.

At the end of the meal, Marin—Sally still couldn't call him Pierre, even not to herself—stood up and pointed to the living room. "Now we'll talk," he stated, and Sally recognized his pointed, tough demeanor underneath the polite veneer. She followed him, her hand holding Jerry's. The moment they entered the living room, the lights switched on, thanks to some automatic mechanism, and they found themselves in a room the size of their apartment, covered with colorful carpets, classic furniture, and soft couches. Pierre pointed to one of them. "Please, sit," he said, and sat across from them on a couch upholstered in leopard skin.

In front of them, on a low mahogany table with golden feet, large art albums lay next to a pile of books about sailing. "These are my two loves," Marin said, and grew silent. Sally waited for him to add "besides my children" or "in addition to Muriel," but he remained silent and just stared at her with concentration.

"Shall we get to the point?" she asked directly.

To her surprise, Marin said, "One moment more. Someone else will join us." Almost immediately a tall and slender man entered the room, his hair strikingly white. The man's face was pleasant and thin, wrinkles around his eyes, making his demeanor seem nice. "I'd like to introduce you to Robert Darmond, my lawyer and a childhood friend," said Marin. "He's up to date on all matters. Now, Madame Sally, tell us what you know."

The living room suddenly felt like a movie set, as Jerry described it earlier; the authoritativeness with which Marin spoke, coupled with his immense richness, augmented that feeling. Sally looked at Jerry. He seemed indifferent, for a moment even bored, but she knew exactly what he was thinking and what he would say to her had they been alone: "This is your project, dear, and you must find a way to manage it."

"All right," began Sally. "I told you that—"

"Let's start with the necklace," he interrupted her bluntly. "My wife said she lost it, and you told my secretary you know who found it."

For a moment, Sally felt embarrassed. "I've already told your secretary that Ben David *received* it."

"Excuse me," Darmond entered the conversation. "Received it from *whom*?"

"From Marin's wife Muriel. She lives not far from him, in Beersheba too," Sally said, feeling Jerry's displeasure next to her. Why does he not interfering if he thinks I'm wrong in my behavior?

"And what is she doing there, in—"

"Beersheba. Israel. She's studying Torah, growing closer to Judaism. There's a rabbi's wife who comes to teach her and brings her food. Ben David controls the process. Muriel adores him and that's probably why she gave him the necklace."

Darmond smirked again. "We have different information."

"It's wrong," asserted Sally with confidence that brought a look of surprise to Marin's face. "I have recordings of Ben David and Vivian Moyal saying that—"

"There are *recordings*?" Darmond interrupted her.

"Yes."

"Here, with you?"

"I have a Hebrew transcript in my room."

"And in Israel it's legal to tap into phones?"

"No," admitted Sally. "Not without a police warrant."

"In other words, you're implicating my client in a crime. You understand that according to Swiss law he must report this immediately, and if the recordings or the transcripts are here with you, you must hand them over to the police as evidence."

A wave of anger flooded Sally. "I think there's a misunderstanding here. I came to help you and—"

Darmond was ready to answer, but Marin stopped him with a wave of his hand. This time his voice was softer. "You understand, Madame Sally, we are trying to understand why you took such a risk upon yourself, coming here with a story that can incriminate you and—" he turned his head to Jerry "—your husband."

"I didn't think of the risks," said Sally frankly. "All I wanted was to let you know you're in the hands of a corrupt man."

"What's your motive?" asked Darmond.

"I've already explained to Mr. Marin."

"Pierre, please," pleaded Marin.

"Then call me Sally, no Madame."

For the first time since the beginning of the conversation, a smile appeared on his face, and immediately vanished. "Why have you come all the way here, Sally? On the phone, you told me that my fund helped you starting out, and that you're furious about a Jew tricking a Jew. Monsieur Darmond here doesn't believe there are people motivated by such things."

"Do *you* believe that?"

Marin hesitated for a moment. "My heart tends to believe, but my brain and my experience, you know—" He nodded his head. "In order to remove this obstacle between us, allow me to ask you most directly: Do you want money?"

"No," said Sally, and immediately remembered Jacob and Diana and her debt to them. "Nothing beyond the expenses I incur."

"Have you paid for the phone tapping?"

"I've done part of it myself, part with a friend, and the last bit was done by a private investigator, who's a friend from my previous job."

"And what exactly is this previous job?" Darmond asked dismissively.

"The Mossad," Jerry said, without batting an eye.

Sally could have jumped on him with a hug. This man, for whom secrecy was sacrosanct, who wouldn't even admit to his parents or her family that he wasn't simply a clerk in a government office, now came to her rescue.

The information made Darmond edgy. "Now I don't understand this at all," he spread his hands to the side. "You're a professional and understand the risks, and have nevertheless decided to help Monsieur Marin, a man whom you've never met, claiming you're doing this for emotional reasons. It doesn't make sense."

"Sometimes emotion is the true logic."

Pierre's face radiated. "You are probably a very special person, Madame Sally—I mean Sally," he said warmly. Darmond, for his part, wouldn't let go. "What else do you have to tell us?"

"I met Muriel."

Both men grew alert. "Where?"

"In Beersheba, not far from the rabbi's house."

"Impossible," said Darmond. "She's in a secret place, at a holiday home Monsieur Marin rented."

"In Portugal," Pierre disclosed.

"What city in Portugal?" Jerry inquired.

"I promised not to inquire. I send a sum of money to a bank account in Cyprus every month, partly to cover the rent and partly to cover her living expenses."

"Does she live there alone?"

"Maybe with one or two maids." He shrugged. "I know this because Monsieur Darmond—" his voice suddenly filled with a note of appreciation "—succeeded in tracking her down, employing an investigations firm to permanently observe the house."

Sally pulled out her mobile phone, flipped to one of the photos Diana took, and placed the phone silently on the table. Marin looked at it first and swallowed hard. His expression grew severe. He passed the phone to Darmond, who peeked at it and said, "It could be her, or not. My people tell me that—"

Marin's anger erupted like a brushfire. "Your people are supposed to guard her and report to me on her every movement." He patted the phone. "There are photos here, and the lady also has transcripts of phone conversations."

"We are employing the best investigations company in Europe," Darmond defended himself.

"One of the things I learned in life is that reputation comes and goes. It's hard to argue with the facts. The lady has photos. Do your investigators have photos that disprove them?"

Darmond didn't answer. He leaned over to the phone and examined the image once more. "It could be Photoshopped. A very professional editing job. Why is there a dog here?"

"It belongs to my friend and came with us." An idea occurred to Sally. "Had the image been edited, do you think a dog would be added?" She brushed her finger over the screen. Another image appeared and another. "That's her," ruled Marin, his face focused on Muriel standing at the gate of the house on Tamar Street. "I know that expression on her face." He glared at Darmond and massaged his temples. "Leave me alone," he ordered. "All of you. I need to think."

Sally and Jerry stood up.

"I suggest we all meet here in an hour."

Darmond stayed seated. Marin stared at him and he stood up as well. The three of them left the room together. Darmond disappeared as soon as they reached the foyer.

The dinner table was again cleared of dishes, and Sally wondered what was done with the leftovers. Natalia emerged out of nowhere and announced, "You haven't drunk your digestif yet. Would you like me to serve you on the porch?"

Sally looked at Jerry inquisitively. In Hibbat Zion, the *moshav* she grew up in, they only drank *Kiddush* wine. "Those are liquors that help your digestion," he explained. "You'll like them."

They followed Natalia to a glassed-in porch. Beyond the windows, a stunning view could be seen. Gigantic spotlights illuminated the mountain across the valley, exposing its green slopes and pristine snow cap. "Sweet, sour or bitter?" asked Natalia.

"Sweet for the lady and bitter for me," replied Jerry.

Sally hugged his arm. "Thanks for coming with me," she said. "There are moments when you're indispensable."

He smiled shyly back at her, and they both silently watched a flock of white rabbits skipping lightly from cliff to cliff.

Natalia returned carrying a tray with four bottles and two glasses. Jerry poured. "Underberg, 44 proof," he said as he served her the glass. He looked around and drew close to her. "Let's speak quietly, far from the window. The glass projects sound waves."

They moved to the corner of the porch. They sank into an inviting couch resting beneath a stone cornice. "I don't like this Darmond," he whispered into her ear. "He's doing all he can to present you as a fraud. I can't tell if he's trying to protect Marin or just lying."

"Jacob discovered that he stayed in a hotel in Geneva at the same as Vivian. I think it's no coincidence. He's on their side."

Jerry shook his head doubtfully. "What reason does he have to prefer an imposter rabbi and a crook to a serious man like Marin who provides him with a living and a secure life?"

"Maybe someone is offering him more? A competitor of Marin's, let's say, or an enemy? In any case, I'm not worried. It's like poker: Any player can bluff, but the person with the really good hand has nothing to worry about."

Natalia appeared at the edge of the porch. She greeted them with a curtsey. "Monsieur Marin would be happy for you to join him in the living room."

"Already? He asked for an hour," commented Sally with her typical directness.

Natalia smiled and said nothing. She placed the bottles and glasses back on the tray and started walking back to the living room. Sally and Jerry followed her. Pierre sat alone on the leopard couch. Darmond was nowhere to be seen. Natalia placed the tray on the coffee table. Sally and Jerry sat down on the couch across from him, with only a thick file separating them.

"Let me begin with a personal confession," Marin said. "I don't trust people. Any person is prone to treason, and since I have money, treason is usually at my expense."

Sally prepared to say something, but he lifted his hand to silence her. "Only in rare cases do I feel secure with people. It's a combination of good energy I pick up, and some information." He opened the file and Sally saw her headshot at the top of a document. Marin noticed her surprise. "I assume you realized I would check everything possible about you and Mr. Amir?"

"This is exactly what worried me," mumbled Jerry.

"I can assure you that nothing of your work was leaked to us. I can also say I was very impressed with what I read about you. If I understand correctly, you lived in Pakistan during the time I was also there for a short visit."

"We saw you at General al-Sharif's ball," Sally said. "I almost came over to say how grateful I am to you."

"Considering the circumstances, that wouldn't have been wise."

"Right. Jerry cooled my enthusiasm. Sometimes I'm too spontaneous."

"And that spontaneity is what makes me trust you. Now, in order for you to understand how much I trust you, and in preparation of the cooperation I'm about to offer you, I'd like to expose the history of my relations with Ben David. The entire story. Each of my people dealing with it knows one bit of it. I'm telling you all of it."

"I really appreciate that," said Sally.

Marin sipped from his glass. "Well, it all began with Muriel. I met her when Vogue held a photoshoot on my yacht. I fell in love with her immediately, and she also didn't remain indifferent to me. We started dating and I discovered a wonderful woman, beautiful, both inside and out, in need of love and security—both of which I could provide her with. Six months later she began studying Judaism and the chief rabbi of Zurich conducted the conversion ceremony. I separated from my first wife, the mother of my two older boys, and married Muriel in the Great Synagogue of Zurich." His eyes went moist, perhaps with compassion for the first wife he abandoned or in memory of his second marriage. "She was a wonderful wife, always taking good care of me and the children, managing the house when I was traveling. She was full of love for me, even admiring."

Sally nodded. She could certainly understand how this man could be admired, so handsome and powerful.

"Then things started to go wrong. I don't know the reason, but she became depressed, started drinking, and became aggressive and bitter. We turned to the doctors, of course. They prescribed medication that had no effect on her condition. Then we tried psychologists. At first only female ones: I wasn't comfortable with my wife sitting in a closed room alone with a strange man. But when nothing helped and I was told that an authoritative male character would do better for her, I agreed to that too." He sighed. "But even the best psychologists couldn't rescue her from the deep depression she experienced. And then I met Vivian Moyal. Her husband was my partner in a few businesses, and after they separated she tried to make, well, intimate contact with me. She knew about Muriel's problems, of course. You couldn't not know. Anyone who knew us spoke about her outbursts; her wanderings around ski and holiday resorts—drunk or drugged. Anyway, when she realized there was no other way to get close to me, she told me she was in touch with a rabbi and Kabbalist who works miracles—Ben David from Beersheba. I am a believer and know that miracles happen, but very rarely. With a heavy heart, I invited this man to me, to Geneva. I can't call him a rabbi any longer. I began the meeting feeling I was about to meet a swindler, and ended it certain I had encountered a real saint. It wasn't just the way he spoke, which entered my heart like a pleasant melody, but also the information he knew about me, my illnesses, my children, the children from my first marriage, my father, my mother. Everything, he said, was written in the sky and clear to him. Years later I realized that he and Vivian simply invested time in a huge investigation about me."

"Such an investigation costs a lot of money," Jerry said.

"They had money. They cheated numerous people before reaching me, and I was a good investment. I was exactly the person they were looking for: A rich man with family problems that only a saint could solve," he chuckled. "I actually believed he was a saint. I opened my heart as well as my wallet to him. I told him about my wife's condition and described the problems of our son Joel, who was thrown out of school after school and also suffered from depressive spells. Ben David consoled and encouraged me. He said with confidence that the problems were indeed very grave, but he could solve them. He added that Muriel and Joel needed urgent treatment, or else their situation would deteriorate beyond repair. Muriel would commit suicide and Joel would become a criminal.

"I could not afford the risk. I agreed to any treatment he could offer. Ben David was willing to help, but explained that in order to make time for my family members he had to postpone previous treatments he had committed to, and reimburse people's down payments. I immediately offered him a sum that seemed respectable to me—one hundred thousand dollars—but he reacted with disdain, even permitting himself to say that I was disrespecting him by offering such a small amount in return for the time he was investing and the fact he was waiving other commitments around the world. In the same breath, he explained that the money was going to charity and being donated to the needy: To orphanages and *yeshivas* in Beersheba*.*" He examined their faces and for a moment seemed much less authoritative and self-confident. "I realize that today, seeing me sitting here surrounded by all this wealth, you find it difficult to understand how worried I was. But at the time, everything I had was in danger and Ben David seemed like the only solution. I signed a check for half a million dollars and he finally agreed to begin treatment."

The large room fell silent. Sally felt extremely sorry for Marin. She glanced at Jerry, but his expression remained cold.

"Can I offer you something stronger than this?" Marin pointed at the liquor bottle. "Maybe we'll switch to cognac?"

Sally shook her head and Jerry nodded. Marin pushed a button and Natalia appeared. "Yes, Monsieur Pierre," she said.

"Cognac," Marin ordered, "the best bottle." He waited for her to leave the room, then continued. "For an entire month, he lived in my guest-house, where you are staying now, having conversations with Muriel and the kids, reciting incantations in the name of saints and writing amulets. At that time, I was diagnosed with a liver inflammation and Ben David reassured me. You wouldn't believe it, but the infection subsided. It didn't pass, but stopped bothering me. Even my doctor said he had no idea how that happened. Then Muriel began improving significantly. She stopped crying at nights, stopped drinking herself drunk. She confirmed him to be a great saint and righteous man, with amazing healing powers. Joel too finally managed to remain in the same school for almost a year. Laughter returned to my home and I was really happy. When Ben David asked Muriel for one hundred thousand dollars as a donation to an orphanage in the holy city of Safed, I gave her two hundred thousand to pass on to him."

Natalia returned with a decorated bottle and three glasses. "A special Remy Martin," said Marin and poured a glass for Sally, who waved it away with her hand. Marin handed it to Jerry.

The two men touched glasses and Marin continued. "A few months later, Ben David returned to Israel and my liver inflammation flared up again. He suggested I come to Jerusalem and stay in a suite at the King David Hotel. He would stay with his wife and children in the next-door suite and give me treatments."

He sipped from the cognac with an expression of pleasure on his face.

"Excellent cognac," Jerry confirmed.

"It's a special Remy Martin. I'm not allowed to drink too much, so the little I can afford to drink must be the best. Let's get back to Ben David. I continued to believe in him. We all traveled to Israel and there, following a one-week stay at the King David, the liver inflammation became an infection. I was hospitalized at Hadassah and was only released three weeks later, eleven pounds thinner. Ben David came every day, drove Muriel to the hospital and took her back to the hotel, also driving the children to the Western Wall and graves of saints. I did not fault him for my relapse despite his spiritual treatment. I knew what caused it." He stared at Sally with a serious expression. "We are all flesh and blood and we all have our weaknesses. My weakness is women. Since we met Ben David, Muriel started observing Jewish law, including the days of separation from me during menstruation. A day before I fell ill, I pressured her to sleep with me, three days into her seven days of prohibition. She cried and said God would punish us, but I couldn't help myself. The following morning, I awoke completely jaundiced and terribly weak. At Hadassah, they told me that had I slept another hour, I would have been found dead in bed."

He sipped from the glass. "We stayed in Jerusalem for another two weeks, and all the while I was paying for Ben David's suite. A day before we were meant to leave, he showed up and asked for another one hundred and fifty thousand dollars for charity. In return, a Torah scroll would be written in my name. I viewed it as a symbolic gesture, a token of gratitude for all the assistance he lent us. I hoped it would help my recovery. I gave him a check and would probably have kept paying had I not discovered— just as we were supposed to leave for the airport—that Muriel was missing. I panicked. She only speaks English and can mumble some prayers in He- brew. Where could she have gone in a foreign country? I knocked on the door of Ben David's suite. There was no reply. I called reception and was told he had checked out, but left me a letter. It was from Muriel. She said she had decided to stay close to Ben David's family in order to be close to a man of God. She was leaving the children with me. If I wanted to contact her, I was to communicate with Ben David's wife, Shlomit. Naturally, I phoned immediately. Shlomit reassured me that Muriel was merely experiencing a bout of depression and the rabbi was treating her. 'We will call you in a few days,' she promised."

His eyes went moist again, and he wiped them with a pristine handkerchief. "What choice did I have? The children and I returned to Switzerland. My older boy's condition started deteriorating again and the younger one cries and waits for his mother to return every day. I've asked Shlomit to make Muriel speak to me, but she said again and again that Muriel is isolated in a house in Portugal, that she is in a process of spiritual purification and religious devoutness and should not be in touch with anyone from her past. However, she added, expenses were significant and the rabbi was asking for an additional two hundred thousand dollars. Here, for the first time, I felt I would not yield to his authority. I didn't pay. I preferred to invest the money in finding Muriel. I asked Monsieur Darmond to search Europe and especially Portugal and… Yes, Sally, we were wrong. We thought we knew where she was: In a small village near Oporto. The investigations company reported that Shlomit was living there with her, along with two maids and Ben David who arrives every now and then on the weekend. Muriel, they argued, never left for a moment. They tried to question the maids when they went shopping, but the maids shut up and disappeared. I don't know if they were wrong, were misled, or deceived me knowingly. We will check that." An expression of fury spread across his face and disappeared. "I called Shlomit's mobile phone every day. She said Muriel was not interested in speaking to me. She was hurt. I was a difficult man, she argued, and inconsiderate, and she was debating whether she should stay with me. Meanwhile, I needed to take care of the children, to send them to school, to see to their emotional needs. I can't do it. I simply can't. They need Muriel back and I wanted her back; if not for me, at least for them."

"May I?" Jerry bent forward toward the cognac bottle.

"Of course," said Marin, and continued. "Therefore, I needed to separate her from Ben David. Monsieur Darmond found a lawyer in Israel who promised to find Ben David, obtain information about him, and file a complaint against him for every possible felony until he lets go of Muriel and releases his wife's supervision of her. I paid the lawyer one hundred and thirty thousand dollars, but he did nothing. He cheated me, too, buying time with various excuses. After six months of suffering, he argued that Ben David violated no law and nothing could be done to him. Now I understand he had colluded with Ben David, and together they began tightening the noose around my neck: Vivian Moyal flooded my office with telephone calls, Ben David sent me messages about the need to give Joel a bar mitzvah, and Shlomit, who returned to Israel meanwhile, said she had left Muriel in the care of a different rabbi's wife who moved into the house in Portugal. Again and again, she insisted that Muriel refuses to speak with me. Turns out I financed a vacation on the beach in Portugal for Shlomit, then another woman, while Muriel was in Beersheba the entire time."

He laughed bitterly. "So many sophisticated businessmen tried to trick me and failed, and this gang succeeded. I can't understand it."

"In business, people are constantly alert to any harm," Sally commented. "Not so in personal life. They hurt your most vulnerable spot, where you were most trusting: Your family."

"Yes," Marin nodded sadly. "That probably explains it." He shook his head. "I have no illusions. She won't return to me. But the children need her, and for their sake I'm prepared for any kind of separation settlement. Sally, you seem like the right person to me. You have experience in intelligence, a sense for detective work, ties, connections, and feminine wisdom. You've succeeded in finding Muriel where a large investigation agency failed. Can you bring her back to the children?" For a moment, his eyes were begging just like those of his younger son, whom Sally met at the entrance to the house.

"I don't know. I need to think." She was already starting to conceive a plan.

"Please. I have lawyers, detectives, assistants—but I need someone like you. I will pay any sum you ask for."

"I'm employed by an insurance company. I will take an unpaid leave of absence, and when everything ends I'll go back to work. All I'm asking you for is to cover the expenses."

He looked at her with astonishment.

"What is so surprising to you about that?"

"No one ever did anything for me for free, and when it came to Israelis, things were much worse. Everyone deceived me, not only Ben David and the lawyer. There were many others."

"That's why I'm willing to help you," said Sally. "To prove to you that not all Israelis are cheats. The only thing I want is free access to any information you have and to meet the lawyer who took care of the matter. And yes, I would like Monsieur Darmond to travel with me and cover my expenses, with your permission. I will give him receipts for everything."

Marin nodded his head.

"We must pay the private investigator I employed, He will contact

Darmond and he will pay him directly. My friend who planted the eaves-dropping equipment also deserves something. Five thousand dollars seems like a fair sum." She looked at her watch. "Tomorrow I will return to Tel Aviv and start acting."

Marin stared at her for a long while, and then a rare smile appeared on his face. "Thank you, Madame Sally, Monsieur Jerry. Tomorrow at lunch you will receive tickets for the eight o'clock flight from Geneva."

Back in the guest room, Jerry asked, "Why do you need Darmond in Israel?"

"So that I don't need to turn to Marin every time I need to pay some-one, and besides, I prefer him on my home turf, close to me, rather than here where he can sabotage things."

"You realize you are playing poker with him?"

"My hand is better."

"True, but even in such a case the game can end badly for you."

"How?"

"Have you never watched a Western?"

"I have, but what can defeat a good hand?"

"A gun," said Jerry.

24.

The following morning, Natalia knocked on their door at the guestroom. "Monsieur Marin would like to know if you are interested in leaving for the airport earlier, and stop at the town for an hour or two."

Jerry looked uncertain. Sally replied, "Yes, of course."

Evening fell early, and as they drove away from Marin's mansion, lights began appearing in the villages and farms dotting the hillsides. The car traveled on country roads whose sides were covered in snow. Glancing through the left wing mirror, Sally noticed a gray Peugeot following them. It would not have drawn her attention were it not the only car on the road, adapting its speed to theirs. As they entered Gstaad, she whispered to Jerry, "Someone is following us."

"I know," he replied. "My side has a mirror too."

"Police?" Sally asked, concerned.

"I don't think so. Police would have pulled us over. Someone following us would have the opposite intention: To obtain information about our actions at any given moment."

"Maybe Marin? He could have woken up in the morning full of doubt."

"Maybe," Jerry retorted, laconically.

The limousine came to a halt near a snow-covered pedestrian street, glowing in the dark. The Peugeot parked a distance away, sticking out among the fancy cars like a sore thumb. The pedestrian street was lined with designer fashion shops, banks, jewelry shops, and ski suppliers. "How do people live here?" wondered Sally aloud as Jacques opened the door for her. "No supermarkets? Hairdressers? Hardware stores?"

The driver laughed. "Not here. Millionaires arrive here from across Europe, and here they buy everything they need. Millionaires, you can imagine, don't shop at supermarkets."

"So where do they shop?" she asked.

"All the food consumed at Mr. Marin's house, for example, is delivered by a supply company."

"And what's done with all the leftover food?"

"Mr. Marin demands that much more than he needs is cooked, so that he can donate to the poor. A special car delivers the food to a soup kitchen he established in Geneva. According to your religion that is a good deed, is it not?"

"It is," Sally affirmed with satisfaction. Marin's generosity required no proof, but she was glad for the confirmation.

Sally spent the next half hour at the Lorenz Bach boutique shop. She bought a silk scarf, a pair of shoes, and a few sets of underwear she was sure Jerry would appreciate. Meanwhile, her husband passed the time at the Alpha Romeo display room nearby. When she arrived at the cashier, the driver awaited her there. "Monsieur Marin insists on paying for the shopping," he declared. "In fact, it's already been paid. He has a tab at this shop."

On the way to the airport, the gray Peugeot could not be seen, if indeed it was still following them. At the terminal, a stewardess awaited them, an exact replay of the reception they had had in Tel Aviv. She swiftly walked them through check-in, security, and passport control, delivering them to their first-class seats. Darmond, however, arrived last, a moment before the flight closed. He sat a few seats away from them, reading newspapers he brought with him. Jerry watched a film and Sally shut her eyes and let her mind wander. While abroad, she often met people with opinions of Jews and Israel similar to those of Marin, and always felt a stab in her heart. Now she finally had the opportunity to prove to an influential man that things weren't so. She was steadfast and undaunted. Who would try to harm her? Ben David was only dangerous to those who fell into his net and believed in him. Monsieur Darmond also seemed harmless, although he remained an enigma to her. He was supposedly loyal to Marin, but Sally couldn't forget Jacob's report that Darmond stayed at the Four Seasons Hotel while Vivian Moyal visited it as an unregistered guest. Did she stay in his room? The information collected by the investigation company hired by Darmond also turned out to be baseless. Was he tricked by the company or did he conspire against his employer? His blatant coldness toward her and Jerry only increased her angst. What was he up to?

She preferred to put her doubts aside and focus on the important matters: First, returning Muriel to her children and second, exposing Ben David so that he couldn't entrap other people. It was clear to her that she was entering an adventure with a known beginning but a mysterious end. She could expect surveillance, eavesdropping, time away from home, work at ungodly hours, and untold dangers. But she was prepared for all of this and saw it as an opportunity to do something meaningful that could save her people's reputation. As far as she was concerned, it was a mitzvah.

After landing in Tel Aviv and rushing through the regular stations with the help of a skilled stewardess, Darmond approached them. "I will go straight to my hotel," he said with a smile that did not correspond with his standoffish behavior during the flight. "We'll talk on the phone and coordinate the meeting with the lawyer."

"What hotel will you stay at?" asked Sally. "Perhaps we can share a taxi."

Darmond led the way to the taxi station. When they arrived, he said, "Ladies first," and helped Sally into the first taxi. Jerry sat next to her. Darmond then said, "There's no point in us squeezing in. I will take the next taxi." He shut the door lightly.

"Did you see that?" asked Sally. "He's avoiding us. What's his story?"

"Maybe those are Marin's instructions. He wouldn't disobey his boss."

They looked through the back window and saw Darmond walk past the row of taxis, cross the street, and approach a car waiting for him. It too was a Peugeot. "He has something with Peugeots," Jerry said.

"He has something with us," murmured Sally as the Peugeot followed them and disappeared at the first interchange.

25.

Late at night, after unpacking her suitcases and distributing gifts to the children, Sally sipped wine in the dim living room. The events of the recent days seemed like a dream to her: The plush site in the Alps, Marin's powerful and tortured personality, the child with golden hair who pleaded for his mother, and the cunning Darmond. She was sure he wouldn't call to coordinate the meeting with the Israeli lawyer and blame her for that as well.

But he did call, and even did so quickly. The next day, at seven a.m., Sally's mobile phone rang. Darmond announced that he had scheduled an appointment with Mr. Ovadia at the Daniel Hotel at ten. "Monsieur Pierre has a suite here," he said, with a candor that contrasted with his elusiveness on the flight and at the airport. "And I'm staying in it."

"I'll be there," said Sally dryly.

At breakfast, she described the conversation to Jerry. "I wonder what he's preparing for me now," she added. After preparing lunch for the children and tidying the house, she put on a dark business suit and high-heeled shoes, and left.

The only parking space near the hotel was a dusty dirt lot, which was not promising for Sally's shoes. When she arrived at the reception, the leather on her heels was already scratched. She asked for the phone number of Mr. Marin's suite, and to her surprise was asked to wait on one of the lobby couches. She watched the clerk pick up the telephone receiver and speak quietly into it. After he was done, he signaled to her to wait some more. A few seconds later, a different clerk approached her and asked her to follow him.

They ascended to the eighth floor and turned onto a long corridor. One of the doors was open and cast a square of light onto the blue carpet. A thundering voice spoke French with a heavy Middle Eastern accent, and a voice replied curtly—Darmond's voice.

The clerk stopped at the open door, knocked on it softly, and disappeared. Darmond appeared wearing white tennis clothes and shook her hand politely. She followed him into a large sitting room that overlooked the sea. The man with the thundering voice was tall, full-bodied, and boasted a potbelly that swayed before him. He wore a large kippah. The hat of a Hassid rested on the table, next to a pile of plastic folders filled with papers. The man glanced at her briefly and said, "Attorney Ovadia, pleased to meet you."

"Pleased to meet you too," she replied, even though she wasn't.

Ovadia collapsed on one of the couches and said in Hebrew, "Mr. Darmond tried to explain your role here, but with little success. Are you a lawyer?"

Sally sat on the couch across from him and watched the sea glistening beyond his shoulder. "I suggest we switch to English," she said pleasantly, "so that Mr. Darmond can also be part of the conversation. No, I'm not a lawyer. Enough lawyers have been meddling in this. I was appointed by Mr. Marin to examine what you've done so far to release his wife from Ben David's influence."

"*Rabbi* Ben David," Ovadia corrected her, "has no connection to Mrs. Marin."

"How do you know?"

"I've used the largest investigation company in Europe. They filed reports on the matter and Mr. Darmond can attest to that."

Sally looked at Darmond, who signaled at a pile of files laying on the table. "It's all here," added Ovadia, "but I doubt you can read it. Most of the documents are in French."

Sally smiled again. "And what exactly do they say?"

"That Mrs. Marin fled her husband to somewhere in Europe. She isn't interested in staying in touch with him—"

"Or with her children?"

Ovadia hesitated for a moment. "That's an issue we weren't asked to look into," he replied, "but I assume that there are problems on that issue too. In any case, the matter has nothing to do with Rabbi Ben David, so there's no option of filing a complaint, as Mr. Darmond requested. Even you can understand that."

Sally nodded. "Even I understand," she said.

"And since you were appointed by Mr. Marin to deal with this, I must remind you that I'm still owed fifty-four thousand dollars for the work I did, plus expenses."

"You deserve what you deserve," said Sally.

Ovadia smiled contently.

"And I would also recommend that Mr. Marin pay immediately."

Ovadia nodded.

"That is, if Mrs. Marin were really in Europe."

"What?" Ovadia jumped up. "What do you mean?"

Sally turned to Darmond. "You haven't told him?"

"He did," Ovadia interrupted, "but I proved to him that it's nonsense." He walked to the table and pulled out a file from one of the folders. "Hermes, a company active in Switzerland and across the EU, with a reputation since 1898, claims that Mrs. Marin lives in Portugal in a village called—"

"Please hand me the report." Sally's voice turned severe. She examined the document for a long while, even though she understood nothing written in it. "Where are the photographs?" she asked.

Ovadia handed her a series of photographs of a fair-haired woman taken from a distance behind a house window. Sally examined them one after the other. Then she pulled out her mobile phone. "Here I have photos that were taken in Beersheba ten days ago. Mr. Marin confirmed beyond all doubt that the woman in them is his wife. When are your photos from?"

The shadow of a doubt crossed Ovadia's face. He hesitated for a moment, a hesitation picked up by Darmond. "You gave them to me a month ago."

"Yes, a month," confirmed Ovadia, "maybe a bit more. She may have come to Beersheba later."

The expression on Darmond's face turned stern. "Before Madame Sally entered, I asked you and you said—"

"Yes, I said there was no chance Mrs. Marin was in Beersheba. But if Mr. Marin says it's definitely his wife…" Small beads of sweat began appearing on Ovadia's forehead. "Maybe she went there after her picture was taken in Portugal."

"And the investigation company didn't report this?" Darmond insisted.

Ovadia squirmed. "It may have. I need to check at the office. I have a number of employees."

Sally reexamined the document. "There's a number here for the Geneva office." She tapped it into her mobile phone and put it to her ear. "There's no reply," she said.

"Maybe the operator is busy," suggested Ovadia.

Sally smiled, hung up, and dialed again. This time she didn't even wait to put the loudspeaker on.

"The number is disconnected," a pleasant voice said in French. "The number is disconnected. The number is disconnected…" She looked at the two men with an expression of bewilderment on her face.

"Maybe they're on vacation?" proposed Ovadia. "A holiday or something?"

"I come from Geneva," Darmond reminded him. "We have no holidays now. If you're out of excuses," he added venomously, "maybe you should tell the truth."

"They must have changed the number," stated Ovadia. "I'll find out the new number and call them today."

"Enough already." Darmond's voice was cold and hostile. "It's all fake, isn't it? The reports, the photos. I assume that during the forgery process you changed the telephone number and maybe even the address so that I wouldn't be able to check, and indeed I didn't. That's how much I trusted you and the person who recommended you." His face was flushed in a mixture of rage and shame. He walked over to the door and locked it. "Please Madame. Sally," he said, and for the first time she could feel his appreciation for her, "call the police. Until it arrives Mr. Ovadia isn't leaving this room."

Sally started dialing.

"This is illegal imprisonment," the lawyer wailed.

"You can complain when the police arrive," Darmond said.

"That's exactly what I'll do," answered Ovadia confidently. Sally glared at him. "Aren't you ashamed of yourself? A man in distress, his wife is sick, crazy with concern, and you forge an investigation, cheat everyone, and have the nerve to ask for money? Once the police are done with you, not only will you never practice law, you won't even be employed as a table cleaner at McDonald's." She switched the call to speaker. After three rings a voice answered. "Police. Hello?"

Ovadia suddenly seemed like a trapped animal. "Please," he said. He got down on his knees. "Maybe I was wrong. I've been misled. One of the employees in my office conducted the communication with Hermes, and I fired him a month ago after catching him stealing. He may have involved me in this too."

"Police. Hello?" the voice sounded again.

"I'm sorry, wrong number," Sally said and hung up. "What's your connection to Ben David?" she asked Ovadia.

"No connection, I swear. Nothing. I ordered an investigation and—"

"You have one last chance to confess," Sally said. "Tell the truth and I'll ask Mr. Marin to forgive you for cheating him."

Ovadia glanced from Darmond to Sally and back again.. "You're right," he said, his lower lip quivering. "I was going through a tough time. I have a heart condition and need a transplant. Hospitals and medication sucked all of my money." He fell to the floor, grasping his chest. "I feel bad."

Sally and Darmond exchanged looks. Darmond was fuming.

"Please," begged Ovadia, "let me out. I need to take my medicine."

Darmond shook his head. Sally felt sorry for the man lying beneath them, useless. "I'll forget about the police complaint on one condition."

"Anything you say," replied Ovadia.

"Do what you were paid for. Persuade Muriel to return to her husband and children."

"That's impossible."

"Why?" asked Sally. "Because Ben David doesn't want her to?"

"He's a difficult man. Difficult and stubborn. You have no idea how much. He won't let her go."

"Schedule a meeting for me with him."

"He won't want to. He's already angry at Marin for stopping the donations."

Sally took her mobile. "Then there's no other choice," she said.

"No, don't call. I'll arrange a meeting."

"For tomorrow," Sally demanded.

"For tomorrow, for tomorrow." Ovadia collected his hat and fled the room. Sally turned to the table and picked up the documents and files he left behind. "I want to go over them," she explained. "They may be fraudulent, but I might find something in them."

To her surprise, she heard the sound of sobbing behind her. She turned and met Darmond's eyes, which were red and teary. "How can I face that wonderful man, Pierre Marin, and tell him I didn't protect him? He maintains a semblance of stability, but I know he's devastated. His wife went crazy and ran away, the children are completely destabilized. What will I tell him? That another Jew tried to trick him out of money? What kind of people are you—a people of swindlers, liars, thieves? Pierre Marin's only crime is being rich. In Switzerland nobody dreams of cheating him, but his Jewish brothers tear the flesh off him. Ben David, Ovadia, and honestly Madame. Sally, I'm not sure where you fit in. Why did you give up on the police? You know that Ovadia won't make the appointment, he will do nothing, maybe even flee the country."

"I've given up on the police because I don't think Mr. Marin would want such publicity," Sally replied. "And as for Ovadia, I don't need him to set up a meeting with Ben David. I want him to tell Ben David about our encounter and cause him to act."

"Why would you want him to act?"

"Because we're stuck. There is nothing we can do to make Muriel to return to her husband. She just doesn't want to. As soon as Ben David acts, he will expose his connection to the story and perhaps also incriminating details."

Darmond shrugged. "I would have filed a complaint against Ben David with the police and ended the matter."

"By doing so you might have fulfilled your obligation to Marin, but not advanced the investigation or brought Muriel home." She sat across from him. "Let's pretend I'm the investigator who received the complaint. What would you like to tell me? An adult woman, legally in Israel, doesn't want to return to her husband and children."

"I want to report that a man named Ben David impersonated a rabbi and extorted huge sums of money from a Swiss billionaire."

"Do you have any proof of extortion?"

"I will sit with Monsieur. Pierre, hear the story from him, go over every document he has, and provide proof. I believe Ben David can be thrown into prison for many years."

"Convicting Ben David isn't our goal at the moment, but bringing back Muriel and maybe retrieving funds that were stolen under false pretenses is. If you want to help your boss, you have no choice but to let me act in my way." She stood up and went back to organizing the documents on the table. "By the way, how did you find Ovadia?"

"A woman, a good friend, connected us. She will also have to answer to me."

Sally could only think of one name. "Vivian Moyal?"

Darmond was taken aback. "How did you know?"

She suddenly realized something else. "Is she the one who picked you up from the airport yesterday?"

Darmond didn't answer.

"She must have told you not to trust me, and probably said I was planning to extort Marin. That's why you had us tailed in Geneva."

Darmond remained silent.

"You must decide what side you're on, Monsieur Darmond. If you want us to work together, you have to trust me. None of what we've said can be passed on to Vivian." She collected the folders and Ovadia's business card from the table.

"What now?" asked Darmond. "What's the plan?"

"We wait," Sally replied. "I'm curious to see what happens."

She didn't have to wait long. Arriving at her car in the dirt parking lot, she found all four tires punctured. Piles of earth were thrown onto her hood; the sharp stones scratched the fancy white veneer.

26.

The waiter at the café was no less angry than Sally. "You should be grateful it's only tires," he said. "I had my car broken into and my multimedia system stolen." He placed a cup of cappuccino and two tiny cookies on her table. Sally looked through the window at the large dirt parking lot. "But this was just vandalism. They didn't try to steal anything." The waiter went to clean a nearby table. "Someone was probably annoyed by your beautiful BMW. There are plenty of those." Sally looked at her car with sadness. She had bought it as a birthday gift for herself just this year, and always kept it polished and shiny. Now the car seemed flawed, violated. She had a childish impulse to abandon the car in the lot and buy a new, unscathed one.

The phone rang. Sally quickly looked at the screen. If the caller was Ovadia, she wouldn't answer but let him try again a few times. But it was Darmond. "Madame Sally," he began without a hello, "I must return to Geneva today. The next flight leaves at four and I've already booked a ticket."

"What?" Sally let out a shout. "I need you here!"

"I've just received a few phone calls, Madame Sally. They threatened my family. They knew exactly where my wife works, where my children study. They placed a condition on me: If I don't let this go, my children will be harmed and my wife murdered. They even explained in detail how it would happen, but I'll spare you that. I just wanted to let you know I'm leaving."

"I'm not far from the hotel," Sally said. She decided not to tell him of the vandalism to her car. "I'll come right back and we'll talk."

"No!" Darmond replied with determination and alarm. "I want nothing to do with this. I will tell Marin this too. They know my address, they described my house, and named my daughters' school."

"And Marin? This 'wonderful man' as you called him? You'll just leave him helpless?"

"I will continue to accompany the case from Geneva. There's a good, large, law firm I will approach for this. Some of its associates specialize in family law. They will be able to help Pierre better than I will."

"And how would you feel if they backed out after being threatened?"

"Madame Sally, I don't have answers to all of your questions," said Darmond, sounding defeated.

"All right," Sally replied, and hung up without saying goodbye.

The attack on her car and the threats to Darmond left her angry and frustrated. She tried to assess the tools at her disposal. At this point, Ben David was uninvolved and protected from the law, but a complaint could still be filed with the police against Ovadia, and the fake documents he left could lead her forward. Was there something else? She scanned her mind, trying to find a way that would lead her to the immediate goal: Bringing

Muriel back to her children, and perhaps to the more distant goal of removing Ben David from the Marin family. No ideas emerged.

The tow truck arrived, sending a cloud of dust into the air. Sally left a money note on the table to cover the coffee and maybe partially console the waiter for the damage caused to his car, and left. "Do you need to get somewhere?" the driver asked her after fastening her car to the towing platform.

"I'll call a taxi," she said calmly.

The driver looked her up and down. "I'll drive you home."

"Thanks, I'll manage." She pulled the phone out of the chaos in her handbag to call a taxi, but at that moment it rang. "Yes," she answered.

"How are you?" Marin's pleasant voice was on the other end of the line.

"Could be better," she admitted. "I assume Darmond already spoke to you."

"He did. I relieved him of his duties. Another lawyer from the same firm will pick it up from here. Do you want to back off as well?"

"Not at all." Sally sat on the edge of a bench. "I don't know how to act yet, but desertion is out of the question."

"I really appreciate that. I trust you to deliver Muriel to Geneva soon." From his mouth, the words sounded like an order.

In the taxi en route to Tel Aviv, Sally reflected on the conversation. The sentence "I trust you to deliver Muriel to Geneva soon" echoed in her mind. "I trust you to deliver Muriel to Geneva soon." The telephone rang again. She put it to her ear. "If you want to see your children grow up, keep your filthy hands off the saint Ben David."

"Is this Ben David speaking, or is he too scared to call and prefers to send one of his lackeys?"

"We know where you live and what—"

"Yes, yes, I know. You'll do this and do that and you've already flattened my tires and poured sand onto my car. You don't expect me to be scared of a toy criminal posing as a rabbi, do you?"

The call disconnected.

Never in her life had Sally felt so exposed to evilness and criminality. She had stumbled across them here and there, but never at the level of sophistication and audacity that Ben David, Ovadia and Moyal were engaged in. She was reminded of Darmond's accusation: "What kind of people are you? A people of cheats, liars and thieves." Was he right? Once again, she felt the urge to prove him wrong. After all, the Jewish people had millions of honest, wonderful members, including many righteous rabbis. It saddened her that one imposter, joined by a conniving woman and a greedy lawyer, could tarnish the reputation of an entire nation.

She recalled a verse from the Second Book of Samuel that her father would quote when she was a child every time he came across an act of wickedness: "The wicked are made speechless in the darkness, for it is not by one's own strength that one prevails." He had his own personal interpretation of the verse. He would hold her little hand and explain, "You can't act against the wicked with power, only with cunning. The wicked are confident of their strength, but the just must trust their minds."

Suddenly Sally knew what she must do. She blew her wise father an imaginary kiss and pulled Ovadia's business card out of her handbag. "This is Sally Amir," she said when he answered.

"I haven't spoken to him yet," he squealed. "We only parted an hour ago."

"I know you already have. He's already threatened me and Darmond and damaged my car. But that's not what this is about. I have an offer for you."

"Yeees?" he responded with suspicion.

"I want to tell you something that must remain between us. I didn't mention it in the hotel because I didn't want Darmond to hear, and if you know what's good for you, you'll tell no one, only Ben David."

"I'm listening."

"There's another rabbi, greater than him and well known in the rabbinic world. A real certified rabbi and with a clean past—"

"You're denouncing a saint and Torah scholar," Ovadia interrupted her.

"I know. I'll be punished in heaven. In any event, I want Mr. Marin to meet that rabbi and be impressed with him. Unlike Ben David, he's not interested in money and doesn't get involved in the lives of the people he supports. He only advises. There's no reason why he shouldn't become Marin's spiritual adviser."

"But Rabbi Ben David is also a Kabbalist and a holy man. There are testimonies. He's made miracles, cured bedridden patients. Mr. Marin himself was cured of cancer thanks to him."

"All right," said Sally, "let's assume he's a saint. There are many saints. If he wants to remain Marin's adviser, I demand three things of him: One, to bring Muriel home. I know she doesn't want to live with Mr. Marin, but I can convince him to rent her a house in Gstaad with all expenses covered, and also provide her a monthly stipend of, say, fifteen thousand dollars."

"And what if she doesn't agree?"

"She will continue to live in Beersheba, penniless and disconnected from her children."

"She wants to live there to be close to the rabbi, who will prepare her son for his bar mitzvah Torah reading."

Sally expected that reaction. "A few months prior to the bar mitzvah, Ben David will be able to come to Gstaad, stay at a hotel, and teach Joel. That solves the problem, doesn't it?"

"I'm writing it all down."

"The second demand is that he stops asking Marin for money. All payments will go through me. He will receive travel money and be paid for the lessons he gives Joel, but nothing beyond that."

"Rabbi Ben David is sought after worldwide. If he travels to Marin, he'll be waiving significant income. Why should he agree to your offer?"

"So that he can continue calling himself Pierre Marin's spiritual adviser. That's worth a lot of money in the holiness market," Sally snickered. "It's the perfect deal. Ben David maintains his fake reputation and doesn't need to return a penny of the money he cheated Marin out of." Ovadia exhaled in protest. Sally ignored it and continued. "And Mr. Marin will have his wife back. In addition, his son will be immersed in Judaism. Marin is a good Jew, who would seriously like a Jewish family. Before you ask why *you* should agree, let me remind you of the felonies you've committed: Forgery, first degree fraud, extortion under false pretexts—"

"You said you had three demands," Ovadia interrupted her, swallowing his pride. "I only heard two: Returning Muriel and stopping the payments from Marin. What is the third?"

"A payment of two hundred thousand dollars."

Ovadia fell silent.

"Are you still there?"

"I just wonder why a rich man like Marin would ask a poor rabbi for two hundred thousand dollars."

Sally waited a moment before dropping the bomb. "It's not for Marin, it's for me. I also deserve part of what Ben David earned from Marin, no?"

Ovadia laughed nervously. "Yes, I mean, I'm not sure the rabbi will agree."

"He's no fool. He knows what's good for him."

"I didn't realize you were also—how should I put it?—like that."

"We're all like that," Sally said and hung up.

PART TWO

27.

A white slope could be seen from the windows, like the slope below Pierre Marin's mansion. The vicinity to the mansion was one of the reasons Sally chose the house at the edge of Gstaad, hoping to reduce Rubi and Joel's sense of detachment from their father.

But the children could not be consoled with all the riches of the land of whipped cream: A network of ski slopes surrounding the tiny, rich town. Rubi sobbed and Joel, his older brother, stared at Sally suspiciously. "Are you sure she'll arrive today?" he asked.

"She should be here any minute."

"Why is she only coming now?" Rubi asked. "Didn't she love us before?"

"She loves you a lot, but she was sick."

"That's not true," Joel said. "She didn't want to live with our father. I heard her shouting before she left. She told him he's a cold man. What is a cold man?"

"Do you want to go out to the garden and wait for her?" Sally evaded the question.

"What is a cold man?" Joel asked again.

A toot sounded outside. Rubi sprung up and leaped to the door. Joel rushed behind him. Sally knocked on the nanny's door, and when she opened it, she signaled her to come out. Sally herself remained in the modest living room, monitoring the entrance to the house through the window.

A large car entered the property with a soft purr of its engine. Only the screeching of tires on gravel could be heard. The moment it stopped, Rubi circled it running, banging on its doors and shouting, "Mommy, Mommy!" A door opened and two long legs draped in an ankle-length dress emerged. Muriel's arms, also fully covered, reached out to hug Rubi. Joel stepped hesitantly toward his mother, and she detached one arm from Rubi and stretched it out toward her elder son, beckoning him to come. Joel stood where he was. Muriel got out of the car and approached him, Rubi still clinging to her thigh. "Come, my dear. I love you."

"You're a bad mother!" Joel shouted. "You left Dad and didn't take us with you. We mean nothing to you!"

Muriel glanced at the driver who was busy extracting her suitcases from the boot, then at the nanny who stood frozen at the door, and burst into tears. Sally withdrew from the window with a heavy heart. She passed quickly through the rooms and left the house through the back door. A silver Bentley flashed its lights at her. Sally got into the car and sat next to Marin. "Is everything okay?" he asked as the car started driving.

"Rubi is happy. Joel is angry at Muriel for not taking them when she left. I hope she can calm him."

"She'll know how to," said Marin with an air of conviction. "She always knew how to deal with them. I'm glad they're with her now. Did you agree on the days when they will come to me?"

"It's all written in the agreement. The children will live here, in Gstaad, and visit you twice a week and every other weekend. In any event, I plan to place twenty-four hour surveillance on the house."

Marin examined the fancy street outside through the car window. "Why? What can go wrong? The children have gotten their mother back; Muriel has a house for herself and lives away from me. Everyone is satisfied, no?"

"Ben David isn't satisfied. I think he hasn't given up on the original goal he had when he took control of Muriel—to reach your money. He lost a lot on this round, but will try to make it up on the next one, when he comes to prepare Joel for his bar mitzvah. There's no telling if he won't try to seduce Muriel into taking another spiritual trip to Israel. This time Rubi and Joel will not let go of her. They will come with her, and you'll have to cooperate if you want to stay in touch with them."

"Maybe we can find another rabbi to prepare Joel?"

"She won't agree. To her, Ben David is God's emissary on earth."

Marin opened the minibar door and poured them both glasses of liquor.

"Therefore," Sally added, "I must know what he's up to so I can act immediately."

"Twenty-four hour surveillance costs money—a lot of money. I want to know the cost in advance, before I find myself committed to a fortune in fees. I still owe you reimbursement for travel, the private investigator, the friend who helped you—"

"She'll be here tomorrow and replace me while I'm in Israel."

"That's another expense. I want to know how much I owe you until now."

"You don't owe me anything."

"Please!" his voice rose with impatience.

"Why are you angry?"

"Because when I'm told I owe nothing for a service, I know I will eventually pay double. There are no free meals. Please explain this game of yours. How much do I owe? How much more will I have to pay?"

Sally laughed. The embarrassment she caused this strong man amused her. "You don't need to know everything."

Marin banged his hand on the seat back. "It's my money and I need to know what is done with it."

"I'm not paying the investigator and my friend with your money."

"Don't play with me," Marin fumed. "I don't like riddles and you're becoming too big of a riddle, Sally. It's true you've only done me good so far, but if you insist on hiding details from me, our story is over."

Sally bit her bottom lip. "All right," she said. "I'll explain. I'm really not proud of what I'm going to tell you, but I considered it a form of justice. I rescued some money from Ben David, a fraction of what he took from you. In my agreement with Ovadia there was an article I didn't tell you about, whereby Ben David gave me two hundred thousand dollars. He's sure I pocketed the sum. In fact, I used it to pay the investigator in Israel and the investigators who follow Muriel, I funded my travel, Diana's salary, and—"

"Wait," Marin said. "You're telling me you managed to get two hundred thousand dollars from Ben David and didn't even take a dollar?"

Sally nodded. "I deposited all of it to an account I opened in Credit

Suisse, and I only withdraw funds related to this case."

"What are you made of, Sally?"

"I'm made of what any person should be—mind, feeling, and conscience."

"I've lived many years without meeting a person like you."

"You're living in the wrong places. You were born into wealth and have lived an affluent life. Affluence is deceiving. When you have enough money, it does good. When you have too much, it becomes harmful and attracts the wrong people."

Marin shook his head trying to understand. "I still don't believe it. You don't want anything in return for all you've done for me?"

"I do this because it's important for me to heal the world around me. I especially want to correct your impression of the Jews, your brethren, and help you to return to your Judaism."

"Ben David is also Jewish."

"Ben David is a Jew who went bad. He gives the Jewish people a bad reputation. That's why I allowed myself to trick him about the money. Deceit is an ugly act, but when it's geared at harming a villain like Ben David and bringing about a result that rectifies the wrong he caused others, it's justified."

The car stopped at the entrance to the mansion. Jacques extended his hand through the window and tapped the entrance code. "Are you comfortable in the guesthouse?" Marin asked suddenly.

Sally was surprised. It was the first time since she started working with him that Marin took interest in her well-being. "Yes, absolutely. It has everything."

"And you don't miss Jerry?" he added with a curious smile.

"Very much," she added. "I wish he could come."

"Money is no issue, you know."

"Time is an issue—his time. He's very busy. That's why I plan to return home a day after tomorrow, to be with him and the kids. My friend and partner Diana will report back to me on developments and oversee the surveillance of the house."

The car continued to the guesthouse entrance. Sally turned to leave, but Marin grasped her wrist, holding her back. She looked at him, embarrassed. He was silent for a long moment, then swallowed hard and said, "Thank you. Thank you for doing this and for who you are. You've saved my life."

Sally smiled. "Maybe this proves that no act of kindness goes unrewarded. You saved my life many years ago in London, and now I'm paying you back."

28.

The large rooms were empty. Sally went to the kitchen to make herself a cup of coffee. On the shelf she only found a jar of instant coffee. She could, of course, phone Natalia, the housekeeper, and ask for a cup of strong, black coffee, but she felt it would be too much bother.

She opened cabinet after cabinet. They were all packed with food, but there was not one package of black coffee. In the gap between two cabinets, her eye caught a glimmer. She moved to the left and investigated the gap from the side. There could be no doubt. It was a tiny camera lens.

She overcame the urge to touch it, took a pack of chocolate from one of the shelves, and continued to walk nonchalantly along the row of cabinets. Her face was calm, but her eyes were searching for another glimmer. Her half hour search revealed three more lenses, which, along with the first, covered the entire kitchen.

From the kitchen she moved to the bedroom, where she found another lens, hidden in the bed's backboard within a fold in the upholstery. Here, again, she made sure not to give the slightest indication that she had found it. But inside she was fuming. Whoever watched the footage captured by the lenses—and watching her now—probably watched her and Jerry make love, eavesdropping on their conversations. She wondered whether the cameras were installed to follow them, or whether they had always been there to satisfy Marin's need for control and information.

The telephone in her pocket rang. "We've just landed," Diana reported. "Where do I find your driver?"

Sally marched quickly toward the front door and left the house.

"Hello?" Diana asked. "Sally, are you there?"

Only once she was deep in the garden did Sally answer. "Wait, don't look for the driver. There's a change of plan. Don't come here. Find a good hotel and book a room. I'll come talk to you."

"You promised me a fancy guesthouse," Diana complained, partly in jest and partly seriously.

"Go to a hotel called d'Angleterre. It's just as fancy. I'll explain everything later."

The sun started setting and the trees in the garden cast long shadows on the grass. Sally returned to her room, making sure not to switch on the lights, and took her handbag from the dresser. She left the house and walked to the backyard, where she opened a small door in the wall to a huge grassy field. She walked across it, feeling the moisture penetrate her shoes. When she arrived at the road, she turned down toward the valley. She could see the lights in the small village in the distance, and she walked there for two hours, thankful for her daily exercise sessions that kept her aerobic abilities up to shape. *Who could be behind the installment of the cameras?* she wondered. Marin owned the property and could make changes to it, no questions asked. But Ben David, or any other hostile element, could have also installed the equipment during the many days when the guesthouse was empty, and Marin's house was abandoned for journeys around the world.

A beer advertisement flashed over a café. Sally pushed the swinging wooden door in and entered. All the patrons went silent as they looked at the stranger. She went up to the counter, which a fat man was wiping with a moist rag. "I need a taxi," Sally said in English.

The man shrugged. "Not English," he said and turned to speak to the clients in charmless, local French. A woman with a wide farmer's face rose from her chair at the corner. "Yes, please?"

"I need a taxi," she repeated. "I need to get to Geneva."

"There are no taxis here, but in another—" she looked at her watch "—in another three minutes a bus will arrive. It reaches the train station in Gstaad. There you can catch a train to Geneva." She looked at her watch again. "The last one leaves at six fifty-three. You'll make it." She held Sally's arm and escorted her to the door. "The bus will stop here, at the entrance to the café."

The bus arrived from around the corner with typical Swiss precision. Sally got on and sat on a hard, wooden bench. The bumpy ride of the vehicle on the country roads made her feel unusually sad not to have more body padding. She arrived at Gstaad twenty minutes before the train's departure and had time to buy herself a bottle of mineral water and a snack. At the Geneva train station, she got in a cab and asked the driver to stop at a distance from the Hotel d'Angleterre. An evening breeze was blowing, cool but pleasant. Sally found a small public garden, sat on a bench, and dialed the series of numbers she had written on a note.

Diana arrived immediately and fell into her arms. "What's this secrecy? What's going on?"

"I want to keep this compartmentalized," said Sally. "It's better that they don't know you at Marin's house, in case someone there is cooperating with Ben David."

"Did something happen? Do you suspect someone?"

Sally attempted to quickly recall everyone she knew at the mansion. Natalia, Jacques the driver, Rubi and Joel's nanny, Darmond, and even Marin himself. She decided to keep the information to herself until things clear up. "I don't know yet. In any case, we need to consider the possibility that we're being followed and prepare ourselves appropriately. Please buy a Swiss sim card and don't connect it to the Internet, where it can be hacked and listened to." Sally pulled an envelope out of her handbag. "Here is ten thousand dollars. Half is a forward on your salary and the rest is for expenses. Take receipts on your first name."

"And where will you be?"

"Tonight, I'll still sleep at Marin's guesthouse. Tomorrow I intend to fly home. Roy's on leave from the army and I won't miss the opportunity to spend a week with him. You'll fill in for me here. Muriel is at the house I rented for her in Gstaad, and I want to know everything that happens there: Where she goes and when, when she returns, does she take the children with her, who comes to visit her, and how long they stay. Tomorrow morning, I'll introduce you to the team of private investigators I hired. They will set up a tent on the hill across from the house and pretend to be skiers. Their mission is to track Muriel using special equipment that includes night vision."

"Why is this needed?"

"Firstly, in order to assure that she doesn't sink back into another bout of alcoholism, that she doesn't break the children's visitation agreement with their father, that she doesn't smuggle the children across the border—in short, that she doesn't go wild. Secondly, to identify any move from Ben David as soon as it takes place. I don't believe one word of his, and I know he'll try to trick me. As far as he's concerned, Muriel is the key to Marin's pocket and I'm sure that his releasing control of her is only temporary, until he comes here to prepare Joel for his bar mitzvah." Sally again rummaged through her bag and produced a few pages covered with dense handwriting. "These are all the telephone numbers and details you need to know: Names of investigators, their tasks, the location of their surveillance posts. I've written it out rather than save it on my computer in case someone manages to hack it. Tomorrow, we'll take the time before my flight to rent a car and tour all the locations you need to know."

Diana smiled. "Wonderful. We'll have adventures, like in Beersheba."

Sally didn't share her excitement. "I really hope not. The Swiss police don't get adventures."

29.

Sally loved returning home from trips and seeing her family again, and the familiar environment of her home. Even the huge pile of laundry Roy brought home from the army, scattered on the floor next to the technician trying in vain to fix the washing machine, didn't dampen the joy of being home. "What happened to the machine?" she asked.

The technician blurted an answer filled with technical language, and Jerry continued. "It's been like this for three days. They can't fix it."

"And where's Roy?"

"He left his clothes and went back to the army. They canceled his vacation. Something operational."

Sally felt sadness mixed with pent up anger at the army, at Roy for not letting her know, and at the washing machine. Her thoughts wandered to the day they bought it, shortly after returning from their last mission in the US. Roy, whose khaki uniforms now filled the laundry room, was a twelve-year-old boy at the time, and Michael was eight. When she first activated the machine, the children rejoiced as they watched their clothes spin around behind the Perspex door.

"Madame," the technician said, interrupting her daydream, "you'll have to buy a new machine. The control is gone and is not worth fixing."

"All right," said Sally. "How much do we owe you for the visit?"

"Why is it all right?" asked Jerry, who didn't like to replace appliances unless they were completely destroyed. "What is this control? Maybe it can be fixed after all."

The technician shook his head. "It's a printed circuit board. They don't fix those."

Jerry paid him with a sour face and demanded a receipt. After he left, Sally hugged him and asked, "Why are you angry? The machine is old and needs to be replaced. There are more annoying things, like that I never got to see Roy."

"Do you want to hear something really annoying?" His face was stern. "Someone called to say you had left the plane and were on your way here, and that if I didn't guard you he would burn you in your car next time you leave the house. He also knew what school Michael goes to and where Roy serves."

"Don't worry, it's just talk. They did the same to Darmond, who really freaked out. You're stronger than that."

"I don't care about Darmond. I do care about my children, and they're in danger. I ask, or rather, I demand that you stop working with Marin."

"You know I love our children no less than you, but I won't be intimidated. There is a creator for this world, and when a person does the right thing, God protects him."

"There you go again with your nonsense!" Jerry said dismissively. "The creator didn't protect many people who did good, or save them from disaster. Your argument makes no sense."

"It's not a matter of making sense, but of faith." She took his hand. "I believe that me, you, and the children are being guarded. So far, things only attest to that. Think of the way we began our lives in England, of how we got married despite everything, surviving all the trials and tribulations of our missions abroad. If nothing happened to us in Pakistan, why fear a toy criminal impersonating a rabbi?"

"Because rabbis, both real and fake, have followers, some of whom are criminals."

Sally cut him short with a kiss. "Enough, I'm dead tired. First class or no first class, you know I can't sleep on planes."

30.

After *Shabbat*, the laundry already lay clean and folded in the closed, a new washing machine placed in the bathroom. The menacing phone calls ceased and life returned to normal, with phone updates arriving twice a day from Gstaad. Diana reported on developments, or more accurately, reported that there was nothing to report. Her surveillance logs showed that Muriel never left the house, while the children traveled to their father on Friday afternoon as agreed, returning to their mother on Saturday night. The nanny would go home during that time, deliverymen brought shopping and laundry, and the postman arrived every day.

"Are you sure he's a postman?"

"He looks like one, at least. The investigators observing the house also confirmed it."

Who uses postal services so often to receive mail every day? wondered Sally. She almost had Diana order the postman to be tailed, but decided not to on second thought, knowing that the Swiss investigators she'd hired weren't as experienced as Jacob's. Observing a house from a distance was relatively simple, but tailing a person required special skill. Followers must change every street, must keep their distance from the subject without losing him, and must blend into the surroundings without raising suspicion. She wondered whether this was important enough to involve Jacob and use more of the funds she had rescued from Ben David, which were beginning to dwindle. Thoughts raced through her mind, and when the phone rang, she answered nervously. "Hello?"

"Sally, it's Gila—"

On another day, Sally would have been happy to hear the voice of her high school friend who now lived two streets away. "Yes, Gila?" she said, feigning niceness.

"What is this 'yes, Gila'? I'm no longer Gilush to you, and you're not happy to hear from me?"

"I just—I just have so much work to do."

"In that case, you need a break. Lunch tomorrow?"

"Actually, yes. That's a good idea. At Elisa's?"

"At Elisa's," Gila repeated.

All evening, and the following day, Sally was bothered by the daily visits of the postman at the house in Gstaad. On her way to the restaurant she reached a decision. She stopped at a kiosk and called Jacob from the pay phone there. "Can you send one of your investigators to Gstaad?"

"I can send an investigator anywhere. It's only a matter of money. I have someone who's just finishing an investigation in Paris. He can be there within a few hours. By the way, I thought you hired local investigators."

"I need a gentle surveillance." She gave him the details and returned to her car. A few minutes later she was parked next to the restaurant.

Elisa's was located on the northern beach of Tel Aviv and served as a meeting place for journalists, models, businesspeople, and senior army and police officers. That wasn't why Sally liked the place, but rather its beachfront location. Sitting there, she could imagine herself at one of those open restaurants she liked in Cannes or Monaco, the sea breeze blowing in her hair.

Immediately upon entering, she recognized Aaron, who was Jerry's handler during the distant London days. She didn't know if he still worked for the Mossad, and remembered the orders she was given in the past: *Never reveal you've identified an agent in case he's there undercover.* She crossed the balcony and sat across from Gila, enjoying the pleasant sun. Gila ordered seafood and Sally—as was her habit in non-kosher restaurants—a salad. "So, what's new with you?" asked Gila. "You disappear, return, and then disappear again. Everything is so mysterious."

"No mystery, just assignments that require plenty of travel."

"What kind of work is this?" Gila insisted.

"You know, computer business. Sometimes I get sent abroad for consulting."

A shadow appeared on the table. Sally leaned backward, allowing the waiter to place the plates on their table. But instead of dishes, a muscular hand landed on it, along with a familiar voice. "I beg your pardon."

Sally and Gila looked up. Aaron's face was as expressive as Sally remembered it, with just the slight addition of some gray in his sideburns. "Can I speak to you for a moment?" he asked, gesturing at the side of the balcony.

Sally exchanged embarrassed looks with her friend.

"It's important," Aaron added, granting his most charming smile to

Gila. "Just a moment or two."

Sally stood up and followed him. He leaned on the banister facing the sea. "Sally, are you getting a divorce?" he fired at her.

"What?" she responded in astonishment. "Why? What makes you think—"

"Shh...speak quietly. There are at least two people here following you."

Sally looked cautiously around. No one seemed interested in her, and everyone was busy with their food. "Second table on the right," Aaron said quietly. "Next to the Tuborg ad. They stare at you every minute, and earlier were wandering around your car." He pointed at the white BMW that glistened in the sun, its scratches and punctured tires all repaired.

"How do you know that's my car?"

"I noticed you as soon as you entered the parking lot. Do you have a lover? Have you fought with Jerry? You don't have to tell me your secrets, but for heaven's sake, be careful."

Sally looked again at the two men. One was drinking coffee while the other was busy with his mobile phone.

"They're not especially professional." Aaron laughed. "They examined your car as though they were thinking of buying it, then entered and ordered coffee, paying the waitress as soon as she delivered it."

That was the ultimate proof of surveillance. Paying in advance allowed the follower to leave the location immediately, if the subject decided to leave. Sally felt embarrassed. During her work with the Mossad, she was followed more than once, acquiring essential precautionary measures. This time, due to her call with Jacob, she hadn't come early to check out the place. *Maybe Jerry was right*, she thought, *maybe dangers are lurking all around me and I'm too complacent, endangering my family and myself.*

"Sally, you haven't answered me. What's going on with you?"

"Jerry didn't send them and we're not getting divorced. I'm involved in a project that causes me to step on some people's toes."

"Are you in danger?"

"I don't know," said Sally candidly. "Up until now I thought I wasn't. I believed I was in control. But things are starting to heat up. These people probably have more audacity than I thought."

"And they also have money," Aaron added. "Take a look at the edge of the parking lot. A young man is leaning on a motorcycle. He hasn't moved for a while. This is a professional surveillance of two men, a car, and a motorcycle, by the book. One hour of this costs a fortune. Someone really wants to know what you're doing."

"Yeah," Sally whispered thoughtfully. "It looks like it."

"I can't leave you like this," Aaron said with concern. "I have a few friends here. We'll escort you home."

Sally laughed. "And what will happen at home?"

"There Jerry will take care of it."

"This has nothing to do with Jerry and I ask you not to tell him a thing. This is my business."

"All right Sally," Aaron shrugged. "I hope you know what you're doing."

"I know very well." Sally stood tall. "And thanks for warning me."

He took her hand and looked at her softly. "If you need anything, you know how to find me."

"Of course," Sally said and returned to the table. Fear made her stomach turn. She decided to pick Michael up from school and send Roy a text message. As soon as she sat down, she pulled her phone out and typed "Is everything OK? I miss you. Mommy."

No answer arrived. Even though she knew that as an officer in an elite unit, Roy sometimes disconnected from his mobile phone for days, she grew fearful.

"Did something happen?" Gila asked.

Michael! A thought crossed Sally's mind. The man who spoke to Jerry on the phone said he knew where Michael went to school. According to her calculation, he was supposed to return home just then. "I have to speak to Michael," she explained as she tapped his number into her phone. "He felt ill this morning."

Michael answered immediately.

"I want to come by and take you home," Sally said.

"What are you talking about? I'm already on the bus," he said, as teenagers shouted in the background.

"Is everything all right?"

"Yes, why wouldn't it be?"

"What are those screams?"

"My friends, you know, they're acting crazy. What happened? Why did you call all of the sudden?"

"As I said, I thought of picking you up on the way home," she said, and hung up.

"Will you please explain to me what's going on here?" Gila asked. "First a stunning man comes to the table and drags you off to a secret conversation. Then, when you return, you hysterically text Roy and call Michael. Let's start by asking who that hunk is and is he available?"

"He's not available and is very married," Sally replied, annoyed. She was angry at herself for acquiescing to Ovadia's miserable behavior, and wondered why Ben David agreed to her conditions, including the financial sanction. She used to think that Ben David wouldn't act before arriving in Gstaad to prepare Joel for his bar mitzvah, and would only try to convince Muriel to return to Israel with him. Now she knew he was much more determined and audacious. She recalled the cameras in Marin's guesthouse and now believed they were installed at Ben David's initiative. For the first time, she considered the possibility that similar cameras were installed in her home in Tel Aviv. She remembered the laundry machine technician. What were the chances that Jerry was right? That the machine wasn't really broken, and actually the technician came to install cameras and microphones all over their home?

"Sally, what are you daydreaming about?"

Sally awoke. "Here, I'm with you," she answered, and for the next half hour she chatted away with Gila as her mind sifted through facts and contrasted different times and places in an attempt to decipher what was happening around her. Right after saying goodbye to Gila, she sent a text message to Diana in Switzerland. "Is everything all right?"

"Of course," came the answer immediately. "Nothing has changed since we spoke this morning."

She left the restaurant and approached her car, looking to both sides. The two men vanished from the balcony. The motorcycle man stayed standing at the edge of the lot, making sure not to look at her. Sally entered her car and started it. When she looked through the rearview mirror to back up, the motorcycle man was gone.

Sally drove home slowly. She had no way of knowing whether she was being tailed, but it wasn't important. Her address was public, and she always drove home on the same route. A loud toot from a truck interrupted her thoughts. Sally was startled and slowed down. The truck rammed into the rear of her car, launching her forward. Instinctively, she turned the steering wheel and drove onto the traffic island without hitting the car in front of her. The truck continued driving, ripping off a piece of the back bumper that landed on the road.

Sally gripped the steering wheel and breathed deeply to relax. The back side of her car protruded onto the road, and the cars slowed down to pass her. From nowhere a policeman emerged to stop traffic and allow Sally to merge back into it.

When she returned home she parked her car in the garage, where its disability set it apart from her neighbors' polished vehicles. Her heart was pounding when she exited the elevator, to find her apartment door open. She pushed it in with anxiety and took one step inside, lifting an umbrella from the rack. "Michael?" she asked.

No answer was heard.

"Michael?" Her voice was now anxious. "Michael?"

A sound of running water came from the bathroom. She knocked on the door. "Michael?"

Again silence, just the sound of running water in the shower. Sally spread her fingers and banged on the door twice. The flow of water ceased. "Who is it?" Michael shouted.

"Mommy. Is everything OK?"

A moment later, which seemed like an eternity to Sally, the door opened, and Michael stood there wrapped in a towel. "What's wrong with you today, Mom? You call me on the bus and now disturb me in the shower, and—" He broke out laughing. "What's that ridiculous umbrella for?"

"You left the front door open and I thought someone broke in."

"I didn't leave the door open. I never leave it open. I'm no child, you know, I'm at least as responsible as Roy—"

"I didn't say you weren't responsible." She breathed in to calm herself. "Never mind. Finish your shower."

She shut the bathroom door, and without letting go of the umbrella toured all the rooms of the apartment. Finally, she returned to the kitchen, picked up her mobile phone, and texted Jacob. "Are you in the country?"

"Yes," he answered.

"Tomorrow, ten o'clock, at the regular place."

"All right," he confirmed.

31.

Sally could recognize the looming confrontation on Jerry's face. This time, his tight lips and slanted eyebrows foretold a real fight. "Aaron spoke to me," he said even before putting down his briefcase and removing his jacket. "He promised you not to tell me, but he's worried, and as a good friend he had to tell me. I justify his decision—"

"All right, someone's following me. So what?"

Jerry sat down on one of the living room couches and leaned forward, distraught and angry. "Three followers—two by car and one by motorcycle. That, in addition to all the threatening telephone calls against our children and us, and maybe other things you never told me. What happened to your car, for example?"

"It has nothing to do with it. A truck collided with me."

"Do you have its details?"

"It drove off."

"You've never had an accident, and suddenly a truck rams into you and flees? And you think I haven't noticed the new tires and the scratches to the paint underneath the polish? Sally, this is getting serious. I demand that you stop. Let Marin know you're quitting this whole thing." He slid his phone to her. "Now!"

"You know I won't do it. I've never run away from something because of threats."

"These aren't threats, don't you get it? They may have already switched to actions without you knowing. Following my conversation with Aaron I checked up on Ben David in the police database and other sources I have access to. He's linked to a criminal organization based in the south, and I'm sure they're using him to get to Marin's money."

"In that case, I'm even more essential. I'm saving Marin from a criminal organization. Give me the details and I'll send them to Jacob."

"I'll give you no details. Stop this at once! I know these types of people. They'll give you no notice before they start hitting. One day you'll come home and find everything destroyed, or worse, someone will harm Michael on his way to school. What will you say then? That you did the right thing for Marin?"

"I won't say anything because nothing will happen. I will take Michael to school every day and bring him back, and—"

"*I'll* take him. You, with your reckless behavior, have become a target. You're endangering everyone around you."

"The target is Marin, not me. And that's also the reason that even if I stop all my activity today, they won't believe I retired and will continue to threaten me. After all, they won't give up Marin's money. So there's no choice. I have to go all the way."

"What is this 'way' exactly? How will you persuade Ben David and the criminal organization behind him to let go of Marin? You don't realize the kind of swamp you've entered." Jerry pointed at the phone again. "Call him," he ordered.

"I will not call him, and I won't stop this work. I've never told you to stop *your* work."

"I've never endangered my family."

"Really? Weren't we all at risk when we went to Pakistan?"

"That was unnecessary. *You* insisted on joining the project—"

"And I passed all the necessary tests, and your bosses authorized me joining. If I was good enough to take the risk back then, why not now when I'm doing a mitzvah, a good deed?"

Jerry stood up, angry. "You and your mitzvahs and beliefs." He took his phone. "Don't bother saying a word to me until you tell Marin you're stopping this."

That was his custom every time they fought, to take a vow of silence. Sally couldn't stand the quiet that would spread through the house. "In that case, I'll go visit my parents. At least they'll speak to me."

Jerry didn't answer.

Sally prepared dinner, as well as breakfast for the following morning, covering it in cling wrap and placing it in the refrigerator. She went to Michael's room, passing by the closed door of Jerry's study. "I'm going to stay with Grandma and Grandpa. I've left food," she told her son, who was preoccupied with his computer. "If you need anything from me, just call. I'll be in touch. Dad will take you to school."

Michael turned around and looked at her with astonishment. "Why Dad? I take the bus for five stops. No big deal."

Sally sat down on his bed and took his hand. "Do you remember how, when you were a child, we lived in Pakistan and we all had to be careful?"

"You know I only have faint memories from that time."

"Anyway, we're in the same situation now. Something in my work forces us all to be very alert. The entire family. I've already told you I'm helping a good man escape from the clutches of someone evil, and the evil person is trying to fight back."

Michael smiled. "You're always fighting evil people."

"Right. I can't stand injustice, and I hope you can't either."

He nodded. "I can't either," he said solemnly, "and neither can Roy, I think. That's why he joined the special unit."

She kissed him on the cheek and left the room.

32.

The familiar smells of the fields dulled the stormy quarrel with Jerry, and Sally's fear of Ben David's long arm. She went off the main road and slowly drove through dirt roads, absorbing the calm of the ancient orchards, the crows of the chickens in their coops, the green surroundings. The back gate of her parents' plot of land was open and inviting. Her father stood there, short and stout, hoeing around the trees. He didn't believe in automatic irrigation or in drip systems, and instead quenched the thirst of his trees with water he poured into trenches he dug around them, as he'd done for fifty years.

Sally tooted lightly. Her father stood up, a smile spreading across his face. She got out of the car and hugged him, soaking up the strength she inherited from him. "What's wrong, Sallinka?" he asked.

"Wrong?" Sally played stupid.

"You know I can feel you…"

Her mother came out of the house and walked over to them with open arms. Sally hugged her, kissed her soft face, and placed her head on her shoulder, seeking solace. Her father walked them both inside to the kitchen. On the large wooden table, where her mother used to serve her sumptuous feasts, a freshly baked cake miraculously appeared next to the ancient coffee pot and three porcelain mugs. "Dad, Mom, I want to tell you something and I'd like your advice."

"Does it have to do with that bandit Dadoshvili?" her father asked.

"Yes," said Sally, and recounted everything that took place in her life recently. When she was done, night had fallen and the sound of crickets was all around them. Her father, as usual, let her mother answer first. "What do you say, Mother?" he asked.

"Don't give up," answered her mother decisively. "You will fight and succeed, bringing nothing but blessings to your family."

"You have the great privilege of stopping the villain," added her father.

"And what about the threats?" Sally asked.

"Once," her father answered calmly, "a rancher had a strong, fast horse that won races and received many prizes."

Sally sat back in her chair. Her father almost always answered people seeking his advice with tales, and as a child she used to love hiding in the corner of the living room and listening to them. Now his voice filled her with a confidence she hadn't known in years.

"One day," he continued, "the horse was lazy leaving the stable and pretended to be ill. The same thing happened the next day, and the day after. Finally, the farmer called a veterinarian to examine the horse. When he left the farm with the farmer he said, 'I'm not sure what's wrong with him, but I'll try to cure him. I'll give him a few injections, and if he doesn't recover, I'll shoot him.'

"As though by demand, a horse neighed in one of the neighboring farms." They both burst out laughing.

"The farmer had a sheep that heard their conversation," her father continued. "After the doctor had gone, the sheep went to the horse and told him everything. Naturally terrified, the horse jumped out of the stable and galloped around the farm. The farmer was very happy. So happy, in fact, that he said, 'This is a wonderful day. We must celebrate! Let's slaughter a lamb.'"

"So you agree with Jerry—that I shouldn't meddle in this business lest I get slaughtered?"

"Yes, if you consider yourself a sheep," her father said. "But since you're no sheep but my daughter, you won't run. You'll do the opposite. You'll fight and win. I believe in you and know you believe in yourself."

Sally's eyes welled up with tears of excitement. "May I stay here?" she asked.

"No," he said, patting her hair. "*Shalom bayit*, peace in the household, may not be mentioned in the Torah, but it's a commandment and should be obeyed. Go back to your husband, cook a good meal, hug and kiss him, and say, 'I'm your loving wife and also my father's daughter. Father said that a believer should have no fear, and I trust him.'"

"You know Jerry. He's stubborn and doesn't believe in anything. He will be mad and won't speak to me."

"He may not speak on the first day or the second, but he will on the third. The important thing is that you remain near him when he does, and don't hide here."

Later that evening, when she returned home carrying fresh fruits and vegetables with the smell of earth still clinging to them, she found Jerry's study shut and the bedroom empty. She lay down on the bed in her clothes, too tired to undress, feeling endlessly lonely and tired. Her mobile phone rang. She answered immediately, expecting to hear Jacob's voice. "Sally Amir," a man said. "I'm warning you. If you don't stop harassing the honorable Rabbi Ben David you won't see the light of day. You have two days left to live."

Sally felt the strength bestowed upon her by her father. "We'll see who has two days left," she said in a harsh voice, and he hung up.

The last thought to cross her mind before falling asleep was that she had forgotten to check if cameras had been installed in her apartment.

33.

Jacob and Sally usually met in a giant parking lot near the national park in Ramat Gan. Jacob, as usual, arrived a little early. Sally recognized his black Jeep and pulled over next to him. Jacob moved into his car's passenger seat and opened the window. Sally's window also slid down. They were now side by side. "We checked out the mailman," said Jacob immediately. "As you suspected, he doesn't work for the postal service. He's just an unemployed man who received a uniform from a woman he didn't know, one hundred euros, and instructions to arrive at a café in central Gstaad, take an envelope, and deliver it to Muriel's home. Every three days, the woman promised, another envelope would await him in the café containing another hundred euros."

"How did you find out about this?"

Jacob laughed. "A good investigator and free beer at the bar."

"And who's the woman?"

"He didn't know. He met her once and she vanished. I placed an investigator at the café and he discovered the letter arrives by fax, and the owner puts it in an envelope. It was only a matter of time before someone came to pay him, and also leave money for the mailman. Yesterday, the woman arrived, but she entered the café through the kitchen, looked over the counter, handed something to the owner and disappeared. My investigator was able to take a blurry photo." He tapped on his phone and Sally's mobile let out a loud ring as the shadow of a woman appeared on her screen. She wore a kerchief over her hair, another scarf covering her neck and part of her face. Something about her seemed familiar to Sally. Ben David's wife? The woman in the photo was too tall. Vivian Moyal? Too thin.

"She's very good," said Jacob apologetically. "What's the chance that some intelligence agency is involved?"

Sally shrugged. "Marin's companies are active in fields that could definitely interest certain countries, but I fail to see how this all relates to Muriel. More likely the letters are Ben David's means of communication. Could you intercept the letters by any chance?"

Jacob shook his head. "We can't do that without exposing ourselves," he said, his voice turning businesslike. "Now tell me, what did you want to talk about?"

"Firstly, send someone over to my house to check that no video equipment was installed there."

"Jerry can't ask his colleagues to take care of that?"

The mention of Jerry's name and the thought of their fight made Sally emotional. "I'd rather he not get involved." She tightened her lips so as not to burst into tears, and told Jacob of the cameras she had found at Marin's house, of the followers in the café, of the threats, and of the truck accident that may or may not have been related.

Jacob remained businesslike. "What would you like to do?"

"There's no choice, sometimes you need to fight back that same way."

"You want me to run Ben David over with a truck?" Jacob's eyes were amused.

Sally didn't laugh. "No, but there are a few other things I'd like you to do." She pulled out a handwritten list of instructions from her handbag, similar to the one she had given Diana, and gave it to Jacob. He took one look at it and said, "These are very serious actions. I'll need to add a risk fee."

"I understand. Tomorrow I'll transfer you another fifty thousand dollars."

"Did Marin give you money?"

"No, Ben David did."

He reacted with surprise, but asked nothing more. Instead he asked, "And you really believe Jerry knows nothing about this?"

"He prefers not to know. He'd like me to stop all of this. He believes I'm dealing with a criminal organization here." Her tone became more impassioned. "You realize there's no way I'm stopping, right? I've come too far not to win. Otherwise it would have all been in vain."

Jacob fixed his eyes on her. "Sally, were I your husband, I'd pressure you to stop."

"He really is pressuring. We're quarreling."

Jacob's face soured. "Too bad. Is Marin worth a fight with Jerry?"

"Not at all, but the fight won't last long. Jerry will come around. I know him."

"I think you should stop here. Everything's becoming too dangerous." Jacob looked at her glumly. "Every war has goals. What are your objectives? Where do you want to go with this? What do you want to achieve?"

"As it seems at the moment, I'd like Ben David to release Muriel from his grasp right after Joel's bar mitzvah. He should also leave Marin alone and return his money."

"What if he is connected to a criminal organization, and worse things happen than your encounter with the truck?"

"There's still a chance it was only an accident. In any event, if a criminal organization is involved, I'll file a complaint with the police."

Jacob burst out laughing. "You're so naïve, Sally. The police can't catch murderers and you expect them to cope with criminal gangs?"

"I'll make them act. I have good friends and connections."

"I don't know how many friends you'll have left after you separate from Jerry." Jacob breathed in deeply and sighed. "Well, it's your project. Or, as Jerry would always tell me when we worked together, it's your funeral."

34.

Loud music greeted Sally when she returned home. It came from Michael's room, but this time she did not knock on his door and ask him to turn it down. She switched into house clothes, entered the kitchen, and opened her private cookbook. It was divided into sections including the best dishes from the countries where the family had served. In the Pakistan section she found the recipes she was looking for, and started to cook. In the afternoon, when Jacob's technician arrived to check for the existence of surveillance equipment in the apartment, her clothes had already absorbed the smells of Jerry's favorite foods: chicken curry, rice with garam masala, and a yellow lentil dahl in a special sauce.

Michael devoured the food and left for his boy scouts meeting. The technician also enjoyed some dinner after declaring the apartment clear of eavesdropping equipment. When Jerry arrived, the table was already set and a chilled bottle of wine was placed on it. He put his briefcase down and sat at his regular seat. Sally served the food and he breathed its aroma in deeply and said, "Curry. Terrific. Thanks."

Those were the only words uttered during the meal. Jerry kept silent and Sally knew there was no point starting a conversation unless it was to tell Jerry she had decided to stop her activities for Marin. Jerry's face was tense and severe, and he ate slowly, as usual. "Very tasty," he said finally, wiped his mouth with a napkin, and repeated his thanks.. On his way to the study he blurted out, "And you shouldn't mislead the children with your tales of heroism. Michael talks about you as though you were Super-woman."

"I did no such thing. I simply shared what's happening with them."

"There are things you shouldn't share with children," he said.

"As far as you're concerned, you should share *nothing* with children. Let me remind you that our lifestyle was never normal, and my way of integrating the children was through full involvement. Michael even joined me when I bought my BMW, and then came on a Jeep trip with me."

"I objected to that too. That's all we needed, four-wheel drive cars and Jeep treks."

"You oppose anything slightly out of the ordinary. Such a stick in the mud."

Sally's phone rang. "Hi Sally," Diana's voice roared. "The cook resigned after the kids complained about her food and she was insulted. I've hired another cook who used to work at a restaurant in Lausanne and came highly recommended."

"All right, I'd like to meet her when I arrive."

"I've also cut the nanny's expenses. We don't need her here when the children are at school. She leaves in the morning when the children leave, and returns in the afternoon."

"Excellent," Sally replied. Every Swiss franc saved to Marin felt as though it was saved to her.

During Roy's visit on the weekend, Sally projected business as usual. She prepared the food he liked, tidied the house, baked, and watched over the maid. Like after every quarrel, relations with Jerry remained cordial but chilly. But this time, the fight lasted longer than usual, perhaps longer than ever. Jerry wasn't planning to relent in his demand, and Sally, for her part, couldn't obey it. She continued to manage the surveillance of Muriel's home from afar, oversee the secret assignments she asked Jacob to carry out, and discuss various issues with Marin at least once a day.

She planned to rest at home for another two weeks, then fly to Geneva two days before the planned arrival of Ben David to prepare Joel for his bar mitzvah. But one Thursday evening, as she tidied the house for *Shabbat*, the phone rang. "We're in trouble," Diana informed her. "Our two men who were staking out the house froze in their tent last night. They crawled to the road, where a passing car took them to the hospital. Their car remained on the scene, with the binoculars, cameras and night vision equipment. The neighbors grew suspicious and called the police, and that's it. We're back in Beersheba." Sally started planning what to ask Jacob and his investigators. "I'll see what I can do and get back to you," she said.

"One moment," Diana added, "there's something else. Regarding the mailman, we can relax. He hasn't arrived in two days."

Sally thought for a long moment. Something was wrong, something to do with the mailman that lay before her eyes the entire time, and that she simply couldn't decipher. Something that could not be managed remotely. "I'm coming over," she said.

35.

As soon as the wheels of the aircraft touched down on the tarmac, Sally grew calm. That's how it always was. When problems happened far away they seemed oppressive and unsolvable, but as soon as she set out to solve them, she felt she could overcome anything.

Diana, on the other hand, was terrified, on the verge of panic. "They've disappeared," she said, her voice rising shrilly. "They simply disappeared."

"Who?"

"Our two investigators."

"Wait," said Sally, "tell me everything from the start."

"As you instructed me, the four Swiss investigators set up camp on the mountain, directly across from Muriel's home. Every day, two of them went skiing while the two others stayed in their tents and observed the house. During the nights, only two remained in the tent and watched the house using night vision equipment. You know the rest. They froze, were hospitalized, and the car was discovered by the police. Tomorrow they're supposed to go to the police and give a testimony. Two hours ago I came to the hospital to pay for the treatment and debrief them for the testimony, but when I arrived they said they'd paid themselves and then left. Now we have a double problem: Explaining what the car was doing on the hill across from Gstaad packed with surveillance equipment, and making the two patients give their testimony."

"Why is that our problem?" wondered Sally.

"Because your name is on the summons for questioning. The police will contact the investigations company and—"

"And there they'll be told that a woman named Sally Amir ordered an investigation of a certain house in Gstaad, never requesting illegal means to be used. I don't understand why you see a problem where there is none."

Diana was silent for a moment. "Why do you talk to me like that? All right—I may have overreacted about the danger, but I did it out of concern for you and your project."

Sally hugged her. "I'm sorry. I'm a bit nervous, that's all. Forgive me." She got into Diana's car. "There's one thing that worries me," she told Diana as they sped on the highway to town. "The postman."

Diana braced herself. "How come?"

"I assume he brought Muriel letters and maybe instructions from Ben David, bypassing the disconnect we imposed on them. The fact he stopped coming means only one thing—that there's another mode of communication that we're unaware of. Since Ben David is afraid of talking on the phone or sending e-mails, and the mail stopped coming—" Something in the back of Sally's mind cut her sentence short. "As I said, the mail stopped coming," she repeated.

"What did you mean to say?"

"That we don't really understand what's happening. Ben David acts in all kinds of ways, maybe even controlling others, and through them, us."

Diana seemed preoccupied. "What makes you think that?"

"I don't know. A feeling. Can you take me to your hotel?"

"Aren't you going to Gstaad, to Marin?"

"No," said Sally. "I have a few meetings in Geneva."

Diana stared at her for a long while. "Why do I have a feeling you're not telling me everything?"

Sally smiled bitterly. "Believe me, it's for your own good."

36.

A moment after the porter placed the suitcases in her room, Sally collected her handbag and left. She took the service elevator to the floor above the lobby and took the stairs out of the hotel to a back carpark. On the street, Jacob was waiting for her in a black Ford, as he had told her on the phone. "How was the flight?" he asked.

"Like any flight. The best part is arriving."

He snickered. "The best part is still to come, but before I present it I'd like to understand the arrangement with Ben David. When does he arrive? Where will he stay, and how long will he spend with the boy?"

"He's supposed to arrive in ten days, live at Marin's expense in any hotel he wants, and teach the boy the Torah reading and *haftarah* for two hours a day, as well as some Jewish law."

Jacob placed a photo in Sally's lap. Sally examined it carefully. "Do you think they're—" she asked.

"Yes," he replied curtly.

"Any others?"

Jacob handed her more and more photos. They all depicted a dark-skinned man frolicking in bed with a blonde woman. They were both naked, captured in various positions. "How long has this been going on?" Sally asked.

"Two days."

"That's what I suspected. Those are exactly the two days that passed since the postman disappeared. He was no longer needed when the real thing arrived." She looked at the photos again. "How did he enter the house?"

"That's a question your Swiss detectives need to answer," Jacob smiled. "On my shift, it wouldn't have happened."

"My Swiss detectives froze two nights ago, and disappeared from the hospital this morning."

"How convenient."

"I still need to ask their office what exactly happened. At the moment, it seems like someone paid them off so that we don't know that Ben David is already here." She focused her gaze on the short and extremely hairy man. "I never imagined he could seduce her, such a Nordic princess."

"I've realized there are two types of men," Jacob said. "Those who look good and those who are sweet talkers. He probably belongs to the second category."

Sally handed him the photos back. "Keep these in a safe, and meanwhile I'd like you to continue photographing anything taking place inside the house for twenty-four hours."

Jacob shook his head. "That's dangerous. You got what you wanted, and now I want to take the system apart. The punishment here is five years in prison and they cut you no slack."

"I told you that I found cameras in Marin's house too."

"Marin films in his own place. It's not nice, but it's legal. We're photographing other people, which is forbidden."

"I have to know what's going on in there," Sally said. "I have no other source but your cameras. Were it not for them, I wouldn't have known Ben David was here, and worse, I wouldn't have known he's having an affair with Muriel."

Jacob shook his head decisively. "No more filming. The frozen detective business makes me suspect that someone is double-crossing you Sally, and that someone can take me down too. He knows everything you do. The immediate suspect is, of course, the detective agency you hired. Unlike me, they're not committed to you personally, and anyone can buy them. I only hope you haven't given them any information about me."

Sally was grateful for her decision to compartmentalize her contacts. "They don't know you exist. Neither does Diana."

"Diana is the woman who installed the eavesdropping equipment at Ben David's home? The one who used to work for the Mossad?"

"Yes. Jerry has known her for many years."

Jacob nodded, reflective, and put the photos in the glove compartment. "What do you plan to do next?"

Sally thought for a moment. "I think," she said, "I'm going to have a painful conversation with Pierre Marin."

37.

Natalia's face wore an expression of amazement. "Madame Sally, why didn't you ask to be picked up? A taxi from Geneva must have cost you a fortune." She opened the boot and extracted Sally's small suitcase. "You've only come for a day or two?" she asked.

"That's what I thought," Sally replied. "Now I'm not so sure any more."

Natalia nodded with understanding. "Yes, that's how it works, things change. There have been changes here too. Monsieur Marin will tell you. He just finished eating and went to wait for you in the lounge when you called at the gate."

Marin was indeed waiting for her, seated tall and elegant on one of the couches. On a small table next to him stood a coffee pot and small cup. He gestured to the couch across from him. "I don't want you to surprise me again, Sally. If I weren't home they wouldn't have let the taxi in, you know."

"I know," said Sally calmly. "If they hadn't let me in, I would have waited in the taxi until you arrived."

"And what if I were abroad?"

"I would have asked when you return, then gone back to Geneva and waited."

He looked at her with amazement. "All that to save a simple phone call?"

"I don't know who listens in on your phone lines," she said tiredly. "The detective agency I hired in Geneva probably double-crossed me, and a few other things have happened, so at the moment I trust no one."

"Wait, wait." He held up his palm to stop her. "Tell me everything from the beginning."

"Yesterday I was informed that the investigators watching the house in Gstaad froze in the cold and were evacuated to hospital at night. I was also told that the postman, who would arrive at the house every day to deliver a letter to Muriel, stopped coming. I felt something was wrong. I immediately flew to Geneva, and when I arrived I realized that as soon as the surveillance stopped, Ben David came to the house. I'm certain the detective agency colluded with him."

Marin frowned. "He was supposed to arrive only next week to prepare Joel for his bar mitzvah."

"Yes, and you're probably wondering why he came early."

"Exactly."

"Well, there's no pleasant way to say this." Sally hesitated. "It's no coincidence that he arrived early or that somehow he removed the surveillance on the house. He—he's having an affair with Muriel."

A nervous muscle twitched in Marin's face. "How did you find out?"

"I can't say."

"Do you have proof?"

"Photos. Lots of them. I can show you one or two, but I'll need to take them right back."

"You don't trust me?" he asked coldly.

"The law here forbids hidden photography, and if I leave them with you you'll have become an accomplice."

Suddenly, without warning, he slapped the table. "You're lying!" His lips quivered. "You don't want to give me the photos because there are none. You're going to show me a blurry photo and immediately take it away, and so prove that Muriel is betraying me? Is that the plot? Finally, your true colors are revealed Madame Sally Amir. You don't want money or any other reimbursement, but instead you want to destroy me with a lie. That's why you arrived by surprise and this time you're also staying in a hotel, aren't you? You knew that if your lie was discovered I'd banish you immediately. Well, you were right. Natalia!" he shouted.

The housekeeper arrived immediately.

"Order a taxi for Madame Amir, and have her wait in the waiting room until it arrives," Marin bellowed.

Natalia dawdled for a moment, embarrassed.

"Now!"

Natalia curtsied.

"I do have photos," Sally said coldly, "and when you recompose yourself I may be able to show you one or two. You can find me at the Hotel d'Angleterre in Geneva."

"Even if you show me photos I won't believe it," Marin said, sullen. "You're tricking me! You've all conspired against me. It's Photoshopped. Someone here is trying to deceive me. I want nothing more to do with you."

"Why, because I ended the illusion that you control all aspects of your life? Because I didn't tell you everything is OK like everyone else around you?"

Marin turned his back to her and didn't answer. His shoulders shook with anger, or perhaps with tears.

"Madame Sally," Natalia said softly. "Come with me, please."

38.

When she arrived at the hotel, Jacob was already waiting for her on a couch in the lobby. They went up to her room, where she told him the details of her visit with Marin. "Did you bring the photos?" she asked finally.

"Yes," he pulled the envelope out of his briefcase. "The less we wander around with these, the less likely we get into trouble," he said. "They should be kept in a vault."

"Soon you'll be able to put them there. I just want to take a photo or two out of the package—it won't be too embarrassing on the one hand, but on the other will reflect reality and can be shown to Marin."

"That's very dangerous. If he leaks them we're in trouble."

"Don't worry," said Sally and opened the envelope. Within half an hour, dozens of surveillance photos were spread out on her large bed. Dark- and fair-skinned limbs intermingled, and the backdrop moved from a pink sheet to dark couches and even to the wooden kitchen counter. Sally grouped them according to their level of offensiveness. She finally chose three photos that could serve as decisive proof—but not too blunt—

of the sexual nature of Ben David and Muriel's relationship. "Tomorrow I'll pick one to show Marin," she said.

"Your self-confidence never ceases to surprise me." Jacob smiled. "How do you know he'll want to see them?"

"I know people. He trusts me and secretly knows I haven't tricked him. When he comes to his senses he'll want to know the truth."

She was right. The following morning at nine a.m., the phone rang in her room. "Madame Amir?" asked an official voice. "This is Marie Calderon, Pierre Marin's office manager. He would like to speak to you."

"Please," replied Sally.

Marin's apology was short and to the point. An hour after he ended the conversation with, "I really appreciate the fact you aren't holding a grudge," one of his cars pulled up at the hotel. This time it wasn't Jacques who was driving, and when Sally asked about him, the new driver said he didn't know the man.

By noon she was sitting across from Marin, who placed himself behind his large wooden desk at his hilltop palace. "I'd like to apologize again," he began.

"There's no need," said Sally as she pulled the chosen photo from her handbag. Silently, she placed it on the table in front of him. He stared at it for a long while. He intertwined his fingers, his knuckles whitening, but his speech was subdued. "I gather there are more," he said.

"Many more. A few CDs of non-stop footage."

"Could you leave the photo with me anyway?" he asked. "I'd like Joel to see it and know the truth about his mother. She convinced him that I had banished her to find myself a younger woman."

"You'll have to convince him some other way," Sally said decisively.

"The photo must return with me to Geneva."

He thought for a moment before saying, "I want Ben David eliminated."

"You mean physically killed?"

"Yes. I want nothing to be left of him."

Sally swallowed with amazement. "He did sleep with your wife, but that's no reason to murder him."

"He hurt my honor. No one ever hurt my honor without punishment. I want him dead, and you, with your connections, can get it done."

"No way," she said.

To her surprise, Marin seemed disappointed. "You said you wanted to help me get rid of Ben David, and now that the moment has come you become evasive."

"I didn't mean to get rid of him in that sense." She pulled the photo back to her. "You're so used to having things your own way that you've lost perspective."

"All right," he said. "I understand. You won't help me."

"Pierre," she said, looking into his blue eyes. "Even if you ask someone else to knock off Ben David, that's murder, and it gets you sent to jail. If I hear that Ben David died and suspect that someone killed him on your orders, I will not remain silent."

He looked at her with astonishment. "You'll tell on me?"

"I have my red lines, Pierre, and once you kill a man you will no longer be the Pierre I appreciate so much. You'll just be a criminal, even if you did not carry out the crime yourself." She sent an encouraging smile in his direction. "You're upset right now. Once you calm down, we'll plan how to finish Ben David in our own way."

He shook his head. "You don't understand. *He's* the real murderer. When you were away, a few things happened. A car hit my limousine on the road heading down to the village. Jacques couldn't brake and plunged into the ravine. After the funeral, we discovered a recording device in the apartment above the garage. We followed the wires and found cameras broadcasting to there from across the mansion. You understand, Jacques, my driver—" he hit the armrest with rage "—he knew all the places I went, some of the people who traveled with me, not to mention the women…"

Sally too felt betrayed. Jacques, the charming man who was always willing to help, was the one behind the system of cameras that invaded her privacy? "Why do you think he was killed?"

"I don't know. He may have asked for too much money or became unneeded. In any case, I went to the police and told them everything. As usual, they're investigating and investigating and investigating."

"You don't have any other conflicts? Business rivals?"

"I do, but not the kind that would push my driver into a ravine."

"That's odd," said Sally, contemplative. "A truck rammed into me about ten days ago, in Tel Aviv. I'm also being followed and phone threats are being made to my house. Jerry claims a criminal gang is behind all of this, a group that wants your money and invests significant resources for that. He believes Ben David is just the tip of the iceberg."

"That makes sense and fits with what happened to Jacques," said Marin, then added excitedly, "Can you understand why she prefers a small and ugly man to me?"

"I presume something was lacking in her life with you." She remembered Joel asking her what "a cold man" meant. "Something emotional," she added. "Maybe warmth."

Marin nodded in approval. "I may be difficult, but that's no reason to betray me." He shook his head. "It's hard to live in an environment where you can't trust anyone," he said with a sigh.

Sally put her hand on his in a gesture of consolation. "You can trust *me*."

He placed his other hand on hers. "I thank God for sending you to me," he said emotionally. "Were it not for you, they would devour everything I have."

"We won't let them," said Sally and stood up. "Now please forgive me. I need a shower."

Marin looked at his gold watch. "I suggest we meet again in the dining room in an hour."

39.

Even though she knew the surveillance cameras in the guest quarters were no longer active, Sally covered the lenses with pieces of sticky tape she found in her purse. Then she undressed, changing from her travel clothes to a suit. At five minutes to one, she walked along the path leading to Marin's house, arriving at the dining room at one o'clock sharp. Marin was already waiting there, seated on his chair. He examined her with a long, mournful look. Sally had to stop herself from walking over and hugging him. She suddenly realized that she wasn't looking to console him, but rather to comfort herself for all the tribulations she and her family had experienced, and for Jerry's alienation.

Overwhelmed by the discovery, she sat across from him with measured movements. Natalia rushed to serve chilled white wine, and the regular parade of waiters arrived with various dishes. "Do you eat all these delicacies even when you're alone?"

"This meal is for you." Marin poured wine for both of them and raised his glass with feigned joviality. "To the brave woman sitting across from me!"

Sally smiled, embarrassed. "And to you as well."

Marin grew serious. "I've been thinking a lot about Muriel." He cut a piece of fish on his plate. "In times of crisis, I tend to redefine my goals, or more precisely the things I want to attain. In this case, I realize I've lost Muriel, so all I want is a fair divorce where the children will live with me. Muriel has proven she's irresponsible and certainly can't raise our children," he asserted.

"We're left with Ben David. As I told you, I want to destroy him," he said, raising his arm in a gesture of reassurance. "Don't worry. I won't do anything silly. But I want him to return everything he stole from me, even if that means he and his family will live on the street. The thought that he tricked *me*, one of the biggest businessmen in Europe, won't leave me. As a first step, I want him out of that house. I've already spoken to my lawyers. They're working on a restraining order, and think it shouldn't be a problem. After all, I pay the rent and have signed the contract."

"Who will prepare Joel for his Torah reading?"

Marin was silent.

"You won't deprive him of the big event of becoming a Jewish adult?"

"I'll tell you the truth." Marin wiped his mouth with a napkin. "There was a moment where I decided that my son will be a citizen of the world, with no religion. All this Judaism, what good is it if Jews aren't loyal to each other? Do you know why I donated to Israel all these years?"

"Because you have a Jewish soul."

Marin laughed. "You're very romantic, Sally. The reason is much simpler. I donated because I can't forget the day we fled Morocco. Muslims ratted on my father that he was a Zionist spy. We left all the lights on and left our home with two suitcases before the secret service arrived. They probably would have released him a few weeks later—after all, we were rich and connected. But he would have come out a broken man. The image of my mother and father sitting terrified in the car to the airport, while our driver was sure we were only leaving for a holiday in Switzerland, haunts me. I believe it's good the Jews have a state and we must protect it." Marin breathed in. "But recently I discovered that swindlers also live in Israel, and some are even considered spiritual authorities." He slapped his forehead. "I thought Judaism would protect my son. My father would say that Jews stand up for one another, but if our people also have imposter rabbis who can sin and sleep with the mothers of the boys they teach, it's better to live among the gentiles. No gentile has ever done to me what Ben David and Ovadia did—"

"But—" Sally cut him off.

Marin signaled to her that she should let him finish. "Yes, there is a 'but' and that's you. I've been thinking about you, and about the fact that Judaism also produced people like you, all love of others, lovingkindness, and honesty. Therefore, I decided that as long as it's up to me, Joel will be Jewish. But I have a condition: You will supervise it. Find me a rabbi to come here, live in the guesthouse, and teach him."

"Meaning Joel will live here?"

"Of course, together with Rubi and me."

"I'm not sure you'll be able to remove the children from Muriel's custody."

"I am. There's nothing that good lawyers can't do, and my lawyers are the best. They claim that if she slept with our children's religious teacher, they can be separated from her. They just—" he hesitated for a moment

"—well, they're somewhat incredulous, and say they need to see proof and maybe present it in court."

"You know this proof can't be presented," Sally said.

Marin didn't lose his confidence. "I believe they'll find a way."

The two ate in silence for a few minutes. "Are you angry with Muriel?" Sally suddenly asked.

Marin thought for a second, then answered, "Not at all. She's unimportant."

"She was important enough to have two children with."

"She was important when we married and had them, but even then, for reasons that had little to do with her—"

"Then with who?"

He shrugged and sipped from his wine. "You see, in the circles I travel in, being married to a beautiful woman is like owning an expensive painting."

"So to you a woman is an object."

"Maybe." He looked at her with surprise. "I haven't thought about it that way. My father took pride in my mother's beauty and elegance, and I took pride in my first wife and then in Muriel. It means something, to marry a supermodel who appears on the covers of the most famous magazines, doesn't it?"

"You see it as an achievement, but in my mind it's a weakness," Sally said.

Marin regarded her doubtfully.

"I'm sorry if I offended you, but that's my opinion."

"No, I wasn't offended at all. I'm simply not used to such critical women," he said. "Most of the women I knew had no complaints toward me. They even admired me."

"Admiration is an empty thing."

"You've never admired a man?"

"I've only appreciated one," she answered.

"Jerry?"

"Yes, as well as my father and a few others."

"And did you want them to appreciate you?"

"Very much so. I'm not so bothered by the opinion of other people, but when it comes to people I appreciate—I could die for their appreciation."

"*I* appreciate you," said Marin, "and I realize that my relationship with Muriel and my offer yesterday to physically knock off Ben David haven't added to your opinion of me."

"On the contrary. It's because I appreciate you that I'm so saddened by your choice to marry a woman simply because she was a famous model and reflected your financial power. Clearly you have other qualities that could draw women. Intelligence, for instance. You need to find a woman who you appreciate and who appreciates you, not one who'll follow you for your money and good looks."

He didn't respond, but Sally could clearly feel his contentment with the compliment imbedded in her words. "You know," he said suddenly, "I've never been in a relationship with a woman who's my equal—someone like you."

Sally pursed her lips with discomfort. His attractive appearance and her sense of loneliness set her mind wandering. "There are many independent women," she said.

"You represent the ideal woman to me," Marin said. "The courage, the power, the liberation. Liberated women in Europe adopt masculine characteristics to display their independence. In Israel, I saw gentle women in uniform carrying rifles. They seemed very sure of themselves. Did you serve in the army?"

"No. I come from a traditional family, and it would have hurt my father. Although I believe he would have agreed today—"

Sally's phone rang and Jerry's name appeared on the screen. Sally froze for a moment. "Excuse me, it's Jerry," she said as she left the room for the closed porch. The view she saw through the glass reminded her of the last time she stood there with Jerry, united in their love and in the knowledge they were doing the right thing."

"When do you return?" asked Jerry in his solid, frigid manner.

Sally's heart leaped. "Do you miss me?" she asked with hope.

"I need you to testify to the police."

"Why the police?"

"My car was set on fire last night parked underneath our house. I filed a complaint with the police, and, of course, couldn't hide your involvement with the Ben David issue. Since it's a Mossad car, the police are investigating all sorts of directions, including security ones. They want explanations."

Every time she was challenged or attacked, a rush of adrenaline surged through her body. "I'll be there in two or three days and sort everything out," she said confidently.

"Why two or three days and not today? There are night flights, and if they're full I'm sure your millionaire can arrange a private jet to take you."

"He's not *my* millionaire."

"He's yours more than your family, which you're endangering to help him. I want you to be here by tomorrow to give your testimony."

Sally tried to remember the things left on her agenda: Finding a rabbi for Joel, banishing Ben David from Muriel's home, and organizing the campaign against him. "I need two days," she said bluntly. "I can't imagine the testimony is that urgent."

"It's urgent *to me.* It's very inconvenient for me to be involved in this even indirectly, and it's only a matter of time until this is publicized. I assume the Mossad's legal adviser will issue a gag order, but you know the Internet doesn't obey such orders. I want you to come here for me and for our family. I consider your cutting ties with Marin and his problems a test of our relationship."

"Why are you so intent on exacerbating this crisis?" Sally asked with anger.

"I expect to see you no later than tomorrow morning," said Jerry and hung up.

Sally remained standing before the view, swallowing her tears and regulating her breath. She waited a few minutes so as not to return to the table with swollen eyes. When she finally returned to the dining room, she discovered that Marin had remained in his seat without touching his food. She guessed the sad expression on her face did not escape him, but he merely asked, "Do you want your dish reheated? Should a new one be brought?"

"I have no appetite," Sally said and sat down. She overflowed with emotion.

"Jerry's angry," he commented.

Sally looked at him with wonder.

"Do you think I don't understand? His wife is involved up to her neck with the affairs of a foreign man, and meanwhile she and her family are being threatened."

"It's worse. His car was burned. It belongs to the Mossad and an investigation was opened." She thought of Aaron and her conversation with him in the café. "Maybe now he'll receive security and I'll be less stressed."

"Do you want to leave immediately, tonight?"

"I like to finish things I start. As soon as we receive the restraining order, I'll make sure Ben David leaves the house. Then I'll leave my Israeli investigators, who I trust, in surveillance, and fly home. I'll look for the man to prepare Joel for his bar mitzvah from Israel, or perhaps *in* Israel."

40.

The lawyer seemed somewhat scared, squeezed in the van between the investigators Jacob had collected half an hour earlier at the airport. They had a very Israeli look—jeans, T-shirts, and windbreakers. Their hair was cropped short, their faces covered in stubble, and their entire look reflected their military backgrounds.

To their left, in the lake, a white boat sailed; a party yacht that filled the air with music every evening. This time it drifted silently, its deck void of celebrators. Sally couldn't rule out the possibility that it had been hired by Marin to track the removal of his foe.

Jacob's men, who observed Muriel's house instead of the Swiss investigators who'd defected, reported that Ben David was inside. Sally looked at her watch. Three hours remained before the children returned from school, and in that time the operation must be completed and the scene left clear. The car turned off the lakeside road and began the descent toward Gstaad. When they reached the house, they stopped before the closed gate. Jacob signaled with a glance and two of his men got out of the car. One of them tested the lock, but the gate didn't open. His friend returned to the van, pulled out a crowbar from underneath the front seat, and jammed it between the two gate doors. The van entered the courtyard and parked in the center of the front lawn. The investigators leaped out of it and quickly surrounded the house. Jacob, accompanied by Sally and a lawyer, rang the doorbell.

The door opened and an elderly woman stood in the doorway. The lawyer turned to her in French, she answered him, and Sally repeated her words in Hebrew for Jacob's sake. "The owner is gone and they could not be let in."

The lawyer showed her the warrant he held. "This warrant allows us to enter the house on behalf of the renter, Monsieur Pierre Marin, and remove any person inside other than his wife and children."

"Who is Pierre Marin?" The servant's voice rose with indignation. "I don't know any Marin. My employer is Muriel and she is currently out."

"Ask her who hired her," Sally said.

The lawyer repeated the question, and the woman answered, "A friend of the owner, and I don't have to answer that."

The lawyer ran out of patience. He marched in with a boldness Sally never guess his small body possessed. The servant reached out her heavy arm to stop him, but Jacob gently moved it aside, led her to the kitchen, and shut the door. A staircase led to the bedrooms, separated by a large landing. An open door revealed a children's room. The other doors were shut. The lawyer stopped and called out in French, "Madame Marin."

No answer was heard.

"Mrs. Marin," he called again in English.

Noises could be heard behind one of the doors, and Sally imagined a man's voice. "What do you want? Who are you?" a woman called out, and Sally recognized Muriel's voice, which was no less terrified than it was during their last conversation at the gate of the apartment Ben David had rented for her in Beersheba. "Go away. This is my house and you have no right to disturb me."

"Madame," the lawyer said, "we have a restraining order for everyone in the house besides Mr. Marin's wife and children. I was permitted to allow the cook and the maid to remain. Anyone else must leave."

Muriel grew silent. Sally could sense her alarm even through the door. Again, whispers were heard and Muriel said, "There's no one with me."

"Then please open the door. The warrant allows me to check all the rooms in the house."

Silence remained for a long while behind the closed door. "Madame," the lawyer finally said, "your children will soon return from school and the situation will become less pleasant. I suggest you open the door. Mr. Ben David will come out, take the warrant banning him from here, and that will end the matter."

Muriel burst out in a wild, uncontrollable cry. The doorknob moved and immediately stopped. A man's voice said in broken English, "They can't force us to open." Muriel sobbed and answered, screaming, "Please, Honorable Rabbi, please leave. I can't have my children discover us. I'm terrified of what Pierre will do to us as it is."

"You've done nothing wrong," Ben David said. "I'm your spiritual teacher and we met in here to discuss your personal problems. What's wrong with that?"

"We have forty more minutes," the lawyer said. "Then you'll have to explain to your children who this man is and why he's holed up in a closed room with you."

Sally assumed the threat wouldn't help. After all, Ben David controlled Muriel and would not allow her to open the door. But to her surprise the doorknob turned. A small crack opened up between the door and the doorframe, then opened wide. Muriel, wrapped in a bathrobe, stood at the entrance. She was skinnier than Sally remembered her, her eyes red from tears and the corners of her mouth turned down. She lowered her eyes. If she recognized Sally, she didn't even hint it.

Behind her stood a slight man with dark skin. The lawyer handed him the warrant, which he grabbed with disdain. Then he stepped forward, stared at Jacob, and stopped in front of Sally. "Hello, Mrs. Amir," he said, extending his hand. "We don't know each other personally, but we've been in touch indirectly."

Sally did not take his hand. "Indirectly, yes."

"Why are you pursuing us? What in God's name have we done?"

"Don't mention God's name in the same place you desecrated by sleeping with the mother of a child you're preparing for his bar mitzvah. Have you no shame?"

The expression of insult on Ben David's face was real, and had she not watched the footage produced by the surveillance cameras, she could believe he was actually offended. "Mrs. Amir, we will sue you for all the damages you caused us, and we won't forget this terrible insult you voiced here in front of all these people." He looked at Jacob, seeking masculine assurance.

Jacob spoke into a microphone hidden in his jacket lapel. "Everyone to the entrance." Ben David scanned the investigators gathering at the bottom of the staircase, turned his face to Muriel, and said in English, "Don't worry, Madam Muriel, I will return and we'll continue our conversation."

"You won't return," Sally said, also in English, "because Mr. Marin is going to appoint a different teacher for his son. A more moral one. Read the warrant in your spare time. It forbids you to be in contact with any member of the Marin family."

"There's an agreement that you yourself drafted with Attorney Ovadia, designating me to prepare the son for his bar mitzvah."

"You know very well *you* breached the agreement. Instead of preparing the son, you slept with his mother."

"You'll have to prove that in court!"

"Don't make me do it," Sally said.

Ben David scoffed at her and left the room. Muriel's body began to shake. She got down on her knees and began shouting incoherent sentences. "Don't touch her," Jacob ordered. "Stay away. Sally, see if you can calm her but without touching, otherwise we'll be accused of assault."

Sally came over to her, and disobeying Jacob's orders, stretched out her hand. "Come on, get up," she said.

Muriel didn't take her hand. She continued to shake, but her shouting stopped. She howled mournfully, mumbling, "How can I live without seeing him again?"

Jacob and his men left the house. Sally asked the cook for a glass of water, which she handed to Muriel. "I have something better," the cook said. She disappeared for a moment, returning with a bottle of Jack Daniels. Muriel grabbed it from her hand and drank from it eagerly. "That's better, isn't it Mrs. Muriel?" the cook asked, and Muriel answered with a long burp.

During the drive back to Geneva, Muriel's phone rang. "Madame Amir," Marin's secretary announced, "I'm sorry to inform you that tonight's flight to Tel Aviv was canceled. The flight inspectors are on strike. Tomorrow afternoon, flights will resume, and a first-class ticket will await you for the 1:50 flight with Swiss."

Sally hung up and rushed to call Jerry. He didn't answer. She redialed him again and again throughout the journey, but to no avail. She continued trying during her meeting with Diana at Café Central, where she paid her the rest of her salary. "Maybe he's in a meeting," Diana suggested. "Send him a text message."

"Later," said Sally. "First the money." She wrote the check and signed it. "The hotel room is paid for until the weekend, and you also have a first-class ticket back to Israel," she said, handing her an envelope.

"Thanks, but I'm leaving for Paris from here."

"A trip?"

"Work. I've been offered a job as head of security for a financial company. I've always loved Paris, and I'm certainly ready for a change."

"And what about your family?" Sally asked hesitantly.

"I'm sure you ask yourself the same question," Diana replied. "We'll talk about it sometime. Now it's all too painful." She stood up. "I need to pack."

Sally stood up as well and hugged her. "Be strong," she said

"You too. We both need strength right now."

Sally followed Diana until she walked out to the street, then tapped a text message: "My flight is delayed, I'll arrive tomorrow."

"Fine," the answer arrived.

41.

Waiting was always destabilizing for Sally. Her need for order, stability, and control made every uncoordinated change in plan a source of self-doubt, which translated into anger.

She stood in the glassed-in balcony, staring at the Alpine view, and drank her third glass of wine. "Monsieur Marin asks if you'd like to join him for dinner out," Natalia asked behind her. "He would like to order a table at Café de la Paix in Geneva. He says they have French, Italian, and Mediterranean dishes, so you have a large variety."

"I…" Sally hesitated. Dining out could pass the frustrating evening more quickly, but spending time with Marin was dangerous in her current state of mind. "I'd rather eat here."

Natalia's eyes rested on her with amazement. What woman would refuse Pierre Marin's invitation? "I think he'll be very disappointed."

"I'm sorry," Sally said.

To her surprise, Natalia added, "He invited a few other people he'd like to introduce to you." Sally's curiosity arose. Why not? When this whole affair ended she'd certainly want to keep active, and she might as well meet people of different professions. A deeper voice whispered to her that perhaps her relationship with Jerry was crawling to its finish, and she should establish a solid financial base rather than remain dependent on his income, like Muriel was dependent on Marin. "Fine," she said.

"Dinner is at eight," Natalia said, adding a smile to confirm that Sally had made the right choice. "Will you be ready at five? Fred, the new driver, will pick you up and take you to Geneva."

Sally spent the next hours trying not to sulk. She spoke to Jacob, who told her he'd placed two of his investigators in a parked car across from Muriel's house, to keep Ben David away. An hour later, he informed her that a taxi had picked Muriel up and taken her to town. An investigator who followed her reported that she met with Ben David at the office of a local lawyer. "Expect legal action," Jacob said, stating the obvious.

Sally rang Marin's personal mobile. He didn't answer. She sent him a text message reporting the developments, then took a shower and dressed. She still only had the single dress she packed in Israel three days earlier, and she knew that at dinner she'd feel like Cinderella at the ball.

At eight sharp, Fred pulled up at Café de la Paix in Geneva. Marin greeted her in the foyer and walked her to a couch nearby. Only as she sat down did she realize her hand was resting naturally in his. She knew she must pull it out, but his touch was so gentle yet fierce that she could not do so. "I want you to meet a few people," he said. "They're all my lawyers. You know one of them, Robert Darmond, and the others are among the leading lawyers in Europe and maybe in the world. We will discuss Ben David and his influence on my business."

"I tried to inform you. Ben David and Muriel were at a lawyer's in—"

"I know. The lawyer refused to represent him and informed me. No serious lawyer in Geneva or the rest of Switzerland will stand up to me. I assume eventually he'll find someone who wants the publicity or needs the money, but he'll be second class and my lawyers will crush him." He let go of her hand and looked at her warmly. "I want you to be involved in everything, Sally. In fact, I wanted to offer you the position of my personal assistant. I know you won't leave Israel, but these days almost anything can be done online or over the phone, and the distance between Tel Aviv and Geneva is relatively small."

Sally struggled to subdue the mounting excitement inside her. Her rational and cautious side prompted her to respond. "Let's first see how we end the Ben David problem."

"There is no Ben David problem. Even if he turns to the court he'll get nothing, and Muriel certainly won't either. Swiss law takes breach of trust by a teacher very seriously, as it does a woman cheating on her husband." Marin stood up, and taking Sally by the hand, led her to a surprisingly simple dining hall. Wooden tables with metal legs were covered with checkered tablecloths and simple white plates lay resting before straight back chairs. He noticed her surprise and said, "Here they invest in the food, not the decoration."

Four men awaited them at a corner table. Darmond greeted her with icy politeness. The others shook her hand. "Gentlemen," said Marin, "I'm pleased to introduce you to Madame Sally Amir, who has been working with me for a while. Thanks to her, a conspiracy to trick me out of money was exposed. Some money has already been taken, and you'll help me get it back. My wife Muriel was involved in this, and you'll take care of her as well. As you know, I've experienced many disappointments and treacheries throughout my professional life, but the combined treachery of a wife and a spiritual guide is worse than any other. However—" he raised his glass "—I am not even slightly sad, because instead of those two traitors who have no more room in my life, I met a wonderful woman who protected me tirelessly for no reward, a true friend."

The others also raised their glasses, though with less enthusiasm. During the meal, Sally's phone buzzed in her purse. Roy's name appeared on the screen. "Excuse me," she told the men, "it's my son. He's in the army."

She left, hearing Marin explain to his guests about the mandatory Israeli military service. "Mom," Roy said, as she sat on the couch next to the cloakroom. "What's going on between you and Dad?"

"Did he say anything to you?"

"He doesn't want to talk. I came home and saw you were gone. Michael said you'd had a fight and you flew abroad. This has never happened before."

"Well, it's happening now."

"This is connected to that man, Pierre Marin, right?"

"Only indirectly."

"Michael told me that one day you wanted to pick him up from school in a complete panic. He thinks the fire in Dad's car and your accident also have something to do with this. Why do you insist on putting us at risk?"

"All of this is between your father and I," Sally insisted. "Michael and you are not connected."

"It's not just between Dad and you. Michael can't sleep at night for fear. Dad is nervous and silent. So I agree with you that the business with Marin is important, and like you I think any Jew in need should be protected, certainly one that helped you so much starting out, but not at the price of ruining our family. Do you understand?"

"I do. Family is very important for me too, but it's not about that, but rather about succumbing to fear. When external pressure is exerted, like the one we're experiencing now, family members should support one another, not demand surrender."

"It's no pressure," Roy said nervously, "it's a threat. Your car was rammed, Dad's car was burned, we receive telephone threats. What are you waiting for, Michael to be kidnapped?"

"It's not like you to fold like this. Dad's guarding Michael, the cars aren't important, and phone threats are only words. However, what I'm doing here is extremely important and I must finish what I started."

"When will you finish?"

Sally looked at the men around the table through the open door, considering the next stages. A long legal battle with Muriel and Ben David, and perhaps other issues Marin would like her to address as his personal assistant. "It will take time," she said, "and as I explained to Dad, there is no turning back. Ben David and his men will not easily give up on Marin's money; they'll try again and again."

"They can be paid off."

"And who says they won't ask for more once they get their money? Listen, Roy, the train has already left the station and we have no choice but to wait until the end of the journey, when all the crooks are in jail."

On Roy's side of the line Sally could hear approaching male voices, and his speech grew terse. "Mom, I need to go. We'll continue this conversation when you arrive."

"Kisses, my son," Sally said, but the phone was already silent.

Two hours later, on the way to the mansion in Gstaad, Sally was deep in thought in the back seat of the long Bentley. Marin too was silent, respecting her need for privacy. As the car climbed toward his house, Sally was overwhelmed with a sense of loneliness, mixed with dread. She shuddered. Marin opened the minibar and pulled out one of his fine bottles of cognac. "I believe this will help you," he said, pouring her a glass.

She gulped it down in one go, feeling the soothing warmth spread through her.

"Is there trouble with your son in the army?" he inquired.

"No," she answered.

At two a.m., they entered the large garden. Marin said, "I don't want to leave in this state. Would you like to have another drink with me?"

The thought of the loneliness she would experience at the guesthouse prevailed. "Yes, thank you," she said.

Natalia greeted them at the entrance. Marin signaled to the living room and walked into the glassed balcony. A cold bottle of wine and a glass were already waiting on the table. Natalia rushed over with another glass. Sally sat down on one of the couches, distancing herself as much as possible from the sofa she sat on with Jerry. Marin sat on the next couch. "I don't want you to fight with Jerry over me," he said.

She looked at him with astonishment.

"I already told you I realize what's going on between you. If I were Jerry, I wouldn't agree that my beautiful and smart wife spends time at another man's house, even if it is just the guest quarters."

"That's not the problem," said Sally, "there's no romantic jealousy here." Actually, the thought suddenly hit her, there is no romance left between us. When was the last time that Jerry hugged her? Kissed her?

Walked with her in places they used to love, like the alleys of Jerusalem's Old City? "Jerry is terrified of what Ben David and the organization manipulating him could do to our children and to his reputation. He may also be concerned for me, I don't know. He's a good man, but so rigid..."

Marin leaned forward and asked her softly, "May I kiss you?"

Sally was silent with astonishment.

"You're a very pretty woman, Sally, very attractive, and I think you like me too. One of us has to make the first move."

Sally felt the urge to cling to the firm hand he was holding out to her. "You seem very tired to me," she said, desperately attempting to postpone the moment of truth.

"I'm not tired at all, nor am I insane." He stood up in front of her. "I'm not going to push you. I know what I'm proposing might complicate things, but if we consider tonight as a one-time thing, as a bit of well-deserved comfort."

Sally stood up into his arms.

42.

It was the saddest flight she had ever experienced. First class was almost empty, adding to the feeling of distress caused by the memory of the night she had spent with Pierre. Her emotions were as strong as they were contradictory: Pierre was a lover of a kind she had never met—smart and sensual, submissive yet dominant. But despite the heights she had reached with him, she felt the depths of the abyss that widened within her, a chasm of guilt and yearning for Jerry.

When she arrived home, it was six in the evening. A new car stood in Jerry's old parking space. Her dented car stood next to it. Sally looked at her mobile, debating whether to call home. Finally, she put it back in her bag and entered the building. She somehow hoped to catch Jerry with another woman, expunging her own sin. At the same time, she knew that was impossible. Jerry was the embodiment of loyalty, and would never betray her with an impulsive act.

She said a brief hello to the doorman and in the elevator, switched her weight from leg to leg impatiently. When she reached her apartment, she gently turned the key and stealthily entered her home. She saw Michael's back in the dining room. Jerry was sitting opposite him. Their plates held cardboard boxes from a well-known meat restaurant. Her gaze caught Jerry's, who didn't say a word.

"Hello," Sally said.

Michael jumped out of his chair, turned around, and ran toward her. She hugged him tightly, as Jerry continued chewing his meal.

"Mom, how long have you come for? Will you stay with us now?" Michael asked.

Sally remembered Rubi's question, the first time she met him, whether she would bring his mother back. Sure, Michael was older and the circumstances of her absence were different from Muriel's, but the fearful tone in the question of both children was the same. She kissed him on the head, to calm him. "I don't know yet. I hope to work from home and be with you a lot."

"They called from your previous workplace, the insurance company," Jerry said gravely. "Your leave of absence is about to end, and they wanted to know if you plan to return."

"I'll speak to them tomorrow," Sally replied, struggling to maintain her light tone. "What's happening here? What's new?"

"Dad is already letting me leave the house alone," Michael chuckled.

"Great."

Jerry responded with a nod of the head. "Would you like to eat?" he asked, polite as always.

"I'm not hungry," she said, sitting in between them.

"Michael needs to finish his roots project," Jerry announced with the tone of an order. "The submission date is approaching."

"Roots project? Has he spoken to my parents?"

"He spoke to whoever he needed to," replied Jerry, signaling with his head to Michael to go to his room.

"Wait, I want to be with Mom for a while!" Michael protested.

"I need to speak to her and you have work to do," Jerry said, glaring at him.

"I'm going, I'm going," said Michael and stood up. After he left, Jerry said with ominous calm, "I understand you've decided to tie your destiny with Marin's."

Sally's heart sank. Did he find out about something? Pierre had promised her last night that he sent Natalia and the other employees to their quarters. Did Natalia figure out what was going on in her employer's bedroom anyway? She may have brought it to Jerry's attention, who she had met during his visit to the mansion. Jacques double-crossed Pierre at the behest of the criminal organization that was backing Ben David. Who's to say Natalia wouldn't do the same?

"Sally?" Jerry asked.

She awoke from her thoughts. "Sorry. I'm still a bit overwhelmed by the flight. So, I understand that aside from the fire nothing unusual happened. The threats have stopped. So, everything is all right, no?"

"We can't carry on like this with your disappearances."

"We've managed all these years with *your* disappearances."

"That was to earn a living. With Marin, you don't even have an income, and we need your salary. I'd like to remind you I'm simply a government employee, and if you stop working for the insurance company—"

"I won't continue working there," Sally said decisively. "It's not the life I wanted, and I refuse to continue it."

"Where will you work then? Will Marin pay you a salary?"

"No, but I have money. I will ask him for permission to transfer six months' salary to our bank account. That should do for now, no?"

"And then?"

"Then we'll see."

Jerry frowned. "You can't lead a life of 'we'll see.' You need a plan, a stable base—"

"*You* need a plan. I don't. And when I see an opportunity, I jump on it."

"What's the big opportunity? To work for Pierre Marin?"

"Yes. He offered me the job of his personal assistant," said Sally as neutrally as possible, suppressing the other things that were said and done.

"And where will you live?"

"Here. Today you can work anywhere," she said, quoting Marin. "You can e-mail, Skype, WhatsApp, video conference…"

"It won't work," Jerry said. "Don't kid yourself. A personal assistant must be close to her boss. You'll have to travel a lot." He leaned back and sighed. "Where are we headed, Sally? I know we're different. I'm an introvert and you're a heart-to-heart type. I'm closed off and you connect with everyone. But we were still always coordinated. What does this Marin have that makes you want to throw away your family and our marriage?"

"I'm not throwing anything away," Sally replied, shaken. "I've been given a chance to lead the life I always wanted and never had a chance to experience, since we started our family. I gave birth, and then constantly traveled to the places where you had work."

"So basically, you're saying you're going to lead an independent life, irrespective of my needs and the children's?"

"I'm considerate. Until you stopped talking to me, I called every night. I come back as often as possible, and when this matter ends I'll be home most of the time. Meanwhile, I'd like you to take my needs into account."

"They're incompatible with normal family life," said Jerry, and stood up angrily. "They're simply incompatible," he repeated and left the room.

Sally remained at the kitchen table, next to the leftovers of the non-kosher meal, and struggled not to succumb to the tears in her eyes.

43.

The drive to the *moshav* the following morning left Sally feeling no better. She drove nervously, maneuvering her car with its destroyed back fender between the scores of cars crawling north. She was half an hour late, and her father and mother were waiting for her at the front gate. "I'm sorry, the traffic was terrible. How long have you been waiting here?" she asked.

"We've just come out," her mother said. "You know Dad can sense you coming."

Inside, all the regular delicacies awaited her on the large table around which the household revolved. She ate slowly, with small bites, to prolong the solace her childhood food gave her. Her parents updated her on news from her brother and sister, events in the *moshav*, and cute sayings from her young nieces and nephews. When she finished eating, silence fell on the room. Her parents' eyes looked on her with anticipation. "You've always taught me that bringing Jews closer to faith is a mitzvah," Sally began.

"True," her father said with a smile, and she knew he could tell where she was going.

"I would like you to prepare a boy for his bar mitzvah. His Torah portion is Beha'alotcha, in a little less than three months."

"It takes at least a year to prepare a boy who doesn't speak Hebrew for his bar mitzvah. Passover and Shavuot take place during this time, and the boy," her father said calmly, "lives far away."

"You can even prepare a gentile for a bar mitzvah," Sally said, "and you can celebrate Passover in his father's home. Mom will come, and if you'd like, the boy's father will fly over additional family members."

"And what about you and Jerry?" her mother asked hopefully.

"I'm not sure," Sally replied.

A tear appeared in the corner of her mother's eye. "So it isn't working out?"

"No," Sally said, "it isn't." She quickly changed the subject. "Is there someone to take care of the farm?"

"We'll leave the farm with Mom," her father said. "The neighbor will help her and we'll pay him for his effort."

"I assume you'll receive a proper salary as compensation," Sally promised.

"I don't care about the salary. The reward for a mitzvah is the mitzvah. Man is repaid for his good deeds from heaven. When do I leave?"

"I'll let you know." Sally hugged him. "And I'm so thankful to both of you for sticking with me on this."

"You're the one who's sticking with *us*, child," her mother said. "After all, you're implementing what your father taught you."

She was much calmer on the ride back. She dialed Marin, who was amazed to hear about the identity of Joel's prospective teacher. "It's a great honor for my son to be taught by the father of the woman who was willing to help me, for heaven's sake," he said. Sally continued driving with a sense of elation, which dissipated the closer she got to home. When she stepped into her apartment, she found it dark. Michael was already asleep and Jerry was holed up in his study. Just a thin strip of light under the door indicated his presence.

The next day was full of silence, as were the following days. Jerry spent his time in the study and Sally in the bedroom, which became hers alone. They met for short, businesslike dinners, where they politely discussed household chores. Meanwhile, her conversations with Marin grew longer. He filled them with expressions of passion and longing, while she was more hesitant, still unsure what she thought about the new situation. "I suggest we put that night in the past," she told him once. "It could be the start of something new, as you say and feel, or it could be a mistake to be forgotten."

"How can you call that night a mistake?" asked Marin. "It contained so much. I've never felt so…"

The intensity of his emotion frightened Sally. She still hadn't processed everything that took place that night, nor the repercussions for her family life if she confessed to Jerry. Now it took all her resources not to be sucked into the whirlpool that Marin created in her. "It could be a mistake, at least as far as our work relationship is concerned."

She could sense the hurt in his voice when he said, "You didn't behave like someone who'd made a mistake."

"I got carried away," she explained, "and so did you. That's why we both need to examine our feelings on our own."

"I know what *I* feel, and if you feel differently, say so immediately. I can't stand being misled."

"Pierre," she pleaded, "you must understand that feelings aren't a business transaction. There's no reality of loss or gain, of leading and misleading. I'm extremely confused; both happy and torn over what happened. Don't pressure me."

Yet in every conversation, Marin continued to invite her to his mansion, or at least to Gstaad or Geneva, so they could see each other. Sally felt herself beginning to recoil. She cherished the memory of the night they spent together and missed him, but also felt burdened by his suffocating neediness and his hunger for control. "I'll stay in Tel Aviv for now," she informed him one evening. "I'll only come if something comes up."

"So you're not interested in me."

"I don't know. You leave me no space to decide."

"All right," Marin promised, "I'll shut up from now on. It will be purely business."

The next day, Sally received an e-mail containing a list of charities requesting Marin's donations, along with a request to visit them and write a report on their activities. Sally started scheduling meetings and traveling across the country. She loved these missions, which brought her back to where it all began, with Marin's generous donation to her studies. They also filled her conversations with Marin with new content. His pleas that she join him in Switzerland died down, and she assumed he had found a new candidate for his courtship. She wasn't indifferent to that, but didn't mourn it either. From the very beginning, Marin was both a prize and a source of embarrassment. His distance sometimes made her uneasy, but also allowed her to repress that wonderful, terrible night of which she never spoke to Jerry.

The repression didn't last long. After her father left for Switzerland, she began to worry. She knew how Marin craved intelligent interlocutors on faith and Judaism, and knew her father's ability to influence others all too well. She had no doubt that the two men were chatting into the night in the cold Alpine climate. She also knew that her father could grasp one thing from the other, put together sayings and hints, and finally discover his daughter's relationship with Marin. Didn't the proximity between his bar mitzvah preparation mission and her secret intimate relationship with Marin place her—even slightly—in Ben David's despicable position? She knew that factually the two were unrelated, but felt emotional distress, which only increased given Marin's high regard for her father. He had warmed up to Joel and little Rubi, who even called him Grandpa, Marin said.

From Jacob's reports, Sally learned that the children were living in Marin's mansion while Muriel was completely out of control. She went out every night, and Jacob's men—who had attached a surveillance device to her car—found it parked next to an apartment in Gstaad that she had secretly rented for Ben David. Her tail revealed that the moment she entered the apartment, the two wouldn't leave. "That's a breach of the restraining order. We could go to the police and argue contempt of court."

"The police won't deal with this," Jacob said. "Not even in Switzerland. Besides, we don't need a newspaper article reporting that a Geneva court won't let two lovers meet, one of whom happens to be Mrs. Marin."

"All right, at least install a system there that will film and record."

"I have no way of doing that. Ben David is there all the time and never leaves. He's scared of the police and perhaps of the criminal organization behind him, which is probably pressuring him to show results and get Marin's money. We've spotted some well-known criminals from Beersheba and the Negev wandering around."

"You're not concerned they'll harm Muriel?"

"They're probably scared of annoying Marin. If they harm Ben David no one will miss him, but Muriel is a different matter, and Marin is rich enough to hunt them down to the end of the world. In short, I need you to pull him out for an hour so that I can install my system. An hour is all I need."

"We could stage a fire in the stairway," Sally suggested.

Jacob sighed. "Sally, Sally. How many times have I told you that I'll do anything but get in trouble with the police?"

"All right," Sally said. "We'll wait. Another idea will come up."

44.

When Sally's first salary from Pierre Marin was deposited in her bank account; she joyfully showed the bank statement to Jerry. "See how everything worked out?"

"Nothing worked out," he said wryly. "Maybe it's just calmed down. Ben David remains, as does the organization behind him, and no one is planning to forgo Marin's money. My problems are also still here."

"What problems? I've been in Israel for six weeks taking care of the house, working, earning money, and you're still angry with me, God knows why."

"I'm angry because you've brought trouble to our doorstep and it's not over yet. You'll see."

Trouble did indeed return when the doorbell rang one evening. Jerry rushed to open it to find a man in his forties holding a briefcase with shiny number locks. Jerry didn't seem surprised. He led him to the dining room and sat across from him. The stranger placed a few forms on the table and started filling them in, as he spoke to Jerry in a muffled voice. Without know what this was about, Sally sensed bad news was coming.

A few minutes later, Jerry called out to her. "Sally, would you care to join us?"

Sitting across from the stranger, Sally took in his severe look under his bushy eyebrows. She noticed his gray stubble left by sloppy shaving. "My name is Yigal," he said with a phony politeness that caused Sally to doubt that was his real name. "I'm investigating the circumstances of the fire in your husband Jerry's car," he added in a formal tone. "It was a government car, as you know, and since this is a criminal act, the SSDS is in the picture."

"What's the SSDS?" asked Sally.

"The Security Supervisor in the Defense System," he said.

"All right. What would you like to know?" Sally asked impatiently.

"I understand you were involved in a private investigation recently concerning a certain group of people."

"I conducted an investigation into an imposter rabbi from Beersheba who harmed a foreign national who is—" she paused for a second, hoping Jerry didn't notice "—my friend."

"And I understand this investigation caused you and your entire family to be threatened."

"You could say that."

The man looked at Jerry, who nodded in confirmation, then moved the forms aside, opened an empty notebook, and said, "I'd like you to tell me everything that happened, from the start. How, why, and where."

Sally tried to stay polite. "Are you serious? It will take hours."

"I have time."

Sally couldn't hold herself back. "I don't. I also don't understand under what right you ask me to reveal private information that—"

"The moment government property is harmed, information on the circumstances is no longer private and I have the legal right to demand of every Israeli—soldier or civilian—to give me a deposition."

Sally turned to Jerry, who nodded. "So I refuse to give you my deposition, as you call it," she said. "What will you do? Arrest me?"

The man jotted something down in his notebook. "Will you sign that you refuse to provide your deposition?"

"I won't sign a thing, and if you keep bugging me, I'll call my lawyer."

He smiled dismissively. "That's all right. We're prepared to deal with lawyers too."

Sally stood up from her chair. "Would you like some coffee? Because otherwise, this meeting is over as far as I'm concerned."

"A glass of water, please," Yigal said nonchalantly.

Sally served him a glass of water, walked to her bedroom, and lay down on her bed in rage. A few moments later, she heard a knock on the door. Jerry entered. "Is that it? Has he left?" she asked.

"He left, but it's not over. They'll want explanations and won't let go."

"I don't owe anyone explanations and besides, why are you involving me in this?"

"Because my car didn't burn itself. You live in your own world, Sally, where you can do whatever you want. You can follow Ben David, you can fly back and forth to Geneva on Marin's money, and you can give up a very lucrative job, like the one you had at the insurance company."

"I've transferred money to our account like I promised," Sally burst out, "and I have a lucrative and very satisfying job at the Marin Foundation."

"I'm not finished yet," Jerry said. "In your world, there's also no commitment to other people. You should know that I'm in trouble. My position is in jeopardy. The man you refused to talk to could remove my security clearance and deny me access to classified material. Without classification, I won't even be able to apply as a janitor, and I'll have to retire."

"And you accept that fate? You won't fight? You won't appeal it? You won't consider another option, like retiring and starting a business? You have such rare skills, you'll be snatched up anywhere."

"Sally, that's where you're mistaken. You can't fight everything."

"You have to try!" Sally fumed. "Your defeatism drives me crazy, Jerry. You're willing to accept any authority, any order, any diktat. Even when that man, Yigal—or whatever his name is—was here, you didn't protect me. You didn't silence him."

"He was doing his job."

"Do you really think I need to tell him everything that happened to me over the past several months just because some puny car was burned?"

"That's the law, and I can't continue my work as long as my wife is involved in a fight with a criminal organization."

"In a *struggle against* a criminal organization!"

"No, Sally, it's the state that struggles against criminal organizations. What you're involved in is a fight. But let's not get bogged down with semantics. I have a more important matter to discuss. Do you want to separate?"

The question hit Sally like a ton of bricks.

"We're already living separately," Jerry explained. "Your life hasn't belonged to the children and me for a while. They're Marin's. Even your father works for him, and your mother will travel to him for Passover along with one of your brothers and his family. If it were not for your certainty that I wouldn't agree, you'd propose that we celebrate there too."

She hugged him. He stood standing and didn't respond.

"I don't want to separate," Sally said. "I also don't want to ruin anything. I want you to understand me, to indulge me, to finally let me live the life I always wanted."

"I can't understand you," Jerry said coldly, and gently removed her hand from his back.

45.

In the coming days, Sally continued to travel across the country for the Pierre Marin Foundation, and although she loved the job and was successful at it, she did not enjoy herself. The alienation from Jerry made everything painful. When she tried to discuss this with him, he didn't change his position one iota: Only if she stopped dealing with Ben David and Marin would their relationship return to normal.

Sally secretly missed Marin, but harshly repressed the memory of the night she'd spent with him. Jacob's reports about Muriel continued: She dined at the fanciest restaurants in Gstaad, ordering the best dishes for her lover. She withdrew cash from her bank account and brought it to his hideaway, stopping on the way to buy him designer clothes he had no use for in the apartment he never left.

Sally also had long conversations with her dad. He told her of the progress Joel had made preparing for his reading of the Torah, of his growing interest in the Jewish religion and its commandments, and of his newfound excellence in school. If he knew anything about Sally's special relationship with Marin, he didn't say a word. But consciously or unconsciously, he divulged the possible reason that Marin stopped mentioning their relationship in their conversations—a beautiful brunette, a model for Dior, who appeared at his mansion.

The jealousy that revelation evoked in Sally was subdued by relief in realizing that life had solved the conflict created by the relationship with Marin. She gave her all in meetings with organization directors who received funding from the Marin Foundation, and in caring for her home. Michael, her younger son, got elaborate breakfasts and a new wardrobe. With Roy, she would speak briefly but lovingly on the phone, her heart going out to meet him. Twice he was supposed to come home for the weekend, but his leave was canceled due to operations or training. They both looked forward to the ten-day vacation he was finally meant to receive.

Ahead of the vacation, Sally cleared her day of meetings and entered the kitchen to make a turkey roll, her son's favorite dish. As she wrapped the filet around a roll of minced meat, her phone rang. "Pierre," her screen informed her. Sally looked at her watch with wonder. It wasn't the regular time for their conversations. She quickly rinsed her hands and slid a wet finger over the screen.

"Sally," Marin's voice emerged from the speaker, "they're unwilling to file the lawsuit. They say the court will throw us out unless we bring proof. They want the photos."

"There are no photos," Sally said deliberately, in case anyone was listening in on their conversation. "There are none. I don't know what made you think there were."

"Can you come?" he asked in a helpless tone. "Only you can get me out of this mess."

Sally looked at the semi-formed roll of meat. "I can't, Pierre. Roy is coming home from the army tomorrow. I haven't seen him since I returned to Israel."

"Bring him with you."

She laughed bitterly. "I can't do that, Pierre. It's the army. He can't leave the country."

"Who must I talk to?" suddenly the powerful Pierre Marin awoke. "After all I've given, I think I deserve Israel to release one officer for a short trip abroad."

Something about Marin's enthusiasm thrilled Sally. The idea of Roy flying with her to Switzerland, where he could see for himself how important the matter she was dealing with was, overtook her. "Don't speak to anyone. *I'll* deal with this."

"Excellent. Two first-class tickets for the eleven o'clock flight will await you at the airport. See you in Geneva."

Over the next two hours Sally spoke to some old friends, and the following morning, at four a.m., she was on her way to her son's base. She waited in the car for him to come out, wearing his work uniform and high army boots. A suitcase with his passport and ironed civilian clothes rested on the backseat. "Mom, I'm dirty after my training."

"Change your clothes, and when we arrive you'll change again."

"Arrive where?"

"In Geneva," Sally said lightheartedly. "Switzerland, you know."

"You can't be serious. I'm not allowed to leave the country."

"I got permission," she said, waving the document.

A glimmer lit in Roy's eye. "Really?"

"Really and truly."

"What a great mom you are."

He quickly changed his clothes as they started to drive away, and as soon as he put his head on the headrest, he fell asleep for the remainder of the ride to the airport. There, he followed her silent and obedient, as he did when he was a child. When they sat in the airplane and Sally started telling him about the purpose of their trip, he fell asleep once again, awaking only when the Alps and Lake Geneva appeared outside the window.

The limousine was parked on the tarmac with Fred, Marin's new driver dressed in a gray uniform, standing beside it. Roy whistled with appreciation. "A Bentley, no less," he said, as Fred opened the door for him. "Mom, is it always like this?"

Only then did Sally realize how used she had become to these conditions. "Yes," she said, "but there's nothing special about it."

"Nothing special at all," Roy repeated ironically. "None of the other passengers have a luxury car waiting for them on the runway."

"None of the other passengers are a soldier whose mother abducted him from his base," said Sally, tapping him on the back.

Roy laughed, his sight fixed on the scenery outside. Sally's phone indicated a text message. "I have to meet you," Jacob wrote.

"I'll meet you in half an hour at the lobby of the Four Seasons," Sally replied.

"How green," Roy declared. "What will I do while you're at your meetings?"

"You'll sit next to me. I want you to understand exactly what I'm doing and why it's so important."

Roy shrugged. "As long as this was a trip that was fine, but I'm not sure I want to be part of your work. That puts me in conflict with Dad."

"You won't be part of my work but part of my life, just like the times Dad told you about himself."

"He never did."

"So it's certainly good that one of your parents opens up to you, isn't it?" Sally asked, and without waiting for his response started explaining the background to her meeting with Jacob and her dilemma of exposing the evidence to the lawyers. When they entered their hotel rooms, he was already up to date about everything. "You have two hours to shower and rest up," Sally added. "Then they'll come and take us to the lawyers' offices."

While Roy was in his room, Sally went down to the lobby, where Jacob was waiting for her. "Is there anyone else working for you here?" he asked directly.

"No." Sally was taken aback. "Since I sacked the Swiss company, only you're in the picture."

"All right, well, Muriel has a shadow. Someone extremely professional who follows her and looks out for her ass."

"It's probably the organization handling Ben David. As far as it's concerned, she's the hen that will lay the golden egg they've been waiting for all this time. What exactly happened?"

He looked around with suspicion. "Yesterday we followed her like every day. She took her regular Gstaad route: Restaurants, delicatessens, etc. Our guy followed her two cars back, as we do, and then a small Peugeot came in between them and started slowing down traffic. Muriel stepped on the accelerator and disappeared. As soon as she vanished, the Peugeot returned to normal speed."

"Do you have a license plate?"

"It's a Geneva car rental company. We even found the rental form. The driver's name is Margarite Delacroix."

"And Muriel?"

"Disappeared. Our people rushed to her home, but she wasn't there. She didn't come home at night either. She only returned to Gstaad the following evening. We found her at a petrol station, filling her tank. She seemed very tired, like after a sleepless night." He looked around once more. "She went with some purpose, that's clear. The only question is who with, and why."

Sally pondered. "And Ben David?"

"He was in the apartment the entire time. The water was running; the electricity was on. No one came in or out. The children were with Marin as usual."

Sally sighed. "All right, we'll deal with this later. Now I have a more complicated matter to solve."

46.

The ancient structure exuded power and distinction. Sally told the uniformed guard in the foyer what office she was invited to. He pointed to a row of gray chairs. "They're on the sixth floor. Please wait here for the woman to escort you."

Sally observed the oil portraits on the wall. They were all of self-satisfied men, probably lawyers or bankers. "There's no woman," she mumbled.

"Who are all these people?" Roy asked, looking at the paintings.

"I don't know, but get used to it. These are the people you'll meet inside."

The minutes went by and no one arrived. Sally looked at the guard, puzzled, but his face remained emotionless. She looked at her watch. Fifteen minutes had gone by. "I think it's too much." She stood up and pressed the elevator button. The guard rushed over, protesting loudly in French. Roy stood in his way and the guard stopped in his tracks. His tone became less authoritarian. The elevator door opened. "*Bonjour,*" said Roy and followed his mother into the elevator.

"*Au revoir* is French for goodbye," Sally said. "Or *adieu*."

Roy smiled. Sally pressed the button and the elevator leaped upward. "I feel so good with you here," she said, and Roy hugged her.

They exited the elevator into a wood-paneled foyer. The receptionist was probably warned by the guard, and didn't protest as Sally marched straight into a meeting room the size of a tennis court; its door wide open. The room's walls were also covered with portraits of well-dressed, important looking men. Four men who looked like clones of the men in the portraits sat at the large table. Sally recognized Darmond among them. Marin sat at the head of the table next to a heavyset man who scolded Sally. "Madame Amir, we're still in the middle of our previous discussion and it really has nothing to do with the matter in which you're—how should I put it?—involved. We can't begin our conversation with you before we finish. That's our custom and that's also why they didn't summon you from downstairs."

"And my custom is to start meetings exactly at the time scheduled, or at most a few minutes late, with an apology."

The man recoiled in his seat. "And who is the gentleman next to you?"

"My son," Sally said, staring at Marin, who nodded his approval. All the others looked curiously at her and Roy. "Shall we begin?" Sally asked.

The man at the head of the table didn't respond, nor did the others. An uncomfortable silence spread across the room. Roy tapped on the table with his fingernails. Marin suddenly said, "The problem, Madame Amir, is that these men believe there is no possibility to file for divorce using the evidence you've produced." He hesitated for a moment. "They need photos."

"There are no photos," said Sally, wondering whether Marin was in such distress that he didn't understand what she had told him on the phone, or didn't remember it. "Even if they existed, I wouldn't give them to you. Covert recordings and photography are illegal in this country. Whoever would do that for you would get in trouble, and you'd get much unwanted negative publicity."

"In any event, without solid evidence there's no suit," said Darmond. "If you want to separate Madame Marin from that man, you'll have to provide better evidence."

"Or maybe I should find better lawyers, lawyers with enough gumption to find the appropriate articles in the law rather than expect to receive the case readymade."

Marin swallowed hard. "Sall...Madame Amir, Attorney Darmond has been my friend for twenty-five years, and I know his partners very well, too."

"In other words, this beautiful room, the plush office, and perhaps even the entire building, are all a product of your money."

One of the men burst out, "Madame, I don't know who you are, but even if Monsieur Marin is prepared to listen to you for whatever reason—I won't have it. I ask that you leave immediately."

"Why, because you won't admit that had you worked a bit harder and been more original and creative you could have found a way to file the suit long ago?"

"Monsieur Marin," said the man. "*You* pay us for our time. *You* decide how we proceed."

Marin hesitated, and Sally responded combatively. "You are paying, but have you received the return you deserve? I think they're more interested in your money than in your success."

The lawyers squirmed in their fancy suits. One of them whispered to his neighbor, "She's against us because we're not Jewish." Sally heard the comment and shot back, "I don't divide people into Jews and non-Jews but into honest and dishonest. I'll leave it to you to decide where I place lawyers who charge by the hour and don't do their work. We have everything we need to win the suit—depositions, testimonies, documents."

To her surprise, Marin said, "Madame Amir, the laws here are different than in Israel, and they know them. If they say the evidence we have won't do, they probably won't—"

Roy placed his hand on his mouth and mumbled to Sally, "He's trying to save their honor. Let him."

Sally signaled to Marin with her eyes toward the door. He stood up. "I'll be right back," she said to Roy in Hebrew. "Guard the fort."

Marin walked her to the next room and pointed to a sitting area. Sally remained standing. "How much did you pay them this year?" she challenged him.

"A lot of money. They're worth it. They care about me. They've been my friends for thirty years."

"Where are your brains?" she demanded. "You're Jewish, aren't you? So be a bit wiser. Do you really believe that twenty-year-old supermodels have fun with you because you're good-looking, and that these lawyers are your friends? Wake up! They all have one goal: They want your money, just like Ben David. The men in the meeting room didn't do their jobs. I take risks for you, my men take risks for you, and you let this group of pretentious men tell me that all our findings, all our surveillance reports, all the witnesses who signed depositions for us concerning the relationship between Ben David and Muriel—all this is worthless?"

"They claim it's not enough. Why do you think you know better than them?"

"I don't know better, I *care* more. I *want* you to be freed from Muriel and Ben David." She collapsed on the seat. "Do you know what? OK. I'm willing to give you the photos and sign an affidavit confirming I took them so that you don't get in trouble. An hour later I'll be out of Switzerland, and out of Europe entirely."

"You're giving up on the possibility of ever returning to Europe only so I can use the photos?"

"Yes, and I'm completely fine with that. So decide. If you leave the matter to them, I'll give them the photos and take off. If you trust me, let me refer this case to someone who will really handle it for you honestly and professionally."

"Let me check with them, maybe they—"

Sally couldn't stand it. "I won't work with them. I don't trust them. We either look for different lawyers who will find a solution, or I leave and let them take care of you."

Marin considered the matter and finally said, "Don't bail on me. Let's go back and see what can be done."

At the entrance to the conference room, Roy gave Sally a handwritten note. "Mom, I'm proud of you. You rock. They were shaking here while you were in the other room. Now calm down and be softer with them." The expression of the man at the head of the table was indeed more pleasant. He smiled at Sally. "We've discussed this. It will be hard to operate without conclusive evidence, but I'm sure we can find a solution. Starting tomorrow morning, our entire office will work to review court rulings and interpretations of the law."

Marin looked at her with relief, but Sally wasn't planning to relent. "How many hours will you give this and what is your hourly price?"

The leader fell silent. Sally waited. He leaned toward his colleagues and exchanged a few whispered words. Finally, he sat up and said, "Given the longstanding relationship between us and Monsieur Marin, and given the—how should I put this?—personal and sad aspect of the case, we'll give this service free of charge."

Sally was unimpressed by the gesture. "Free gifts are worth nothing," she said, quoting an old saying her father used to repeat in Aramaic. "I want you to provide a service you imagine was paid for in full. By the middle of next week, I expect to receive a detailed and well-founded divorce request for Muriel Marin."

The chief lawyer looked at Marin quizzically, who said, "Starting now, she manages everything to do with my divorce from Muriel. She will also report to me on the progress made."

"Mom, I'm proud of you," Roy repeated as they left the room, and Sally, for the first time in weeks, felt happy. They waited for Marin in the foyer, and when he arrived he gave Roy a fatherly pat on the back. "I heard that you're a soldier in the IDF," he said. "Allow me to treat you to the many luxuries Geneva has to offer, and to buy your mother a special gift as a token of my appreciation for what she did earlier in the conference room."

"I won't have it," Sally said. "If you want to pamper him, be my guest. He came here straight from operational activity and he deserves it. Don't buy me any gifts."

Like magic, the limousine approached the curb and now Joel and

Rubi looked at them through the window. Roy mumbled, "Where did these children come from and how did the driver know we were done?"

"Get used to it," Sally said. "This is how it works here." She stepped into the car first, then entered Roy and finally Marin, who pointed at Joel and told Roy, "This is the man your grandfather is preparing for his bar mitzvah."

Roy extended his hand to the boy and said in English, "I'm Roy, pleased to meet you."

"He's an officer in the Israeli army," said Marin proudly, "and Sally's son."

The children looked at Roy admiringly and Marin momentarily lowered the partition between him in the driver and said, "To the Armani shop, please."

Following a shopping spree—where Roy objected to almost all of Marin's suggestions, which included expensive watches, perfumes, and high-heeled shoes ("Does he think I'm gay?" he whispered to Sally)—Sally and her son returned to the hotel with bags filled with Armani polo shirts and a pair of Prada jeans. An hour later, they were back in the backseat of the Bentley, heading toward Marin's mansion in Gstaad.

"Have you shot at people?" Joel suddenly asked, and Sally noted with surprise that his English was almost unaccented.

Roy choked with surprise. "Yes," he said finally. "Soldiers shoot at people. That's what they must do. But they only shoot at those who shoot at them."

Joel wouldn't let it rest. "Have you killed anyone?" he asked with sparkly eyes.

"Sometimes. It doesn't feel good."

"When I grow up I'll go to Israel and be a soldier."

"By the time you grow up there will be peace, and no need for an army," Roy said, and Sally could sense that he himself didn't believe that. To her surprise, Marin grew curious. "Do you think so?" he asked.

Roy shrugged. "I hope so."

Marin relentlessly questioned Roy about his life as a soldier and an officer, on operations he took part in—an issue Roy evaded—and on his feelings about fighting for a Jewish army. "I feel privileged to serve in the army," said Roy without a hint of pathos. "It's an honor to ensure the future of the Jewish people."

Marin laughed. "The young people I know don't think about such things. They just want to have fun. Are there many like you in Israel?"

"I don't know. I never checked. I can only say that all my friends feel the same. Otherwise they wouldn't have ended up in my unit. We eat a lot of dust and sweat, and sometimes more."

"How close is your friendship?"

"Close enough to take risks for each other."

The two children hung off his every word. Sally looked at Marin, whose face was sour. "I suppose you think my friends, the lawyers, are disloyal."

"Every society has different notions of loyalty," said Roy with cautious politeness. "To us, in Israel, friendship and family are especially important values. Here, things may be different."

"Don't be afraid to tell me the truth. What do you think of them?"

"I'm a commander," Roy said. "I manage people who are also my friends. Those people aren't your friends. A person should fight for his friends, and your lawyers show no will to fight. You're going through a hard time right now. Everyone's at your throat. Ben David, your wife, the organization behind Ben David. This is the moment you discover who's truly your friend and who isn't."

Marin looked into Sally's eyes. "This is how I want your father to educate Joel, and also Rubi when the day comes. I want them to become human beings, like your son."

When the limousine entered Marin's mansion, Sally could see light in the guesthouse, and her heart filled with yearning for her father and her previous life.

47.

She was tall and incredibly tanned, and when she saw Sally she smiled at her, revealing white teeth.

It took Sally a few seconds to realize she wasn't smiling at her but at Roy, who was walking a few steps behind her and embracing Marin's two sons, who looked on him with the admiration of younger brothers. "This is Sally, a good friend and my personal assistant. And that's her son Roy," Marin said in an official tone. "Melody, why don't you take Roy for a ride in the new Maserati I bought you?"

Melody took the amazed Roy by the hand. "Come," she said, "the car is here, in the garage."

"You don't mind that they drive together?" Sally asked.

"Not at all. I don't do anything with her anyway."

"And yet you bought her a Maserati."

"Yes," he moaned. "That's the price I must pay to keep her, and considering my financial situation, it's really not high. I also demand nothing in return. Before she was a model, Melody wanted to be an actress, and had to indulge the demands of all sorts of men to get parts, until I met her and freed her from that life."

Sally was repulsed. "Why do you need this pretending?"

"It's part of my status, I've already explained that."

"And I've already told you that there's more to you than just money. You need to find a woman who'll love you for who you are, not for buying her a Maserati. This way, you'll end up with a Muriel again."

Marin stared at her for a long while. "I want a woman like you."

She giggled. "We've discussed this. I'm not available, and even if I were, I don't conform to your standards. I'm critical, independent, and I don't have the perfect figure of a model. You'd get tired of me, and then we'd lose the friendship we have today."

He took her hand softly. "I'll never be tried of you, my dear Sally. I promise that if we can't live together, I'll give you—"

"Money again?" She pulled her hand away, as if he hurt her. "Pierre, when will you learn?"

"I beg your pardon," Marin said, just as Natalia appeared at the door. Her hand, which was just starting to signal dinner, froze midair as she heard her boss apologize profusely in a manner she'd never heard before.

48.

In the evening, as Sally sat in her room watching a light French film, the grandfather clock on the downstairs floor struck eight. Where was Roy? She tried to calculate when he'd left. Three o'clock? Four? She dialed him. The phone rang, but Roy didn't answer. She left her room in panic and found Marin in the large living room. "My son hasn't returned."

"Don't worry. They're in my chalet in the mountains, near Montreux."

"He isn't answering me," Sally said, close to tears.

"Reception there is no good, as the chalet is in a ravine between two mountains. Sometimes I climb one of them to make a call." He poured a glass from his now-familiar bottle of cognac. "Come, drink with me. It's sad to drink alone."

Sally sat down on the sofa, but rejected the drink. "You set this up on purpose, didn't you?"

"No, I didn't. I only allowed it to happen." He smiled. "They returned while you were in your room and seemed to have had a very nice time together. I offered her to head over to the chalet to see make sure everything is OK, and gave her a key." He grew serious. "Do you realize how much I wanted to be with you?"

Sally got up. "It won't work, Pierre. You're a charming, intelligent, experienced, and wealthy man, but you're bad news. Any woman who ties her destiny to yours will eventually be hurt. You consider women a resource, and treat them with the same possessiveness with which you treat your other assets, and even your children. It's true that your wife neglects them in favor of some imposter rabbi, but you're not much better than her when it comes to your relationship with the children. You flood them with gifts, but when have you ever had dinner with them? When did *you* prepare dinner, and showed you care about them?"

Marin sank into a long silence. Finally, he said, "Regarding the children, you're right. I don't know how to speak to them, I don't know how to take care of them, and honestly speaking, they're a burden to me. I had children with two women as a way of binding them to me. Then, I lost interest in them and in their children. But with you—" he suddenly came to life "—I don't want children, nor do I need you for my pride or to impress others. I simply want to be with you. You make me believe in my real self, freeing me from all of my accessories: My cars, my houses, my money. You don't believe me, do you? You think I'm just talking."

"No, I feel you're honest, but I'm not sure you'll think the same tomorrow. Besides, I have feelings for Jerry. They're confused, but they're there."

Marin nodded in understanding. "I won't pester you," he said. "We'll stay friends, we'll work together, and I won't say another word. But know that I'll always be waiting and dreaming of the night we had, and hoping…"

Later that evening, Sally called Roy again. Again, there was no an-swer. She was so angry—although she knew her anger was unjustifiable. It was the first time that Roy had had a leave of absence in many weeks, and when she arranged for him to come with her, she had hoped for much more quality time together.

She called Natalia and asked for a bottle of wine, which she gulped down sitting on her bed, shoeless. She suddenly missed Marin, his faint scent of cologne, his touch—both comforting and stirring, which she re-membered from the only night they'd spent together.

And he was so close. Only a path separated her house from his. Sally put on her shoes and walked out to the corridor, and from there to the garden. She tried to stroll along the lawn, but it was damp and wet her shoes. She returned to the path, which beckoned her along, until she ar-rived at the open, inviting door of the mansion. She entered, breathing in the smell of antique furniture and delicate cleaning agents. The wooden stairs creaked under her feet. She reached the second floor, took off her shoes again, and walked barefoot along the corridor. The touch of the car-pet on her feet aroused her. She stood at his bedroom door and hesitated. "Come," Marin's voice sounded from inside, and she entered.

Roy and Melody arrived the following afternoon with the engine of the Maserati roaring. Marin welcomed them both with a tight hug. Sally hugged Roy. "I'm sorry, Mom," he said, a mischievous glimmer in his eye.

"Nothing to apologize for," she said. "Nothing at all. Now gather your things or you'll be late for your flight."

En route to Geneva, in the backseat of the limousine, he suddenly put his head on her shoulder and said, "I thought about our meeting with the lawyers yesterday. Mom, you're doing holy work." She caressed the short hair on the back of his neck, as she did when he was a child. When they parted at the first-class desk at the airport, she held back her tears.

Only when she was alone in the car, behind the partition separating her from the driver, did she allow herself to cry. She cried over the sense of missed opportunity in Roy's short visit, over her family that was crumbling before her eyes, over her need for justice that was ruining her life. On television, a man and woman were rambling on about global warming. She turned up the volume so that the driver wouldn't hear even the distant echo of her crying. On the side of the screen, an ominous thermometer climbed to the temperature of 40 degrees Celsius. "Within a few years, temperatures in Geneva will reach forty degrees during the summer," the woman said. "The ski slopes will melt and a wave of water will flood the valleys."

The man was less frightened. "The summer will be hot and there may be slight melting, but on the peaks, the heat isn't as substantial because the ice continues to cool the air."

The phone rang. Sally breathed in deeply, straining to erase all traces of crying from her voice. Nevertheless, Marin sensed that something was wrong. "Are you all right?"

"A bit under the weather. I'm on my way to your office."

"Could you meet me at Darmond's office? There's something I want to consult with you about."

Sally looked at the back of the driver's neck. "OK. I also have some materials for him. Tell Fred to drive me there."

"You tell him," Marin said. "He has instructions to drive you anywhere you want to go."

Sally picked up the receiver of the internal phone and gave Fred his new destination. The doorman at the office building rushed to open the car door.. She passed by him quickly and entered the elevator. The receptionist stood up to greet her. "Hello, Madame Amir. They're waiting for you in Mr. Darmond's office," she quickly said, walking Sally to a corner room overlooking the both the lake and street below.

Darmond sat behind a decorated desk across from Marin. "Thank you for coming," Marin said. He stood up and escorted her to a sofa next to the table. "As my personal assistant dealing with all my private affairs, I need your advice. We are drafting my will," he said with a smile. "Monsieur Darmond suggests that I open a bank account in Muriel's name and deposit fifty million dollars in it, so that she can care for our children if something happens to me. The rest of my estate will go to a special fund managed by Darmond and you in cooperation. Funds will be distributed to my children from both marriages as need be—"

"What need?" Sally stopped him.

"For example—" he thought for a moment "—Emil, my eldest son who you've never met, manages a small software business that he created with his own two hands." Sally could hear the pride and sorrow in his voice. "You see, his mother has incited him against me. He's never asked for help and I never volunteered mine, of course. Perhaps after I die—" he hesitated "—he will agree to accept a sum that will allow him to develop his business. I trust your wisdom as managers of the estate to know how much to give him and under which conditions."

"And what if we disagree?"

"A Canton of Geneva judge will decide," Darmond said, glaring at Sally.

"What if Muriel dies?" Sally continued her questioning.

"Ten million dollars will go to her parents in Canada and the rest will be managed by you," Marin explained.

Sally contemplated the matter for a long while. Her eyes were fixed on a photograph resting on the back table, of Darmond in the company of a woman and two children. She analyzed the information she had just heard.

"Is anything wrong?" Darmond asked.

"I don't understand why so much money must be given to an unstable woman."

Darmond crossed his arms like a lecturer. "Let's assume Monsieur Marin passes away tomorrow, God forbid. The children are minors and their guardian is Madame Marin, who doesn't own a cent except the stipend she receives from Monsieur Marin—a stipend that ends with his death. We must give her a sum of money that she can use at least during the initial period until the will goes into legal affect, don't we?"

"But why fifty million? Why not one hundred million?"

"Monsieur Marin's businesses and assets are so numerous that realizing the will can take a long time."

"Then one million, or five, but why fifty?"

Darmond's shell of politeness slightly cracked. "Madame, that's the law here. The will cannot be valid unless we submit it to the court soon after it's written. No court will approve it unless we set aside an adequate sum for the use of Madame Marin and her children."

"And Ben David? How do you ensure he doesn't take hold of the money? You need an article forbidding her to give power of attorney to anyone else."

"We can't," Darmond asserted. "As owner of the account she has the right to do whatever she wishes with it."

"We can add an article to the will stating that as soon as a power of attorney is given in the account, Muriel's rights in it are null and void."

"That's not allowed either," Darmond replied. "In Switzerland, you can't limit the owner of an account with a document signed outside the bank. We have no choice. We'll have to trust Muriel's love for Joel and Rubi."

Sally scoffed. "She's already abandoned them twice."

Marin looked at Darmond, seeking advice. Darmond didn't respond and Marin shrugged. "We have no choice. I'm willing to risk the money for the children." He smiled at Sally. "That's what any good father would do, isn't it?" he said, alluding to their conversation the previous evening.

Sally held herself back from telling him how wrong he was, trying again to express his fatherhood using money. But this was neither the time nor the place. "We have another matter to deal with," she said. "A divorce claim—"

"Certainly," Darmond said. "Here's the document you requested." He placed a number of documents stapled together in front of her. She read them quickly, and realized this was exactly what she was hoping for: A detailed plan, including a number of legal steps to free Pierre Marin from his marriage to Muriel. "What are the chances?" she asked Darmond.

"Good," he answered her coldly.

She searched her handbag and produced an envelope. "Here's something to make them very good," she said, placing it on the table. Marin looked at her quizzically, and she responded with an encouraging nod. Darmond ripped the top of the envelope and pulled out a bunch of papers. He spread them out on the table and read the top document. His expression went from one of curiosity to surprise, and then to anxiety. "How did you get this?"

"You have nothing to worry about. I didn't steal them. The original letters remain where they were, in a box in Muriel's home in Gstaad. I presume she'll have no trouble identifying the photocopies, and Ben David will also have to admit he sent the original letters. I have a legal opinion stating that as long as the original wasn't stolen and no one knows who made the photocopies, they're legal."

"But we'll still need to explain how we obtained these photocopies," Darmond insisted.

"I found them on the sidewalk next to Madame Marin's house," Sally said, using the explanation she contrived together with Jacob. "It happened on the day I arrived there with a warrant to remove Ben David. He escaped hastily and I assume he lost the envelope."

Marin nodded with appreciation. Darmond hissed, "You've thought of everything..."

"*They* thought of everything. You'll find there a detailed plan they came up with to extract sums of money from Monsieur Marin and fund their life together in Canada, in the town Muriel was born in and where she lived before becoming a model. They planned to buy a farm and raise horses."

Darmond turned the page. "There are explicit sexual descriptions here. Did Monsieur Marin see all this?"

Sally looked at Marin who shrugged nonchalantly. "He's not interested in knowing a thing about Muriel and Ben David. He simply wants the divorce and trusts me to deal with it."

Darmond nodded. "This does help us a lot," he admitted, "and yet

Ben David can deny the letters. Since it's a photocopy, we can't use a graphological examination proving he is the author."

Sally sighed. "A person I consult with often taught me a legal expression, 'a waterfall of evidence.' When lots of evidence comes together to support one claim, the claimant has a good chance of winning, even if some of the evidence is inconclusive. There are the letters you just received, affidavits of witnesses concerning the close relations between Ben David and Muriel, Muriel's abandoning her home and moving to Israel to be with Ben David, and the photos and recordings we took in Beersheba that cannot be challenged here. What more do we need?"

"You're right. There's lots of evidence, but the final decision is the court's, and we can never know what it will rule."

"I believe justice will prevail," Sally said confidently.

Darmond stared at her. "I thought you were more sophisticated. Those who are right don't necessarily win the case."

"I am sophisticated but also believe in God, and that he despises injustice. That's what I learned from my father. He is a very sophisticated man, but when it comes to believing in God he's as innocent as a child. He believes in him and places his destiny in his hands."

Darmond smiled bitterly. "I've spent many years in court. I've seen very little justice there, and in this trial Monsieur Marin is engaged in there's no certainty that—"

"We shall win this trial," Sally cut him off, "and also the next trial I'm planning." She stood up and extended her hand to Darmond. "I ask that you prepare another lawsuit, this time against Ben David, demanding that he return the funds he extorted from Mr. Marin while impersonating a rabbi. In this matter too, I expect to see an indictment within two days."

The room fell silent. A few seconds later, that lasted an eternity to Sally, Marin said, "She's right. I'll have no peace and quiet until I settle our score, and since there's no other way, I'll make do with money."

Sally glanced at her watch. The time of Jacob's daily update approached. "You'll have to excuse me, I have other matters to tend to," she said and stood up. The two men also stood up and shook her hand. "We'll speak later," she said to Marin and left the room.

At the lobby, the doorman rushed to open the door for her. "One moment, Madame," he said politely, "I'll call your driver. You can sit here for a moment." He pointed to the couches she had sat on with Roy. "It's very hot outside."

Sally froze. She suddenly thought of an idea.

49.

The air-conditioning salesman spoke very basic French with a strange accent. "Are you Israeli?" Muriel asked.

"Lebanese," said Jacob, "from Zahlé. They make the best *arak* in the world there. Zahlawi *arak*."

"Nice," said Muriel absentmindedly, focused on the advertisement flier lying before her. Her gaze wandered across the various photos of air conditioners. "How long have you been working for Monsieur Marin?"

"I don't work for Monsieur Marin but for Cosmos Holdings, which belongs to him. It's the first time they hired me." He sent a hopeful look toward her. "I promise to do a good job."

She scratched her forehead nervously. Jacob noticed that she bit her nails. "And how long will it take you to install the air conditioners?"

"Usually two days. Air conditioners in three rooms—including motors, drainage, and connection to electricity—that's a big job. If it's important for you to get it done sooner, we can bring more workers and have it done in a day."

"All right, but the workers—I mean, are they OK? The man who lives there isn't so well. They must be quiet and trustworthy."

"There? I thought I was supposed to install the air conditioners here, where you live? They told me that Monsieur. Marin's children live with you and he doesn't want them to suffer from the heat."

Muriel placed a wad of one-hundred-euro notes on the table. "It's all right. Install it here, as you were instructed. I want a similar system somewhere else. I'll tell you where."

"All right Madame, I want you to be satisfied."

"If you do the second job, I'll be very satisfied."

"I'll do everything," said the salesman obediently. "What's the second address?"

"Come here and I'll lead you. You'll follow me."

"Yes, Madame," the man said again, collected his papers, and left.

A few streets away he stopped and dialed on his phone. "It's happening," he said, "and it was easier than I thought. I didn't have to convince her. She herself asked me to install the same air conditioners over there. Actually, how did you know?"

"I know something about women in love," Sally said, trying to distract herself from Marin.

50.

The first images appeared in Jacob's computer right after his men, who came along with the air conditioner technicians, switched on the cameras. A tiny hole in the front of every air conditioner was meant to pick up the activity in the room, and Sally, scarred from the surveillance equipment she discovered in Marin's guesthouse, was scared of being exposed. "If they discover the cameras, we're finished. Marin doesn't know a thing about this and he'll never forgive us."

"Don't worry," Jacob promised. "The lenses and microphones are so tiny that even if one feels the air-conditioning unit, he won't find them."

Sally looked at the computer screen. Ben David examined the new air conditioner in one of the rooms. Muriel appeared next to him, holding a bottle of alcohol. "Southern Comfort," Jacob said. "She has good taste."

"Burn me a CD every day," ordered Sally, "and then immediately delete all the footage on the computer."

"All right." Jacob was fixated on the screen. "I love the first moments of hidden camera footage. Here, Muriel is all over Ben David." He turned

266 | Married to the Mossad

the volume up. "Are you happy with my little gift?" Muriel asked. Her voice was as clear as though she was with them in the same room.

"We're very grateful. Very."

Jacob enlarged the image. "Now we'll see how grateful he is." The door shut, and Muriel was seen crossing the room and heading toward the bedroom. "Shall we move over there?" Jacob asked.

"Thanks, but that time was enough," Sally said, remembering the image of Ben David lying on Muriel's perfect body.

"One moment," Jacob said. "Something strange is happening. Why does she need that big bowl?"

Muriel exited the bathroom carrying a large bowl and two towels folded on her arm. Jacob hit a key and the image switched to the interior of the bedroom. Ben David was sitting barefoot on the bed, his trousers folded up. Muriel knelt beneath him, spread a powder into the water, and then gently placed Ben David's feet in the bowl. "What are they doing?" Sally wondered out loud.

"Sex," Jacob answered.

"If that's the sex you know…" Sally began and immediately fell silent as Muriel dipped her hands in the water and started rubbing Ben David's left foot. "That's good," his voice echoed through the speaker, "that's so good…"

"Look how he thanks her, the pig," Jacob commented.

Muriel placed a towel on her thighs, pulled Ben David's foot out of the water, and put it on the towel. She wrapped the foot and dried it, and then repeated the process with the other foot. Sally and Jacob found themselves hypnotized by the images they were seeing. "There's so much love in the way she's treating him," Sally said.

"I'll ask again: What is it about him that does it for her?" Jacob said. "Look how ugly he is. Skin and bones. I've been trying to keep fit since I was fifteen, and no woman ever pampered me like that."

Sally smiled. "Do you know what the most important muscle a man has for a woman?"

Jacob looked at her surprised. "I didn't expect to hear you talk like that."

"It's not what you think. It's the brain. Men win women over through their brains. Something about him plays on her emotions, on her spiritual side."

"His spirituality is a sham," Jacob said scornfully. "And he has a criminal mind."

Sally realized that as soon as the following day, when she arrived at Jacob's hotel room to receive the daily CD. The envelope also contained a few printed pages. "After you left, they had a conversation you'd find interesting," he said. "We've transcribed it, and I suggest we read it together and think of what we can do." He spread the pages out on the table and pointed to one of them. "Look here," he said, and Sally started reading.

Ben David: "…his papers. It's very important. Where did he put them?"

Mrs. Marin: "In the Geneva office. He has a steel vault."

Ben David: "With a code?"

Mrs. Marin: "No, only a key. But it's made of reinforced steel."

Ben David: "What's 'reinforced'?"

Mrs. Marin: "Strong."

Ben David: "Oh, I see. And where does he put the key at night?"

Mrs. Marin: "He has many keys. He can't put them all in his pocket, so he puts them in the briefcase."

Ben David: "And where's the briefcase?"

Mrs. Marin: "In his study."

Ben David: "Here's what you'll do. Go to his apartment. Say you left things you like over there."

Mrs. Marin: "I didn't leave anything important."

Ben David: "He doesn't know that, does he?"

Mrs. Marin: "No, he doesn't. But..." [silence]

Ben David: "So where's the problem?"

Mrs. Marin: "He won't believe me."

Ben David: "He will. If you say it nicely enough, he will. You'll come to take your things while he's home, and go to his room. Do you recognize the office key?"

Mrs. Marin: "Yes."

Ben David: "And the key to his room in the office?"

Mrs. Marin: "That too."

Ben David: "And the key to the vault?"

Mrs. Marin: "Yes. It's different than the other keys."

Ben David: "We'll give you six boxes with soft material. Plasticine. You take the key and press both sides of it into the material. First the one, then the other. That way we have the shape to make a copy. After you do it for all three keys, bring us the boxes."

Mrs. Marin: "Why get into trouble?"

Ben David: "Because we need money and your husband won't give you what you deserve, which is half of what he has, so we'll have to take it from him. I'm sure we'll find things in his office that will make him pay a lot to keep the police away. You can't be rich without committing felonies.

Therefore, rich people have secrets, lots of secrets about things they did."

Mrs. Marin: "That's theft and extortion. I'm scared."

Ben David: "You're not stealing or blackmailing, just taking your half, which he won't give you. You'll copy the keys, then we'll enter his office. I have a friend, a business expert; he'll choose the material we'll take. Then, my beauty, you and I will build ourselves a new life."

Sally lifted her eyes from the page. "Are you thinking what I'm thinking?"

"Something else illegal to get me in trouble?"

"No, something completely legal. Something even the police could be involved in."

51.

Sally scanned the passengers exiting the Geneva airport arrivals terminal, searching for Diana's black bob cut. When she picked up her phone to call her, a voice sounded right next to her. "You didn't recognize me, did you?"

Sally turned her head with alarm. Diana's hair was long and blond, out of sync with her brown eyes and olive skin.

"You don't like it?" Diana asked.

"I need to get used to it."

"Yeah, that's what people say when they don't like something. So, where to now?"

"As usual, Hotel d'Angleterre. But first I want to find a café or small snack bar where I can give you all the details without fear of surveillance."

"You've become paranoid." Diana laughed.

Sally walked to a small bistro at the edge of the building. Most of the clients sat next to its large windows, soaking up the sun. Sally chose a distant table, inside the large empty space. Diana sat down and dug through her handbag. "My phone," she said, alarmed. "Could I have left it on the plane?"

Sally was apprehensive. Something about Diana's behavior wasn't right. "Is everything OK?" she asked.

"Yes, of course. Here, it was at the bottom of my bag." She placed the phone on the table. "So what's going on?"

"First tell me what Paris was like," Sally inquired.

"You know, work. Information security, the constant fear that our computers are being hacked. As soon as you called asking me to come, I took time off."

"And your family?"

A cloud came over Diana's face. "I don't think I have one. The children are grown, you know. Both are in the army, one signed on, and my husband wasn't very interested in me even back home. How about you?"

"Complicated," Sally admitted. "Very complicated."

"You and Jerry were always the perfect couple to me. What happened?"

Sally fell silent.

"Marin?"

Sally said nothing.

"Is something going on between you? Don't deny it. He's super-hot and you're a pretty woman."

Sally used the first excuse that came to mind. "He loves young women and I'm too old for him."

"Nonsense. Look at yourself—you're ageless."

"Stop." Sally laughed. "That's not why we're here." She began telling Diana about Ben David's plan to break into Marin's office and steal or photocopy materials to be used for extortion.

"How do you know about this plan?"

"We know." Sally tightened her lips and moved her fingers over them, imitating the closing of a zipper.

"I get it. So where do I fit in?"

"We're going to let her copy the keys, and as soon as we find out when he plans to enter the office, we'll wait there with the police."

"Hmmm…" Diana said. "And why do you need me?"

"I need you because Jacob only employs men and a few former female police special agents. There's a good chance she doesn't like me after I arrived at her home with a warrant banishing Ben David. You, on the other hand, dealt with all the matters of the Gstaad house and never confronted her. On the contrary, you hired a cook, you supervised the nanny. You effectively managed her life. Your relationship with her was pretty decent, wasn't it?"

"Decent, no more than that."

"That's good enough. In addition, you know what to expect and how she'll respond. I assume she'll start screaming and going wild like the last time we removed Ben David from the house. If we try to calm her and the surveillance cameras in the office pick up something that even comes close to assault, the entire operation is doomed."

"Why do you fear she'll go wild?"

"We're about to call the police and Muriel won't sit idly by while the man she admires goes to jail."

Diana sighed. "I wish I had such an admirer. I thought something would happen to me in Paris, but Paris isn't what it used to be. It's filled with Arabs and Africans. So tell me, what exactly is happening between you and Marin?"

"I didn't say anything was happening. You decided that," Sally answered warily. The sense of unease she picked up from Diana was only growing stronger. She wasn't the same easygoing friend who waited for her in the back alley in Beersheba while she penetrated the police station yard, nor the woman who managed the surveillance on Ben David when they just started out. Her naughtiness had vanished, replaced with a restrained, even forced behavior. She looked into the eyes of her friend. "Something about you has changed."

Diana smoothed over her hair. "I've gone blond."

"You're different. It's hard for me to put my finger on it. Did something happen?"

"Life happened." Diana smiled grimly. "I need to worry about money, always money. That's why your offer came at a good time."

Sally put her arm around Diana's shoulder. "You know you can always come to me."

"Thanks," said Diana in a muted voice. "You're a good friend."

Sitting in the back seat of the limousine on her way to Marin's home in Gstaad, Sally felt pity for Diana and her financial and romantic troubles. She was also sorry for herself over her estrangement from Jerry. She didn't want to admit to herself the tightening relationship with Marin. Every night they spent together was "only one night," and every time Marin tried to talk about the future of their relations, suggesting they formalize them, Sally stopped the conversation.

Marin graciously stopped pressuring. "I'll settle for the present," he said. "Let's live in the moment." Those moments and nights were magical and filled with gentleness and intimacy. In the morning, she would return to her room at the guesthouse. Natalia and the rest of the staff made sure not to meet her, but surely picked up what was going on. She knew there was something pathetic and dangerous in the way their relationship played out in plain eyesight, but every night, again, her legs would carry her to his bedroom.

Evening fell. The limousine entered the courtyard, capturing with its headlights a sturdy man seated upright on a bench next to the guesthouse. Next to him sat Joel and Rubi. Sally asked the driver to stop and sat down next to her father. "You'll catch a cold, Dad," she said.

"The nights in this season are no different than the nights in the land of Israel during my youth," the father said. "It's nice to reminisce. Where are you headed, my daughter?"

"What do you mean? I'm here."

He knew she understood his intention and continued. "I think you're headed for a cul-de-sac. At the end, you'll lose both your worlds: The one you had, and the one you never will."

As usual, he perfectly articulated her deepest fears. Sally breathed in deeply. "I don't know, Dad. All sides involved are content living in the moment, not defining the situation, not deciding."

"You and Jerry are free to decide or not decide. But this situation affects your children. They suffer from it."

"Roy understands me, and Michael will understand when he grows up, and as I said—nothing is set in stone."

"Doors close suddenly, and it's not always you who closes them. Sometimes they can close on your hand. You have to decide rather than let reality carry you away. Both of you."

"There's a big operation happening soon, that will probably end the whole Ben David project. It takes up my entire being. When this ends, I'll be free to decide." She put her head on her father's shoulder, and he said, "Tell me."

She told him of the trap she plans to set for Ben David. When she finished, he was silent. "You seem displeased, Dad. Am I doing something wrong?"

"It's written in Psalms chapter 7: 'He made a pit, and dug it, and is fallen into the ditch which he made.' Do you understand the verse?"

"I do, but what does it have to do with me?"

"Like anyone who digs a pit to entrap another, you too only see your little plan. But there's a larger plan set elsewhere, where it may be that the digger of the pit will fall into it."

Sally grew apprehensive. "What's the larger plan that I can't see?"

"For example, what if they realize you're listening to them and arrive a day early?"

"They won't know that. Besides, it won't help them. The files are in Pierre's study." She pointed at the house.

Her father fell deep into thought. "I'll tell you what the bigger plan is." He immediately stood up. "Come on in. I want you to write down a few things."

Later that evening Sally returned to the main house. The door to Marin's room was open a crack. She pushed it and entered. Marin was seated on a couch, next to the window. He held his habitual glass of cognac and a small box wrapped in a ribbon lying on the table in front of him. He looked at her and gestured at the box. "For you."

Sally folded her arms behind her back. "I told you, no gifts."

"You can't be so extreme, on the one hand contributing so much to my life—arranging a plan to entrap Ben David, preventing Muriel from sucking my blood, forging ties with institutions in Israel for me to donate to, and all this for a modest salary—and on the other hand, not accept even a modest gift."

"Your gifts are never modest, Pierre, that's the problem."

"My gifts reflect my gratitude."

Sally undid the ribbon and opened the box. A diamond the size of a pea shone at her from within a delicate ring of white gold.

"I haven't exaggerated, have I? There were larger ones where it came from."

Sally shut the box with a click. "Thanks," she mumbled, "but I can't wear this."

"Jerry?"

Sally nodded. "Maybe one day."

52.

The following day, a spring rain fell on western Switzerland, melting the snow on the sidewalks and roads and turning it to black slush. Jacob sounded perturbed on the phone. "I have three things to tell you. First, something weird is happening. Ben David spoke to Attorney Ovadia and asked for an expert to be sent over."

"What kind of expert?"

"He didn't specify, just said, 'You know.' Ovadia didn't understand at first, but Ben David wouldn't explain, only said something I couldn't understand." He went silent for a moment and Sally heard the sound of pages turning before Jacob added, "'They have eyes but cannot see, ears…'"

Sally smiled. "And then Ovadia got it?"

"I think so. He said, 'I'll take care of it.'"

Sally's smile turned into laughter. "Well, it's a corruption of the verse 'they have eyes but cannot see, ears but cannot hear.' In our family, we also use this joke to refer to someone who can't see what's before him."

"So what is it that Ovadia didn't understand at first, and I can't understand now?"

"I think Ben David needs an expert to check whether any cameras were installed in his apartment."

"How do you know?" Jacob asked with an air of surprise, almost insult.

Sally thought for a moment. "I don't know. A feeling."

"So why now? Any ideas?"

"Yes," Sally said. "I have my suspicions. Anyway, what can you do about that?"

"Our cameras are tiny and well-hidden. I don't think they can physically be found. I'll stop the broadcast and then they'll be undetectable with a frequency scanner."

"All right, you do that. What else?"

"I also think we have a date for their operation. Sunday, two days from now. Speaking to Ovadia, Ben David asked the expert to arrive tomorrow at the latest, because something is happening on Sunday and he wants the coast to be clear."

"Okay, we have some changes. My dad's idea. I'll update you. What's the third thing?"

"Ben David and Muriel are speaking about opening a bank account in her name. Fifty million dollars will be deposited there and only she will be able to withdraw money from it. Ben David is insisting that she give him power of attorney and she explains that she can't."

Sally tried to calculate the time that passed since her meeting with Marin and Darmond. One day. There was no way the will and accompanying documents were drafted so quickly, and that the issue of the bank account was officially conveyed to Muriel. Who leaked it then? Darmond?

Someone in his office?"

"Sally?" Jacob said.

"Sorry, I was daydreaming. Are you in Geneva?"

"Yes."

"Take care of the camera business. I'm coming over to you and we'll finalize the operation issue. As for the account, I need to examine it."

Sally spent the next few hours in the space that had almost become her home—the backseat of the limousine. By the time she arrived in Geneva, she had written the details of the operation as a flowchart on a yellow notepad. When she was done, she looked at the chart. It didn't seem right. She ripped the pages out and started everything again. This time, the operation was divided in two. She read everything again and smiled contentedly.

At the café on Lake Geneva, she presented the plan to Jacob and explained every stage of it. He listed with concentration, and when she was done, he said, "Very sophisticated. I'm trying to think of something you haven't covered."

"There's no such thing, Sally said confidently. Her finger quickly passed over the flowchart. "If A happens, we have a response. If B happens—" she pointed at another part of the chart "—we have another response, and if neither of these happen, we haven't lost anything, and we'll wait to pick up the next date of their operation on your systems."

"That reminds me. Ben David's guy has arrived. One of my men knows him. He's an expert in eavesdropping and sells surveillance equipment in Tel Aviv. Your guess was inaccurate," he said, a glimmer of triumph in his eye. "He isn't trying to check whether we installed surveillance equipment, but is installing his own. Based on the noises we're picking up on our distance microphone, he isn't trying too hard to hide it, but is drilling in the walls and pulling wires through the holes. What I don't get is why he needs cameras in his home."

"He doesn't need cameras nor is he installing them. He's using them as a blocking means, to render our equipment useless."

Jacob nodded with appreciation. "You have a point. When you get tired of working on Marin's issues, you have a job with me."

Three hours later, a system was installed in Ben David's apartment, creating a powerful masking shield. Jacob reactivated the cameras and typed a few commands into his computer. A tight wave of lines appeared on the screens. "That's their masking. It won't allow radio signals to enter or exit Ben David's apartment."

"How will you overcome it?"

"Masking works on a certain frequency range," Jacob explained. "It's the range usually used by surveillance equipment. But there are other frequencies, more remote ones. Over the course of the evening we'll use our frequency scanners and cause every camera to capture a frequency that isn't interrupted."

"I trust you," Sally said, distracted. Her mind was already preparing for the operation.

In the evening, at the plush lounge of Hotel d'Angleterre, Diana was waiting. Sally noticed her from a distance, sitting at a table and speaking on the phone. When she came close, Diana abruptly ended the conversation. "You haven't ordered your regular coffee?" Sally inquired when she sat down.

Diana seemed more flummoxed than ever. "No, I haven't had the chance. I needed to finish a phone call first."

Sally examined her face. "You don't involve me in your issues, which is fine. It's your right. But I think I could help you."

Diana waved her hand in dismissal. "No one can help me. I'm in over my head." She wiped a tear from the corner of her eye. "I want us not to talk about this ever, okay? Promise me that when these times end, we'll forget all about them. Both of us."

"That bad?"

"Yes. After we finish our job, I'm out of here. I may go to South America, maybe somewhere else. I need to get out of this life, do you understand?"

"No," Sally confessed. "Explain it to me."

"Let it go," Diana blurted out, suddenly angry. "Just leave it. OK? Now tell me what I'm supposed to do."

"OK," Sally said in a tone of acquiescence. "The day after tomorrow, on Saturday, we'll wait at Marin's office at seven a.m. I don't suppose they'll arrive earlier, because the building is shut. We'll hide and let them approach the metal vault, break in, and extract the files. Then we'll come out, take them over, and call the police. The surveillance cameras will be used as proof of the crime, and Ben David will finally go to jail, where he belongs."

Diana nodded mechanically, and Sally wondered whether she grasped what was just said. "So when are you picking me up?" Diana asked.

"A day after tomorrow, at the entrance to the hotel."

Diana stood up. "Forgive me," she said in a voice on the verge of tears. "I need to go now."

For a moment, Sally considered asking one of Jacob's men to follow Diana and see where she was headed, but then felt it would be unfair to expose the man to her heartbreak. She waved to the waiter and ordered a cup of coffee. After finishing it, she called Fred the driver and walked to the front of the hotel. En route to Gstaad, she noticed that, unlike Jacques, he never exchanged a word with her. *Better that way,* she said to herself and started reviewing the plains she had made, the overt and covert ones. Somewhere along the way, she had an epiphany. She realized clearly where the rotten apple was in her small organization. Everything seemed to come together and make sense, and the more she thought about it, the more she realized how much she had been misled. When she arrived at Marin's mansion, she went right to her room and spent the night thinking and noting her conclusions on the yellow notepad. When she was finished, she called Jacob.

"Do you know what time it is?"

"I do. Now listen. There are a few testimonies we need to collect immediately tomorrow morning, without delay."

53.

It was four a.m. when she accompanied Marin to his car. He was drowsy. "What a terrible time," he muttered, "I can't function at such an hour."

"You'll sleep on the plane," she said.

"On a flight to Brussels? You take off, have a drink, and land."

She didn't allow herself to kiss him in front of the driver, just shook his hand. "Good luck to all of us," she said, and he lifted his thumb in response.

The car drove away. Sally passed through the rooms in the house to make sure no one was left. All the employees were sent on a day of leisure organized by their employer. She cautiously collected her handbag with the yellow notepad from her room, went down to the garage, and got into the Land Rover, the simplest car in Marin's fleet. The roads were empty and she drove quickly. At 6:50 a.m., she parked her car at the parking lot of Hotel d'Angleterre and approached the front of the building. Diana was already there, holding a paper cup of coffee. Jacob arrived at seven

284 | Married to the Mossad

sharp, driving a van with two other men she didn't know who had Slavic features. As soon as they sat down, Jacob stretched out his hand. "Your mobile phones."

Sally gave him her phone. "I've switched mine off," Diana said.

Jacob looked at the device on the top of his dashboard. "That's a frequency scanner," he explained, "and your phone is still giving off a signal."

Diana reluctantly handed him a small, silver mobile. "Keep it safe," she said. "It's a gift from a dear man and I only use it to communicate with him."

Jacob nodded his thanks. "These phones are dangerous to us. They're connected to the Internet and can be used for eavesdropping. I promise not to answer any incoming call."

A metal shutter covered the entrance to the parking lot in the building where the offices of Cosmos Holdings were located. Jacob used a magnetic card and the shutter moved up. "How will Ben David's people enter the building?" Sally wondered. "At the street entrance there's a doorman, and here, a shutter."

"I assume they were able to steal and duplicate a card, or pay off some secretary," Jacob replied.

The parking spaces were empty with the exception of one car, perhaps the doorman's. They took the elevator directly up to the desolate offices. The air conditioners were off, and there was a stuffy smell in the air. Jacob stopped at the foyer and began explaining. "We want to let them in and catch them red-handed. That's why Sally will enter this room—" he pointed to the room next to the reception desk "—and you'll enter this room." He gestured at one of the silent men toward a room next to the entrance. "As soon as they enter, secure the office door so they can't leave.

Diana, go in with him so you can act immediately if Muriel goes wild."
He nodded at Diana, then pointed at the second silent man. "Meanwhile,
me and you will wait in the room with the metal vault. I will confront the
burglars and call the police."

Sally went in to the room allocated to her. The only window in it
would not open, and an insufferable scent of cheap perfume stood in the
air. It was embedded in the walls and furniture, and Sally searched the
desk for indications of who inhabited the office during the week. Based
on the objects lying on it, it was a secretary's desk: A drawer for incoming mail, a drawer for outgoing mail, a computer screen and keyboard, a
mouse, and desk calendar. She moved the keyboard aside and opened her
yellow notepad. The more time passed and Ben David didn't arrive, the
more the assumptions she'd written down over night became a certainty.
She read them again and again and felt both proud for cracking the mystery and great sadness.

At 11:10 a.m., Jacob's voice sounded. "Everyone to the foyer, please."

Sally left the room, breathing a sigh of relief. The others also arrived
one after the other. "You're free to go," Jacob told the two silent men as he
escorted them to the door, locking up after them and pocketing the key.
"We'll move to the conference room," he told Sally and Diana.

They followed him there. "Is the operation off?" Diana asked.

"One second," said Jacob, turning the handle of the window, which
opened immediately. A fresh breeze blew in. Jacob sat at the head of the table and waited for the women to sit down as well. "Ben David and his men
haven't arrived," he said, "which on the one hand is bad because we waited
for them, and on the other is good because that was actually the plan."

"What do you mean?" Diana asked.

Sally was silent as she examined her face.

"We didn't think they'd come here," Jacob said. "We waited for them somewhere else, where they did indeed arrive." He looked at Diana. "Maybe I'll let Sally explain. It was her idea."

Sally hesitated. She knew the next moments would be difficult. For a moment, she wanted to ask Jacob to speak, but immediately decided to go forward. She cleared her throat. "The idea belonged to someone smarter than me," she said. "The original plan was to wait here for Ben David, as we did. But when I told my father about it, he asked who knew about the plan. I mentioned the people and when I reached five he stopped me and said, 'That's too many. Once two people know, it's no secret. Five people are already the whole world.' Using his advice, I devised another plan in case this one was discovered. So while we waited here, a more serious contingent waited in Marin's mansion, while he advertised his trip to Brussels."

Diana swallowed hard.

Jacob pointed to his phone. "I've been told that Ben David arrived there with Muriel and a number of other men from the organization that operates with him. Muriel was immediately removed from the scene so as not to get Marin and the family in trouble. Ben David and the others were placed under citizen's arrest until the police arrived. They are all under arrest now and will soon be investigated."

Silence fell in the room. Jacob and Sally were silent, looking worriedly at Diana who asked, "What?"

"For a while now we've been suspecting that someone working with us, someone we trusted and even befriended was double-crossing us," Sally said. "Clearly someone told Ben David that the files he was looking for weren't here but in the house, where he did indeed arrive—"

"All right." Diana stood up. "My job here is done now, isn't it?"

"Right," Sally said, "but we need to discuss the matter I just mentioned."

"I'm not in the mood to discuss anything right now. I want to go."

"You can go," Jacob said, "no one's stopping you. But I suggest you consider your situation. You have two alternatives: Either give us a detailed testimony incriminating Ben David, or I'll file a complaint against you with the Geneva police."

"Against me? You have nothing against me."

"We have lots," Sally said. "As soon as we realized that someone inside us was acting against us, we began investigating." She pulled out her yellow notepad and started reading. "We've deciphered the photo of the woman handling the disguised mailman who brought a letter from Muriel to Ben David every day. We received an eighty-two percent likeness to you. Then we interviewed the chef who you'd fired. Unlike what you told us, the children never complained about the food. She was simply dismissed without warning and replaced with a chef who reported to you about everything happening in the house. During the last hour, one of our lawyers took statements from both the women and had them sign depositions."

"She was sacked because she was no good. The children would spit out the meals she cooked."

"That's not what they say," Sally continued. "And then there's the nanny whose position you cut because she wouldn't inform you on what the children were saying about their mother and Ben David. She testified too. I assume you didn't fire her because you were scared you wouldn't find anyone to take care of those children, who are slightly problematic."

"Sally, these are all speculations. You will erase our friendship over this?"

"And when Ben David wanted to reach Muriel before the scheduled time, you sent the Swiss investigators to hospital and told me they'd disappeared that morning, before I arrived."

"This morning we examined their medical records." Jacob looked at his phone and read out, "Weakness and diarrhea. Light treatment was given, and the patients were sent home."

"Still speculations." Diana remained adamant. "So I was wrong, I thought they froze, and then I was wrong again for thinking they fled the hospital. That doesn't make me Ben David's accomplice."

Jacob scrolled through his phone. "We've received the original car rental form for the Peugeot that allowed Muriel to flee my detectives and disappear for over a day. Your fingerprints are all over it, front and back. If the Geneva police examine the passport shown when the car was rented, I'm almost certain they'll find it was stolen. I'm also sure that sums of money were transferred to your bank account from sources other than Sally, which you'll have to explain to the police. You'll also have to explain a few things to the Paris police, such as your connection to Vivian Moyal, who will be arrested in the coming hours on suspicion of theft, fraud, and money collecting from Pierre Marin under false pretexts." Jacob said those last words with the official air of a prosecutor, and the first crack appeared in Diana's mask. Jacob immediately widened it. "As we speak, my men are examining security footage in the locations where you two would meet, and as soon as we have enough evidence, we'll hand it over to the police, as required."

Diana was silent.

"What hurts me," Sally said, "was that I thought you really were suffering from unrequited love or a financial crisis, and truly wanted to help."

"I really am suffering a financial crisis," Diana said harshly. "I owe lots of money. It's hard to live alone and maintain a lifestyle; it's also hard to get old without plastic surgery and cosmetics that cost a fortune. While I was still working with you, Vivian Moyal turned to me and offered me work with a real estate company in Paris. I knew, of course, about her ties to Ben David, so I told her I was busy. But she never stopped calling and speaking of the wonderful work one could do online from home, and the fantastic pay."

A tear appeared on the corner of her eye. "I needed money, so I agreed. At first I did survey asset prices in Paris by going over real estate ads. You were in Israel, and I was only here to loosely supervise things, so I had time. Two weeks later, I received a check, and right after depositing it, Vivian turned to me again and started asking me about you. She told me how nastily you've been persecuting Ben David and how much Marin was paying you. She asked me how much you were paying me. I didn't want to say, but she claimed that whatever it was, it was a pittance compared to the sums you were raking in. Real estate work was finished, she said, but I could help her another way and make lots of money. I immediately realized what it was, and said, 'No, I won't betray Sally.'"

Sally snickered.

"And what then?" Jacob asked. "You still betrayed us, your friends."

"Twenty thousand dollars a week," Diana said, beginning to cry. "Who can withstand such money? I calculated the amount I would have five weeks later, ten weeks, twenty. For the first time in my life, I'd be rich and free!"

Sally suddenly recalled the phone call between Ben David and Vivian Moyal staying at the Four Seasons that Jacob recorded. A man's voice could be heard there, and the hotel records had Darmond staying there as a guest. She decided to take a chance. "Darmond," she said. "Tell us about his part."

Diana's body language exposed her. Her shoulders slouched and she shrank in her seat. "What does he have to do with this?"

Sally wouldn't let go. "Well, it's both money and a man."

Diana didn't reply.

"He won't defend you," Sally added, pushing onward. "He'll protect himself and claim he has nothing to do with this, and you'll find yourself alone to face the allegations. He'll even claim that nothing happened between you."

"He can't. Too many people saw us together in Paris," Diana shot back.

Sally chuckled. "You have no idea what men can come up with when they're under pressure. He has a family, a wife and two children. I've seen their photos in his office. He won't leave them for you."

"He doesn't live with them. They live in a mansion in Provence and he lives in Geneva."

Sally clicked her tongue. "All married men say they don't really live with their families, that their wives don't understand them, and that they plan to leave them. I thought you were smarter than that."

This time, Sally's words struck right at Diana's heart. "I would never come on to a married man," she defended herself, "but he's so special and sexy. One evening, after a meeting we had with you on Skype, he offered to bring me to his hotel."

Sally wrote the word "Darmond" on her notepad, wondering whether Marin would also respond to this act of treason with an outburst of emotion, as he did with Muriel's.

"Can we count on you to testify?" Jacob's voice bellowed.

"No." Diana was unequivocal in her response. "No. I want to get out of here now and stay away from all of this. I don't care about Ben David or about Marin. I know an island in the Pacific, off the coast of Chile. Its beaches are pristine and its men young and beautiful. The money Vivian paid me will suffice for a good life there. So, if you'll excuse me, our conversation ends here."

Jacob chuckled. "Did you ever consider you were an accomplice to a crime? Breaking and entering, attempted extortion, conspiracy to commit a crime, and a few others?"

"I'm not an accomplice to anything. Vivian wouldn't tell on me because she'd be incriminating herself. Darmond too will say you're crazy. So there's no problem, is there?"

"You'd have a problem with this." Jacob pointed upward.

"God? Do me a favor. Have you caught Sally's bug?"

"Microphones," said Jacob peacefully. "Cameras. It's all being taped and filmed, and sent to my computers in real time."

"You can't do that."

"We've received permission from Marin, the owner of this office, to document Ben David's capture."

Diana stood up. "I don't care. I'm leaving. I'll be somewhere else in a few hours."

"The world is very small today," Jacob said. "Prepare for your photo to appear in every airport in Europe within the hour. The money you earned will be spent on lawyers, and if you plan to flee to a third world country, on bribes as well."

Diana sat back down. "So what do you want?" she asked tiredly.

"This situation is as follows," Jacob said. "Ben David and a few others will have now been arrested by the Gstaad police, and will be transferred to Geneva. I don't know how they'll explain breaking into Marin's home, but we need your testimony to establish a case for conspiracy to commit a crime. We will make sure you'll be indicted for nothing. You will appear before an investigator judge, tell him everything that was already recorded, and can then leave Switzerland and Europe altogether." He dialed his phone. "Can you come here?" he asked someone in his broken French. "A woman needs to give testimony on Ben David's case."

After hanging up, he turned back to Diana, as though the conversation was never interrupted. "Before the police arrive, I have a few more questions. Where did Muriel go that day you stalled my investigators?"

"I don't know."

He glared at her.

"I really don't. Robert—I mean Attorney Darmond—asked if I could do it. I said I could easily do it, and he asked me to, and..." She fell silent.

"Is that all? You have nothing more to tell us?"

"Any information you give us will make it easier for us to get you off the hook," Sally added. "And don't worry about him. He'll abandon you anyway."

Diana laid her head and arms on the table and broke out sobbing. "I think they traveled together," she said in a broken voice, "on the day she left Gstaad, he left Geneva. He traveled with her because he wanted her. I was never sure he really loved me."

Outside the conference room, loud knocks could be heard on the locked office door. "I'll open for them." Jacob stood up and told Diana, "Think well if there isn't anything else you'd like to add."

There was nothing of the sort, or perhaps Diana preferred to remain quiet. Her face remained glued to the table, and her blond head of hair quivered. Two policewomen entered the room and held Diana's arms. Diana said to Sally without turning her head, "You have no idea how lucky you are."

"What did she mean?" Jacob said after Diana had gone.

Sally shrugged. "Who knows? Now tell me," she said, wanting to change the subject, "how did you find the car rental slip and how did you persuade the Paris police to arrest Vivian Moyal?"

"I never saw the slip, nor did I reach Vivian Moyal." He smiled. "Do you know what I did in the army?"

"No, you were already working for the Mossad when I met you."

"I was a military police investigator. I learned a few tricks there."

"I feel sorry for Diana," Sally said.

"Are you crazy? She double-crossed you!"

"She's a good woman searching for love and money, and Vivian Moyal entrapped her. Darmond is the real villain in this story. You should have heard him rant about the treacherous, thieving Jews when we met Attorney Ovadia. All the while, he was deceiving Pierre and betraying him. Then he put on a show, as though he were being threatened, and fled Israel, probably to scare me. Now I understand why he wanted to get the photos we took in Muriel's apartment. I'm sure he would have handed them over to Ben David, who would have gone straight to the police. Now I also realize he told Ben David about the account Pierre was going to open for Muriel, and maybe even planned how to withdraw lots of money from it."

"Wait, that's only the beginning," Jacob said. "Many things will become clearer in the coming days." He collected his briefcase and Sally too collected her affairs. "Victory is sweet, isn't it?" he suddenly asked.

She smiled. "Very, but if I know anything about Ben David, the story isn't over yet."

PART THREE

54.

They sat side by side, silently. Darmond, wearing no tie, his hair disheveled, lowered his eyes. Ben David, on the other hand, was full of confidence, smiling defiantly at his surroundings. Cameras flashed. "Diana was wise to cooperate," Jacob whispered to Sally. "Imagine if she was sitting here too, her photo splashed across the papers."

Sally shrank back. "As long as they don't photograph us."

"Come on, relax. You're seated in the fourth row, on the side. Do you really think someone will notice?"

Sally scanned the hall, which was entirely full. More and more people crowded near the entrance, waiting to get in. It seemed like everyone in Geneva wanted to witness the two swindlers who almost took down the billionaire Marin, leaping into to the newspaper and television broadcast headlines. Muriel's name was absent from all the stories. On the day of the break-in, even before the police arrived at Ben David's estate, she was rushed to a mental health institution in Lausanne, where she completely collapsed. Vivian Moyal was mentioned as a side story, as someone investigated by Paris police. She too, like Diana, agreed to serve as a state witness in the upcoming trial.

A side door opened and the investigator judge entered the hall. He was elderly, with a fatigued look, and Sally couldn't help but think about the dozens or hundreds of criminals he'd judged. He read out the short list of indictments, and Darmond responded with long-winded, effusive phrases. The judge turned his gaze on Ben David, repeating the same clauses. A bald, well-dressed man stood before the bench, replying for Ben David. "A lawyer?" Sally asked.

"Yes. From Paris. No Swiss lawyer would stand alongside someone who harmed Marin."

"There are actually many unemployed lawyers in Geneva. Darmond's entire firm. Marin sacked them the moment Diana signed the affidavit implicating Darmond as an accomplice to the activity against him."

"Where is she now?" Jacob asked. "On the island she dreamed of?"

"Maybe." Sally smiled.

"What do you mean by 'maybe'? Yes or no?"

Sally wouldn't answer.

"How much did you pay her?"

"Who told you I paid her?"

"I already know you. You're obsessively generous."

Sally laughed out loud. A few heads turned to look at her. She covered her mouth with her hand.

"I hope she doesn't get into trouble again."

"I think she learned her lesson."

"There are people who never learn," Jacob started, then went silent as Ben David's lawyer ended his speech. The judge looked through the documents before him. The court was silent. A phone rang at the back of the hall, and the judge frowned as he surveyed the audience, beginning to speak into the microphone before him. "After hearing the response of the people brought before me today," he said, "I believe they should be indicted on the charges mentioned in writing by the Geneva police. They are suspects and will remain under house arrest in the Canton of Geneva with an electronic bracelet ensuring they do not leave."

"Commit to house arrest? Has Ben David ever stood up to a commitment?"

"I forgot to warn you. That's what's done here."

"Don't they have prisons?"

"They have a small prison in Champ-Dollon, not far from Geneva, where only prisoners considered a menace to society are kept."

"Ben David is a con man and imposter—isn't that considered dangerous?"

"He's neither a murderer nor a rapist, and in Switzerland they take their electronic bracelets very seriously."

Policemen led Darmond and Ben David out of the hall.

"I want close surveillance of Ben David's apartment," Sally said, frustrated. "Take into account how cunning he is."

"He may be cunning, but he has nowhere to run. He can't return to Israel, because the organization that handled him will give him no rest, and he can't hide anywhere in Europe."

The entrance to the courtroom was buzzing with people. Ben David's lawyer gave interviews on the steps to an army of reporters. None of them knew that the short man and the elegant woman standing next to him were the only ones to know about the entire affair. "Who will take care of Ben David now that he's under house arrest and Muriel is in a mental institution? Who will bring him food, or visit him?"

"Don't worry." Jacob smiled, waving his phone in front of her face. "My people in Israel tell me his wife is on her way over. Have I already asked you what it is about him that makes women fall at his feet?"

"You asked and I answered," Sally answered bitterly, and added, "I'm willing to admit that Diana, Muriel, and Mrs. Ben David don't add to women's reputations."

They continued walking along the street, and when they arrived at a small parking lot, Jacob stopped. "Can I take you anywhere?" he asked.

"Thanks," she said, pointing at a red Avis sign. "I've hired a car."

"Has something happened?" He looked at her curiously. "Something I don't know about?"

Sally smiled. "No, not at all. I just didn't want Marin's car to arrive here and run into some journalist." She patted Jacob's back. "We'll speak on the phone."

A beige Volkswagen Passat awaited her at the car rental company. Sally got in and quickly drove to the lakeside road. She passed by Ariana Park with the Palais des Nations at its center, white and imposing among the wandering peacocks. She thought how ironic it was for the United Nations—former League of Nations—to be situated among a flock of peacocks.

At the next intersection, Sally turned onto a narrower road that climbed into the mountains. The air became cooler, and she wound up the window. A French radio station broadcast classical music and colorful flowerbeds smiled at her. But all that was not enough to make her happy. The meeting she was headed to was too painful, too difficult.

After a drive of over an hour, she entered a parking lot adjacent to a building with a red tile roof. "Oberge des Chasseurs," read a copper sign attached to a short flight of stairs. She climbed them and entered a wood-decked reception hall. Taxidermied animal heads were hanging on the wall, befitting an establishment celebrating hunters. The receptionist smiled at her. "Can I help you?"

Sally looked at the wall behind the woman. It was covered with hooks, some of which held keys attached to wooden bars containing room numbers. "Yes," the lady said, "we are a rustic business. We have no locks activating by magnetic cards. Which room, please?"

"No, I haven't ordered a room. I have a meeting. Can you please call Dr. Moore?"

The clerk looked through her room cards. "Dr. Moore, yes." She picked up the old receiver and said, "Dr. Moore, you have a guest." The echo of a man's voice could be heard through the phone. She put the receiver down and said, "He'll be with you in a moment."

Sally looked up at the staircase. A pair of shiny shoes appeared on the top landing, followed by gray trousers, an ironed shirt and jacket, and finally Jerry's strict face. She walked toward him, her arms spread out to the sides, either seeking a hug or in greeting. Jerry held one of them and shook it formally. Then he walked Sally to the edge of the lobby and waited patiently for her to take her seat on the couch. He pulled up a chair and sat across from her. "We have an hour," he said. "No more. I need to reach the airport and travel on to New York."

"I could have met you at the airport and spared myself this ride. That way we'd have more time to talk."

"Yes, of course," he said in a low voice. "I saw the circus you made in court this morning. I certainly need no part of that. After all that's happened, the questioning by Mossad, the telephone threats, Michael's anxiety, all I needed was to be seen with you at the airport and my entire cover would be blown."

"I'm sorry for all the pain caused to you," Sally said, placing her hand on her chest. I'm really sorry and I want everything to be as before."

A dark shadow of anger crossed his eyes. "Are you sure you're emotionally prepared for that?"

Sally hesitated.

"I'm no idiot; I know exactly what happened between you and Pierre Marin. I also have to confess to my part in that. I'm even ready to consider trying to start again together and fix everything that went wrong between us. But I need to know that you're completely available for that, meaning that you will entirely disconnect from him and his business."

Sally swallowed hard. "With him, yes," she said. "But his business… I've spent my entire life trying to do good for people who need it, and finally, I've found a job I really like. Why do you want to send me back behind the computer screen? Are you trying to punish me?"

"Not at all," Jerry said calmly. "I just know that to end a relationship you need complete detachment. If you want to come home, you'll need to give up on both Marin and the job. I'm not telling you to go back to working for the insurance company. I understand you're far beyond that now. I also believe you can find interesting work in Israel, where you can do good for people." He leaned back and his face softened a little. "Come back. We'll have a big Passover *Seder* at your parents' house like every year, and everything will be back to normal."

"My father won't be home," Sally said faintly. "He's celebrating the

Seder here. So are my mother and brother. I was planning to ask the children to come, and I was hoping you would too."

Jerry's face grew stern again. "I won't celebrate the *Seder* with Marin," he said decisively.

Sally nodded with understanding. She admitted to herself that she would react similarly.

"You can still come home," Jerry said, and she knew how difficult it was for him. "If your father is staying here, we can have a small *Seder* at home, with the children."

"I can't disappoint Dad, Mom, my brother. I owe it to Marin too."

"You don't owe it to Marin—you want to be with Marin." He sat up rigidly. "Stay here. The children will come to you, if they want. I don't intend to settle scores with you through them. As I said, I know—" he swallowed hard "—I know I haven't been the perfect partner. I've thought about it a lot recently. I'm closed, I speak little, I may not be very emotional or easy to compliment. I know living with me was emotionally like living in the desert, and I'll change. I promise."

Sally wiped away the tears of emotion from the corners of her eyes. "I—I really don't know what to say."

"Say you're coming back. I love you and want us to be a family again. That's why I stopped my trip and came here, to meet you."

Sally was overwhelmed with emotion. She'd never heard a confession of love from him. She held his arm, expecting him to shake her off, but he didn't. "Please understand. I can't leave my entire family in Gstaad after bringing them there."

"They'll do just fine on their own. Your father is at ease anywhere, and if your mother and the rest of the family are with him, he'll bloom."

Sally didn't reply. After a long silence, Jerry said, "I understand." Without adding a word, he turned around and walked to the stairway. Sally watched with an aching heart as he moved away, until only his shiny shoes remained on the landing, before they too disappeared.

304 | Married to the Mossad

55.

She chose a small but quality hotel next outside the city, next to the lake. "A chef restaurant and heated pool," the online ad declared. Sally wasn't interested in the restaurant or in the pool. She needed distance from developments, to plan her next moves.

As she entered the room, the phone in her pocket rang. "I thought you'd come here," Marin's pleasant voice said. "It's a great day, after all. We won."

"Yes, we won," said Sally joylessly, which he immediately noticed. "What happened?"

"The big matter is solved, and now I have to face my personal crisis."

"Did you speak to Jerry?"

"Yes," she said, but immediately added cautiously, "on the phone." All of Jerry's movements were secret and under cover. He couldn't reveal his real name while traveling, and certainly not meet with her.

"I don't want to bug you, but just wanted to know you're all right. Do you have somewhere decent to sleep? To eat?"

"I'm at a hotel in Geneva."

"Somewhere comfortable?"

She scanned the room. The furniture was somewhat old fashioned, but exuded homely warmth. "Yeah. Looks good."

"Rest. It's been a long day." He paused for a moment, then added, "May I call tomorrow?" His speech was polite, cautious.

Sally replied, "You may call whenever you like. We'll remain friends. I just need to decide where to go from here." A wave of nostalgia overcame her and she rushed to hang up. Her decision to forgo her wonderful, generous lover was painful. She turned on the TV to serve as company. After flipping through a few boring channels, she settled for a fashion show, watching young women strut up and down the catwalk, as her mind drifted to where it always would when she was in distress: Her parents' home.

The home was far, but her father was nearby, at Marin's guesthouse, three hours' drive away. For a second she wanted to ask Fred, Marin's driver, to bring him to Geneva; but immediately decided it wouldn't be fair to ask her elderly father to take to the road only because of her mood swings. She had to solve her problems alone. She took a piece of paper with the hotel's emblem, and jotted down the options she had: Her dream job versus her family. Another wave of nostalgia for Marin overcame her. Perhaps she should follow her heart?

A dark, slender figure marched down a red carpet on the screen. She smiled to the camera, and Sally identified her immediately. Melody. She immediately recalled the things Marin said about her, treating her as nothing more than a luxurious accessory. But Sally also remembered him declaring how different she was to him, and wanting to stay with her. She walked to the bathroom and examined her image in the mirror.

She didn't have Melody's youthfulness, but she was still presentable, even pretty. Her large, blue eyes glowed over pronounced cheekbones, a small nose, and full lips. Her blond hair flowed softly onto her shoulders. How much longer would she remain pretty, and how long would Marin find her attractive? She thought of her mother, whose face remained pretty but also full of wrinkles. Would Marin remain by her side in her old age? She knew he wouldn't. In women, as in business, he was motivated by the same impulse—hunting. If Jerry was the flowing river of her life, Marin was the froth on top of the water. She returned to her room and let her mind wander in circles, until she fell asleep.

A loud ring awoke her from her troubled sleep. She looked at the screen. Marin was the caller and the time was 1:13 a.m. "Yes?" she answered in a sleepy voice.

"Muriel is gone," Marin said with alarm. "The driver arrived at the mental institution for a visit with the children, and she wasn't there. The management and staff were stressed. First they asked them to wait, then asked them to leave and return in an hour because she wasn't feeling well. When they returned, they stalled further, but finally confessed that she simply took off without saying a word to anyone. I went there. The room looked as if she were about to return in a moment, but she didn't."

"Any idea how she left?"

"It's a closed institution, but not a prison. There's a gate with a guard, but he mostly prevents unwarranted entry. There are psychologists, cooks, waiters, repairmen on staff, as well as invited guests. Anyone can leave."

"Maybe she went for a walk in the area and got lost."

"I don't think this was a short stroll. She took the only thing that ties a model to her home: Her makeup kit. Now, the only question is where she went and whether Ben David is connected to this."

"Ben David can't accept guests and his wife is with him. In addition, there's my investigator by the house. If Muriel were to arrive, I'd be informed." Sally sighed. "All right, how are the children reacting?"

"Terribly. Rubi is crying and Joel won't talk. Even your father was unable to cheer him up."

Sally's thoughts raced. "Have you already opened her account?"

"Yes." Marin's tone became tense. "Do you think she'll withdraw money from it?"

"I hope not," said Sally, with no certainty.

"She knows the money is meant for the children, if something happened to me," he said, as if trying to convince himself.

"That never stopped her before. When Ben David is in the picture, she loses all her will power."

"Do you think he's connected to her disappearance?"

"If not him, the organization behind him. Following her appearance with the investigator judge this morning, they may have realized he's finished and chosen an independent course of action."

"And kidnapped her?"

"I'm not sure they kidnapped her, but she may have cooperated after being told they needed money to free the holy man she loves. In any event, I suggest that the police ask the bank to inform it of any withdrawal from the account. I'll ask my men to tighten their surveillance on Ben David's home, in case her disappearance is part of a larger plan, which also includes his escaping…"

Marin was silent.

"Are you there?"

"Yes. I'm simply concerned."

Sally understood him, but couldn't offer words of encouragement. She resorted to the area she was best at—operations. "OK, I'll start working on my side. Goodbye."

"Wait, Sally, I know I've already told you this, but thanks for caring. I have other assistants in different areas, but no one works with such devotion."

"You know I'm not like your assistants. I'm a friend," Sally said, doing her best to remain formal. She hung up the phone and immediately called Jacob.

56.

Two sad-looking children sat at the long table, completely oblivious to their surroundings. Natalia, the housekeeper, walked between the guests and filled their glasses with wine. Sally's father stood up, and with him stood all the guests: Her brother and sister-in-law, their children, various guests, and of course Marin, who nudged Rubi to stand up too. Joel, who sat across from him, stood up last. "Blessed be God, who made us live to witness this time," Sally's father said.

"Amen," answered the people gathered around the table.

After the hand washing, everyone ate bitter herbs and chanted the ancient Aramaic words "Ha Lachma Anya." Her father signaled to Rubi, who began singing "Ma Nishtana," but broke into tears. Marin looked at Sally helplessly. She signaled to the door with her eyes. He stood up, placed a comforting hand on his son's shoulder, and walked him out.

The *Seder* continued in a somber mood. Everyone gathered knew why Rubi was crying and felt sympathy for his older brother, Joel, who filled in for him and sang in a broken voice. He would be celebrating his bar mitzvah in a few weeks, and his mother, who had again vanished from his life, would not be there. Sally's father joined him in singing. The others joined in the refrain, but it was not enough to clear the air.

Sally's father turned to Joel and said, "Here, let me answer you. We were slaves to Pharaoh in Egypt, and God removed us from there with a mighty hand." He went silent, signaling to Sally's brother, who continued running the Seder, then passed it over to one of his sons. It was the point where Sally's sons would also take part in the ceremony, but they weren't there. She felt the pain of their absence, but part of her understood and even appreciated the fact that they chose to remain with their father and alleviate his loneliness on this night.

Natalia appeared quietly behind her, handing her a note with just one word on it: JACOB. Sally met her father's eyes, which blinked their approval. She quietly apologized and left the room. In the foyer, Marin and his son sat in an embrace. Sally passed by them and went up to her room, where she pulled out her mobile phone and dialed Jacob's number.

"I'm afraid we've failed," he said, cutting straight to the point, with no niceties.

Sally was alarmed. "Was she found dead?"

"No, no one died, thank God. But Ben David is also gone."

"How, with an electric bracelet and your surveillance on the apartment?"

"An electric bracelet can be removed, and our guard... Well, it's a long story."

"Tell it to me," Sally insisted.

"According to our surveillance log, two policemen arrived at the house and left an hour later. We assume one of them was Ben David. It's hard to believe the Geneva police are corrupt. More likely, the uniform was stolen or rented from a theatre warehouse."

"And Ben David's wife?"

"She went shopping and never returned. That's the moment we realized we'd been had. We called the police, who found the apartment empty and the electronic bracelet on the table, flashing as usual."

"Where did the second policeman go, the one whose clothes Ben David took?"

"After a long search, he was found tied up in one of the closets. He's a stripper who claims he was hired to entertain a group of women who were meant to undress him."

Sally exhaled with exasperation. "So we have nothing now."

Jacob, pessimistic as usual, agreed with her. "We have nothing. I assume that Ben David, his wife, his children and Muriel agreed to meet somewhere, and we don't even have a lead. Any ideas?"

Sally felt extremely tired and could only think of one thing: To disconnect, to sail far away from the war on Ben David that now ended in utter defeat, far away from the family crisis and the heavy burdens on her shoulders. "No," she said, "I have no ideas. If something comes up, I'll get back to you."

She went down to the dining room. Marin and Rubi were back in their seats, and the *Seder* had reached an advanced point. Her father said the words, "He raises the poor from the dirt, and lifts up the needy from the garbage pile, that he might seat them with princes, with the princes of his people. He makes the barren woman of the family a happy mother of children," and he sent a loving glance to his wife, as he did every year. Her mother smiled calmly, and Sally felt grateful for having at least one constant in her life: Her parents.

Then she thought of the idea. She held it inside until the start of the meal, then ran upstairs to her room. "Her parents," she said, out of breath, into the phone. "We need to find Muriel's parents."

"They live in some remote farm in Canada and are unhappy that she converted to Judaism. What could we find there?" Jacob asked.

"The same thing I find with my parents when I feel life is overwhelming me—support. Robert Frost once wrote, 'Home is the place where, when *you* have to go there, they have to take *you* in.'"

"Who is this Frost?"

"An American poet. Never mind, let's focus on Muriel. Think about the state she's in: Ben David has become a fugitive and he needs money. He won't turn to his admirers, because he has none left. The entire world knows he's a con man. He only has one admirer left: Muriel. And she only has her parents."

Jacob reacted with skeptical silence. "I know you hate losing, but now you're expressing wishful thinking, not logic, and what's worse, you're going to invest lots of money in this pipe dream. You need to send someone to track down her parents in Canada, which is a huge country. Assuming we find them, send more people there, settle in, stake out the house...all based on your hunch that she's back in her childhood home."

"An informed hunch," Sally corrected him. "A combination of logic and life experience, and finding Muriel won't be that difficult. Do we have her profile? Education, hobbies, CV?"

"No, we never needed all that."

"I'll prepare it tonight and send it over, along with more specific guidelines for our search."

Jacob laughed. "Your optimism is endless."

"It's better than despair, isn't it?" she replied and hung up. Sally went online and tapped in Muriel's name. Her phone displayed headlines linking her to Marin, to upscale fashion houses, and to a Paris modeling agency. She called Jacob again and gave him the name and address of the agency. "Try to get her portfolio, or at least early photos from before she became famous. That's where the authentic Muriel is, and perhaps also clues to where she came from."

When she returned to the table, the *Seder* was almost over. Her father and the other guests were singing "Had Gadia" and the atmosphere seemed slightly happier. Sally sat at the table and Natalia rushed to serve her. "You haven't eaten dinner, Madame Sally," she whispered.

"Thanks, but I'm not hungry. Only coffee, please," Sally replied in a low voice. Her eyes met Marin's and his face was inquisitive. Sally mouthed the word "later." The thought of having disappointing, perhaps disheartening, news and not conveying it to Marin immediately made her uneasy. She became less and less comfortable the longer her father took conducting the *Shabbat* songs they used to sing at home when she was young. This time, she couldn't enjoy them or join in. Ben David's flight erased all her achievements in one go, and she was terribly frustrated. She desperately wondered whether there was something she could have done and didn't do to prevent his escape, and what she now needed to do to find him.

She impatiently waited for the last of the guests to retire to their rooms in the guesthouse, and for the two children to go to bed. Marin sat in the wide lounge and poured himself a glass of his favorite cognac. "Did something happen?" he asked when she appeared, still buzzing from the singing.

"Ben David escaped," Sally said, unloading the stone on her heart in one fell swoop.

Marin's eyes expanded with astonishment. He didn't say a word, just slowly drank from his glass. Sally told him of the two uniformed men who entered the apartment and left, the electronic bracelet left inside, and the stripper found in the closet. "What torments me most is knowing I've disappointed you. I failed. I managed an operation costing hundreds of thousands of dollars that came to nothing."

Marin struggled to smile. "You did your best."

Sally frowned. "Thanks, but I know you don't mean it. You've been in business your entire life, where you don't reward people for doing their best but for the result. I promised you Ben David would be punished, but he got away at the last minute. I failed."

His eyes looked into hers, and she saw in them a glint of honesty. "Not only haven't you failed, but you've greatly succeeded. You've given me faith that some people have a kernel of good that only needs to be exposed." He put his hand on her arm. "No one has ever worked for me so caringly."

Sally placed her hand on his. "That doesn't comfort me."

Marin looked at her with pity. "Sally the perfectionist," he said, pouring her a glass of cognac. "You won't have anything but a big, heroic triumph."

Sally stood up, tears in her eyes, and went out to the garden. The fragrant spring breeze enveloped her. She shivered as she walked to the guesthouse. On the bench at the entrance sat her father, as he did every evening. She collapsed on the bench next to him. Without saying a word, he stretched out his hand and caressed her hair. "Dad," she said.

"I know." He stopped her. "It's already in the news."

"Everything is destroyed. Everything I've done, all I've worked for in the last few months, sacrificing my time and my relationship with Jerry…"

"I don't think so," her father said peacefully. "Ben David can run, but he can't hide. He has no profession but imposter rabbi, he has no money, and the criminal organization you told me about will demand results."

"He can just disappear. Change his name; find a menial job that requires no professionalism. Clerk, vendor…"

"Do you think he can hold a job? Come every morning at nine o'clock and work seriously until five in the afternoon? He'll have to return to crime in order to maintain the lifestyle he's used to."

"So, you're saying he has to be caught?"

"Yes," he said confidently, "he'll be caught." After a few silent moments, he added, "But it will be accompanied with tragedy, and there's nothing you can do to prevent it."

316 | Married to the Mossad

57.

The information trickled in like Chinese water torture. A month after Ben David's disappearance, a diplomat from the Canadian embassy in Bern called Marin's home in Gstaad and then to the offices of Cosmos Holdings in Geneva, presenting himself as Herbert Zucker, and asked to speak with Mr. Marin.

Marin was in Africa negotiating the purchase of a mine, and Marie Calderon, the office manager who just a few months earlier refused to transfer Sally's first call, now naturally gave her the man's contact details.

When Sally called him, he began by inquiring about her identity and position, and after she faxed him her letter of appointment signed by Marin, he bombarded her with questions about Marin's ties with Muriel, asking for their wedding certificate to be faxed to them.

Sally refused. She didn't have the wedding certificate, and also feared he was a nosy journalist. After checking the phone number and going over the employee directory at the embassy, she discovered that he was indeed an overzealous civil servant. After consulting Marin's new lawyers, an international Israeli firm she hired following Darmond's arrest, she threatened Zucker to turn to the court and force Canada to respect her appointment. A day later, he called back and agreed to tell Sally that Muriel's condition was critical, and she was hospitalized in a hospital in Regina, Saskatchewan. He didn't want to answer Sally's questions about how she got there, or perhaps he didn't have the answers. "I've received clear instructions: To find Mrs. Marin's family and tell them she's hospitalized. I can also add that part of the problem stems from the fact that we had to identify her based on her Canadian identity number, and then check that there was no identity theft. She didn't register as Muriel Marin, nor did she use her maiden name, but rather a new pseudonym she invented."

"What name?"

"Miriaam," he said, drawing out the last vowel. He could hardly pronounce the last part; "Bat Avraham."

Ben David's fingerprints were clearly visible here too. Sally asked Zucker for more details, but when she didn't receive those, insisted on speaking to his superior. She was transferred to the consul, and from him to the deputy ambassador, who slowly explained to her as though she were an idiot that "Canada is a large country, and every province in it is also an independent entity, so information travels slowly between government agencies." If Sally wanted, she could send her questions to the foreign ministry in Ottawa, where they would check with the authorities in Saskatchewan and get back to him.

There was, of course, a faster way of getting information—turning to Jerry. His men in the Mossad could obtain the information within hours, but she felt it unfair to ask such a thing of him. She called Jacob, who was somewhere in the world, after the team he assembled for Switzerland was dismantled following Ben David's flight. After a number of failed phone calls, she found him at a wedding celebration. "I have no information on Muriel or Ben David yet," he shouted, trying to overcome the sound of the orchestra.

"*I* do. Go somewhere more quiet where we can talk."

She heard the sounds grow distant. Jacob's speech could be heard more clearly. "What information do you have?"

"Find Muriel at the hospital in Regina, Saskatchewan. She's admitted under the name Miriam Bat Avraham. Check how she's doing, how she became sick or injured, and whether Ben David is around."

There was silence on the other end of the line.

"Are you there?"

"I'm surprised, that's all. You were right. She returned to her parents."

"I wish I were wrong. She has children here who need her."

The band's music grew louder. "All right, I have to get back. They'll deal with it immediately."

Sally spent a nervous night in front of the television. When dawn broke, her computer made a sound. She ran to it, drowsy, and banged her foot on a chair. A long e-mail from Jacob explained that Miriam Bat Avraham fell off a horse in a farm 150 miles north of Regina. The injury wasn't severe, but it caused a hemorrhage in her brain stem, which turned lethal for the lack of immediate care. According to the doctor who admitted her, the injury was three days old. The medical team tried to get more information from the man who brought her, but he disappeared.

Muriel's hospital forms were attached to the e-mail, mentioning injuries all over her body. Sally wrote to Jacob: "It looks like she's been beaten."

Half an hour later, a reply arrived. "They claim here that these are typical injures for someone who fell off a horse. They assume she was caught in the stirrup trying to climb up, and the horse dragged her a few hundred feet. They say it happens a lot here, and we're still investigating. One of my men left for the farm where her parents live."

At noon, when she arrived at her Geneva office, one of the employees was able to connect her to Marin, who was, it turned out, visiting a mine in Sierra Leone. "I don't understand," he said. "What happened to Muriel?"

"She's in a hospital in Canada," Sally explained, but wind or other interruptions on the line distorted her speech. She repeated herself, and this time he understood. "Do the children know?" he asked.

"Not yet."

"Very good," he said, sounding as businesslike as ever. "I'm going to finish up here and return tomorrow evening. Until then, collect all the information you can find, and I'll explain it to them."

The conversation ended. Sally walked to the window and looked at the street and the Geneva residents walking carelessly through it. Her computer sounded an incoming message, and she hurried to her desk, where she saw it was from Jacob. The headline read: THE TRUE STORY.

"Muriel arrived at her parents' farm not far from Nipawin, Saskatchewan. While still in Switzerland, she sent her parents money, with which they hired two assistants and built a new stable for three horses that Muriel bought (it's possible that the time when she escaped us with Diana's help has to do with this money transfer). Muriel lived in a small apartment above the stable with a dark-skinned man they called 'the Arab.' He spoke a bit of English, relatively good French, and what sounded to them like Arabic. At first they didn't like the romance between him and their daughter, especially since he was married and had a family in nearby Nipawin. But

Muriel told them he made her happy, and indeed she seemed calm and contented as she never had since marrying Marin (whom, by the way, they really don't like, and consider a vindictive, moneygrubbing Jew—or so at least their daughter portrayed him). Every day, Muriel went on a long ride with the two assistants on the three horses. 'The Arab' opposed this. She heeded his plea, stopped riding, and only had the horses gallop in the field near the house. But that came with a price. Muriel went back to drinking. Her sister, who lives in a different farm in the area, told us that 'the Arab' encouraged her drinking habit, and would regularly bring her alcohol from Nipawin.

"Nine days ago, shouts were heard from the riding field. Muriel's father, who rushed to the scene, found her being dragged by the horse on the ground. The two assistants had disappeared and 'the Arab' was standing there, helpless. The father stopped the horse and discovered that his daughter's foot was tied to the stirrup with a thin metal wire. She was injured all over, but worse: drunk. He asked 'the Arab' why she'd tied herself, why she got on the horse drunk, and where her two assistants were. 'The Arab' claimed they mounted her on the horse, tied her, and then made the horse gallop, all out of spite against Jews. He volunteered to drive her to Nipawin in the family van, and from there pay to fly her out to Regina. The father agreed since his wife was very ill, and he didn't want to leave her alone. But Muriel was not flown to Regina, but rather driven to the hospital there over two days by 'the Arab,' where she was admitted as Miriam Bat Avraham. The van was never returned, and 'the Arab's' family also vanished from the apartment they were living in."

"What's Muriel's condition?" Sally typed.

"I have no idea. I'll have them check."

Sally forwarded the e-mail to Marin's address, and to that of their new lawyer. Then she forced herself to go back to work, and by the time she managed to focus again, her phone rang. "I didn't want to inform you by e-mail. Muriel is dead," Jacob said.

Sally felt a wave of sorrow come over her. "And Ben David?"

"No sign of him for now."

"And the two assistants?"

"Just drifters. I assume he paid them to disappear, and they're probably hundreds of miles away from the scene."

"You must find them. Sift through all of Canada, find them, and scare them with indictment as accomplices to murder. I'm sure Ben David got her drunk and tied her foot to the stirrup with some excuse. They'll testify against him."

Jacob was scornful. "It's useless. We'll never meet Ben David again."

"Oh yes we will, and I think I even know where. Think. Ben David doesn't do anything without a reason. He'll have a plan." She looked at her watch. "I have to get going. Leave Ben David and focus on the two workers. I'll explain everything later."

"I'm still not sure what you're planning to do, but good luck," Jacob said.

"You will in a few hours," Sally said and sighed. "If only you were here now with two of your men."

58.

The police officer was polite and cordial, but completely skeptical about her request. "You're asking us to place undercover detectives at Banque Alimentaire because someone dressed as Mrs. Marin will come to withdraw money?"

"Exactly," Sally confirmed.

"And why would Mrs. Marin send a disguised woman to withdraw money when she can withdraw it herself?"

"Because Mrs. Marin is dead."

"In that case, you have nothing to worry about. The account will be blocked and no one can make a withdrawal."

"She died only an hour ago. The bank doesn't know about it yet, and the murderer will try to withdraw the money."

The officer examined her suspiciously. "How are *you* connected to her death?"

"I'm not," Sally said. "I've only just found out."

"How?"

"A mutual friend told me."

"Madame," the officer said, turning impatiently to his keyboard. "Do you want to give us a testimony or a deposition?"

"No, I want to help you catch the murderer. All you need to do is place undercover policemen at the branch of Banque Alimentaire. The murderer will send over a woman who resembles Mrs. Marin with her passport." She looked at her watch. "The bank opens in half an hour. You shouldn't waste a minute."

"Madame, we don't work on demand. You can give us the information, and if we believe officers must be sent to the bank, we'll do so. It's not me who decides, but the investigations officer of the district."

"I'd like to speak to him." Sally demanded. "Right now."

The officer smiled patiently. "I'll convey your request. Can you leave us a phone number?"

Sally dictated her Swiss phone number to the officer. When he finished writing, he suddenly said, "Why do you think the disguised woman, as you called her, will arrive at this branch in particular? Today you can withdraw money from anywhere in the world."

"It's a small private bank with one branch, which is why Mr. Marin chose it, to ensure that only Mrs. Marin can withdraw the funds."

The officer nodded. "Noted," he said. "If you find out anything else, please let us know."

"Of course," Sally promised, frustrated, and left the station.

59.

The foyer of the bank was small and empty. Two clerks were busy typing behind their desks, and as Sally entered they lifted their eyes and looked at her. She didn't approach either of them, but confidently sat on a narrow couch against the wall. A man in a fancy suit exited a squeaky elevator. He too looked at her, but didn't say a word. After half an hour of being politely ignored, one of the clerks stood up and approached her. "Madame, are you waiting for someone?"

"My friend from Canada is supposed to come here. We agreed to meet at ten, but I was informed that her flight has been slightly delayed."

The clerk nodded understandingly and returned to his seat. Another hour went by, and Sally became a fixture of the antiquated hall, like the couch she was sitting on, the two desks, the old computers, and the squeaky elevator, which every now and again would eject bankers and businessmen who looked like they had been formed in the same mold. By noon, hunger was beginning to bother Sally. The clerk she spoke to earlier also began moving uncomfortably. "We're about to close," he told her.

"We'll be back in an hour. There's a pleasant restaurant down the street. You can wait there and return at one, when we reopen."

Sally never returned. On her way to the restaurant, she discovered a fast food stand overlooking the bank. Next to it, a few benches were hidden from the street by a row of blooming trees. She bought herself a tuna sandwich and a cup of coffee and sat under a chinaberry tree. The weather was pleasant, and even when the bank doors opened, her outlook seemed more agreeable than the dull waiting room.

As time went by, doubts grew in her. The thought that she could trap Ben David and the woman he recruited to withdraw the money all by herself suddenly seemed silly and arrogant. On the other hand, what other options did she have? If she were to use Jacob, it would take hours for him to get organized and place investigators in and around the bank, and Swiss investigators had let her down before. But nevertheless, shouldn't she consult bankers, lawyers, or accountants to check that there was no other way for Ben David to withdraw the money while she was waiting here?

She finished the sandwich and her coffee cup was empty. Next to her, on the bench, people came and went. An elderly man with a brown puppy tried to start conversation with her, two teenagers waited for a woman to pick them up in a small car, a mailman who greeted her with "good day" stretched his legs forward and closed his eyes for a short rest. The apprehension tightened her limbs and sped up her heart rate. To relax, she practiced an exercise she once learned at a guided meditation course, conjuring up the image she expected: Ben David, strolling down the sidewalk with a tall blonde woman, walking like a model. She got up, bought another cup of coffee without removing her eyes from the street, and sat to drink it on another bench, more hidden.

A few moments later, she was grateful for that. A tall woman with blond hair and a slender physique opened the door and entered the bank. She didn't walk like a model, but was familiar to Sally. Very familiar. Sally leaped up and crossed the street running, swerving between the passing cars. When she entered the bank, the woman was already seated across from the bank clerk Sally had spoken to two hours earlier. He lifted his eyes, followed Sally as she made the short distance to his desk, and said nothing when she approached the woman, placed a hand on her shoulder, and said, "Diana, don't get involved in this."

60.

Jerry offered his arm to Sally, which she leaned on. The *Shabbat* elevator was taking its time to arrive. This time Jerry didn't complain about that, nor did he rush to the nearby elevator and take it alone, as he had done in the past. Sally gave him a look of gratitude and he replied with a smile. The reconciliation was good for them, and during the weeks that had passed since Diana was caught in the bank in Geneva, the events of the past year seemed foreign to them, almost unimaginable.

The street was awash with bright June sun. Sally and Jerry walked through a new pedestrian shopping mall and entered the ancient walls of the Old City. The winding street that led them to the Western Wall was packed with people. Most of them were guests of the bar mitzvah celebration of Joel Marin, the son of famous Pierre Marin, who had become even more famous thanks to the recent events. As they approached the Wall, Sally identified her son Roy, standing out in his ironed officer's uniform among the masses in white shirts and suits. Next to him stood his younger brother Michael, and Rubi, Marin's younger son, who looked at Roy with

328 | Married to the Mossad

eyes filled with admiration. Joel, the bar mitzvah boy, stood slouched next to her father, looking sad and restless.

Sally smiled at him to cheer him up, but had no illusions. There was nothing that could comfort him on the absence of his mother on his big day. She was also deeply sorry for Muriel, the weakest link of the Marin saga. She remembered her burial ceremony in Geneva's Jewish cemetery, and Marin's tall figure giving a eulogy that ended with the words, "We can only take comfort in the fact that she died while doing what she loved most: Riding a horse, which was a real friend, without conditions..."

The following day, he left the children with a nanny and returned to his business. Only after Muriel's death did Sally grasp the depths of pain in which Muriel lived, and the mistake she made in searching for love with the wrong man. Slowly, gradually, she realized that she herself had almost deteriorated to the same point. As usual, she spoke about it with her father, who asked, "What are you looking for in life, Sallinka?"

"Like everyone else," she replied, "happiness."

Her father thought for a bit and said, "The problem in searching for happiness is that most people get it wrong and believe that in order to be happy they must change the reality they live in."

"Why is that a mistake?" Sally argued. "That's the way—"

"There's another way," he insisted. "Instead of searching for love by changing reality, you can obtain it by changing your demands from reality, or in other words, settling for little and gaining happiness from what you have. And you have a lot, Sallinka."

After a night of thinking, Sally drafted a resignation letter from the Marin Foundation, sent a long e-mail to Marin—who was again in Africa—and called Jerry. "I resigned," she said. "I'm coming back to Israel to look for work."

"Come home," he said curtly.

A day later, when she entered her Tel Aviv apartment, she found a different Jerry; more attentive, open and inclusive, who took an interest in her life and accompanied her in the negotiation process with the various companies she applied to. She was offered nice salaries and titles, but all the jobs were commercial and none made her feel she could contribute something to others.

The Western Wall plaza filled up. People flocked to it from the narrow alleyways. Many looked at Sally curiously and some nodded at her, even though they never met her. Jerry moved uncomfortably. "You have no choice," Sally told him. "The whole country saw me on TV, and in Israel, everyone is my friend now."

"You don't work for Marin anymore. Why didn't you tell them that the footage of Ben David being arrested was enough? Why did you give an interview?"

"Because I'm still committed to the matter. Pierre won't interview, Muriel is dead, and Diana received immunity again for incriminating Ben David and was told to shut up. Someone has to tell the world what happened here, don't they? We need positive public opinion."

"Why? Isn't the evidence enough?"

"In some matters, it's our word versus his. Muriel's assistants were arrested and gave an opposite narrative than Ben David. They say he was the one who tied Muriel's foot to the stirrup."

"Maybe he feared she'd fall?"

"In such cases, it's acceptable to tie both feet and the body with a special strap. That's how they tie disabled people on therapeutic rides. When the assistants asked him why he tied just one foot, he said that's how Muriel wanted it. They said she was too drunk to contradict him. Clearly, Ben David's true intention was to cause Muriel to fall and be dragged by the horse, and that point must be proven in court beyond doubt. Jacob is cooperating with Canadian police, and every day new evidence emerges."

"And that means you'll give another interview?"

Sally laughed. "I guess so."

"I don't think so," Jerry said.

Sally grew nervous. "Will you forbid me?"

"Not me, your new workplace." He reached into his jacket pocket and pulled out an envelope. "I was waiting for the right moment to give this to you. Everything you did in recent months really impressed our people, and Aaron also used all of his influence…"

Sally opened the envelope and opened a page with the Mossad emblem on it.

"You realize you won't take part in any operation. They want you mainly for research and strategic planning."

Sally's heart overflowed with joy. "I don't care, as long as I can contribute."

"No." Jerry laughed. "As long as you're finally forced to keep a low profile and—" he patted her hair "—stay in Israel."

Made in the USA
Lexington, KY
27 June 2017